NEW YORK REVIEW BOOKS
CLASSICS

THE STRONGHOLD

DINO BUZZATI (1906–1972) came from a distinguished family that had long been resident in the northern Italian region of the Veneto. His mother was descended from a noble Venetian family; his father was a professor of international law. Buzzati studied law at the University of Milan and, at the age of twenty-two, went to work for *Corriere della Sera*, where he remained for the rest of his life. He served in World War II as a journalist connected to the Italian navy and on his return published the book for which he is most famous, *The Stronghold* (first translated in English as *The Tartar Steppe*). A gifted artist as well as writer, Buzzati was the author of five novels and numerous short stories, as well as a popular children's book, *The Bears' Famous Invasion of Sicily*.

LAWRENCE VENUTI, professor emeritus of English at Temple University, is a translator from Italian, French, and Catalan, as well as a translation theorist and historian. He is, most recently, the author of *Contra Instrumentalism: A Translation Polemic* (2019), the editor of *The Translation Studies Reader* (4th ed., 2021), and the translator of J. V. Foix's *Daybook 1918: Early Fragments* (2019), which won the Global Humanities Translation Prize at Northwestern University.

OTHER BOOKS BY DINO BUZZATI PUBLISHED BY
NEW YORK REVIEW BOOKS

A Love Affair
Translated by Joseph Green

Poem Strip
Translated by Marina Harss

THE STRONGHOLD

DINO BUZZATI

Translated from the Italian by
LAWRENCE VENUTI

NEW YORK REVIEW BOOKS

New York

THIS IS A NEW YORK REVIEW BOOK
PUBLISHED BY THE NEW YORK REVIEW OF BOOKS
207 East 32nd Street, New York, NY 10016
www.nyrb.com

This book was translated thanks to a grant awarded by the Italian Ministry of
Foreign Affairs and International Cooperation.

Originally published in Italian as *Il deserto dei tartari* in 1940.
First published as a New York Review Books Classic in 2023.

Library of Congress Cataloging-in-Publication Data
Names: Buzzati, Dino, 1906–1972, author. | Venuti, Lawrence, translator, writer
   of introduction.
Title: The stronghold / by Dino Buzzati; translated from the Italian with an
   introduction by Lawrence Venuti.
Other titles: Deserto dei tartari. English
Description: First edition. | New York: New York Review Books, [2023] | Series:
   New York Review Books classics | Originally published in Italian as Il deserto
   dei Tartari. Previously translated into English as The Tartar Steppe.
Identifiers: LCCN 2022027454 (print) | LCCN 2022027455 (ebook) | ISBN
   9781681377148 (paperback) | ISBN 9781681377155 (ebook)
Subjects: LCSH: Soldiers—Fiction. | LCGFT: Military fiction. | Novels.
Classification: LCC PQ4807.U83 D43 2023 (print) | LCC PQ4807.U83 (ebook)
   | DDC 853/.912—dc23/eng/20220613
LC record available at https://lccn.loc.gov/2022027454
LC ebook record available at https://lccn.loc.gov/2022027455

ISBN 978-1-68137-714-8
Available as an electronic book; ISBN 978-1-68137-715-5

Printed in the United States of America on acid-free paper.
10 9 8 7 6 5 4 3 2 1

CONTENTS

THE STRONGHOLD · 1

Afterword · 195

I

ONE SEPTEMBER morning, the newly commissioned officer Giovanni Drogo set out from the city for Fortezza Bastiani, his first assignment.

He had himself awakened before dawn and donned his lieutenant's uniform for the first time. When he had finished, he looked in the mirror in the light of an oil lamp, although without finding the joy he had expected. A heavy silence had fallen over the house and only faint sounds could be heard from a nearby room: his mother was waking to see him off.

He had waited years for this day, the start of his true life. He thought of the dreary routines at the military academy and recalled bitter evenings of studying when he would listen to people passing in the street, free and presumably happy. He recalled winter reveilles in frigid dormitories where the nightmare of punishments would rankle. And he recalled the torment of counting the days, one after another, seemingly without end.

Now he was finally commissioned. No more would he have to exhaust himself over books or quake at the sergeant's voice—all this had passed. The days that had seemed so distasteful to him were now gone forever, forming months and years that would never be repeated. Yes, now he was commissioned, he would have money, beautiful women might look in his direction, but in the last analysis—Giovanni Drogo realized—the best time, the prime of his youth, had probably come to an end. As Drogo stared in the mirror, he glimpsed a forced smile on the face he had sought in vain to love.

What nonsense: Why couldn't he muster a smile with the proper spontaneity when he took leave of his mother? Why didn't he pay the least attention to her last bits of advice, going no further than to catch the sound of her voice, so familiar and good natured? Why was he wandering around the room, edgy but unfocused, unable to locate his watch, his crop, his cap—things he wound up finding where he usually left them? He certainly wasn't going to war! At this very hour, dozens of lieutenants like him, his erstwhile companions, were leaving their paternal homes amid cheerful laughter as if they were heading to a party. Why, in his mother's presence, did his mouth issue nothing but generic phrases devoid of meaning instead of soothing, affectionate words? His mind was flooded, not only with the bitterness of leaving the old house for the first time—the house where he was born among the hopes and fears brought by every change—but also with the poignancy of bidding mamma farewell. Yet over all this weighed an insistent thought he couldn't identify, like a vague presentiment of fatal things, as if he were about to begin a journey from which he would never return.

His friend Francesco Vescovi accompanied him on horseback for the first stretch of the way. The animals' tramping echoed in the deserted streets. The day was dawning. The city was still immersed in sleep. A shutter opened here and there on the upper floors and tired faces appeared. For a moment apathetic eyes were fixed on the marvelous sunrise.

The two friends didn't speak. Drogo thought about what Fortezza Bastiani might be like but he couldn't imagine it. He didn't even know where it might be exactly or how far away. Some people had told him one day by horse; others less. None of those he asked had ever actually been there.

At the gates of the city, Vescovi broke into an animated discussion of the usual things as if Drogo were on an outing. Then at a certain point he said:

"See that grassy mountain? Yes, that one precisely. See that structure on top? That's part of the Fortezza, an advanced redoubt. Two years ago I passed by it, I remember, with my uncle. We were hunting."

By now they had left the city. They started to pass cornfields, meadows, red autumnal woods. On the white road, beaten by the sun, they advanced side by side. Giovanni and Francesco were friends, spent long years together, shared the same passions, the same friendships. They had always seen one another, day after day. Then Vescovi grew fat while Drogo became an officer and now he felt as if the other man were far away. That easy, elegant life no longer belonged to him; grave, unknown matters were waiting. Already—he felt—their horses were marking a disparate pace: his own trudged along, less nimble and lively, like an undercurrent of worry and toil, as if even the animal understood that life was on the verge of changing.

They had reached the top of a hill. Drogo turned back to look at the city against the light. Plumes of smoke were rising from roofs. He saw his own house in the distance. He identified the window of his room. It was probably open; the women were tidying up. They would strip the bed, put things away in the closet, then bolt the shutters. For months and months no one would enter, except for the patient dust and on sunny days faint streaks of light. There, shut up in darkness, would lie the little world of his boyhood. His mother would preserve it so that on his return he would find everything the same, enabling him to remain a boy in that room, even after his long absence. She was no doubt deluding herself: she believed she could preserve intact a happiness that had vanished forever, holding back the flight of time, so that when doors and windows were reopened at her son's return, things would revert to the way they were before.

His friend Vescovi now gave him a warm goodbye and Drogo continued alone down the road, drawing closer to the mountains. The sun stood at its height when he reached the mouth of the valley that led to the Fortezza. On the right, on top of a mountain, he could see the redoubt that Vescovi had indicated. It shouldn't be much farther.

Anxious to arrive, Drogo didn't stop to eat. He drove his already-weary horse up the road, which grew steep, enclosed between precipitous ridges. He encountered fewer and fewer people. He asked a carter how much time it would take to reach the Fortezza.

"The fortezza?" replied the man. "What fortezza?"

"Fortezza Bastiani," said Drogo.

"No strongholds in these parts," said the carter. "Never heard tell of any."

He was evidently ill informed. Drogo resumed his journey, becoming aware of a subtle uneasiness as the afternoon advanced. He scanned the sides of the valley to discover the Fortezza. He imagined a kind of ancient castle with vertiginous walls. As the hours passed, he became more and more convinced that Francesco had given him mistaken information. The redoubt he indicated must really be a long way back. And evening was approaching.

Look at how small Giovanni Drogo and his horse appear on the flank of the mountains, which grow increasingly huge and wild. He continues to climb so as to reach the Fortezza before the day ends but the shadows rise more quickly, from the depths, where a torrent roars. At a certain point, they arrive at just Drogo's height on the opposite slope of the gorge and for a moment seem to slow, as if not to discourage him. But then they slip over crags and rocks. The rider is left behind.

The entire ravine was already filled with violet darkness. Only the bare, grassy ridges, incredibly high, were lit by the sun when Drogo suddenly found himself before a military structure that seemed ancient and deserted, looming black and gigantic against the purest evening sky. Giovanni felt his heart pounding. This must be the Fortezza. Everything, from the walls to the landscape, emanated an inhospitable, sinister air.

He wandered around without finding the entrance. Although night had now fallen, no window was lit and no sentries' lamps could be seen on the border of the towering walls. Only a bat wavered against a white cloud. Finally Drogo tried shouting. "Hey!" he called out. "Is anybody here?"

From the shadows that gathered at the foot of the walls emerged a man, some sort of vagrant or beggar, with a gray beard and a little sack in his hand. In the dimness, however, he couldn't be discerned clearly; only the whites of his eyes glowed. Drogo looked at him with gratitude.

"Who are you trying to find, sir?" asked the man.

"I'm searching for the Fortezza. Is this it?"

"There's no fort anymore," said the stranger in a friendly voice. "Everything's shut up. Nobody's been here for some ten years."

"Where is the Fortezza then?" asked Drogo, suddenly irritated with the man.

"What fortezza? You mean that one?" As the stranger spoke, he held out an arm to point at something.

Through a chink among the nearby crags already shrouded in darkness, behind a chaotic progression of peaks, Giovanni Drogo spotted a bare hill at an incalculable distance, still immersed in the crimson light of sunset, as if conjured by a spell. On its crest appeared a regular, geometric strip in an unusual shade of yellow: the profile of the Fortezza.

How far away it still was! Who knows how many hours of travel lay ahead, and his horse was spent. Drogo stared, fascinated. He wondered whether anything desirable might be lodged in that solitary castle, nearly inaccessible, so sequestered from the world. What secrets did it conceal? Yet the moment was fleeting. Already the last ray of sunlight was slowly withdrawing from the remote hill. And up over the yellow ramparts burst the baleful wind of night's abrupt arrival.

2

Darkness overtook Drogo while he was still making his way. The valley had narrowed and the Fortezza had disappeared behind the impending mountains. Lights were nonexistent. Not even the voices of nocturnal birds could be heard. Nothing but the sound of distant water now and then.

He tried calling out but the echoes returned his voice with a hostile tone. He tied his horse to a stump by the side of the road, where it could find some grass. He sat himself down, his back against the escarpment, waiting for sleep to come, and he thought of the distance that remained, the people he would meet at the Fortezza, his future life, although without finding any cause for joy. The horse kept stamping on the ground in an odd, annoying manner.

At dawn, as he resumed his journey, he noticed another road on the opposite slope of the ravine, at the same height, and just beyond he glimpsed something moving. The sun wasn't yet shining down that far, so shadows filled the recesses, preventing him from making out things clearly. Still, stepping up his pace, Drogo managed to reach a parallel point and ascertained it was a man: an officer on horseback.

A man like him, finally, a sympathetic creature with whom he might laugh and joke and talk about the life they would soon be sharing, about hunting, women, the city. To Drogo the city now seemed to be relegated to a world that was very far away.

Meanwhile the valley narrowed further, the two roads drew closer, and Giovanni Drogo perceived that the other man was a captain. At first he didn't feel he should shout: it would seem pointless and disrespectful. He saluted, however, more than once, lifting his right hand to his cap. But the other man didn't respond. Evidently he hadn't noticed Drogo.

"Captain, sir!" Giovanni finally shouted, overcome with impatience. And he saluted again.

"What is it?" replied a voice from the other side. The captain, having stopped, had given a proper salute and was now asking Drogo why he had shouted. The request wasn't harsh in the least but the captain had clearly been taken aback.

"What is it?" the captain's voice echoed, this time with slight irritation.

Giovanni stopped, cupped his hands to his mouth, and replied at the top of his lungs, "Nothing! I just wanted to salute you, sir!"

It was a stupid explanation that bordered on offensive since it could be construed as a joke. Drogo immediately regretted it. What a ridiculous mess he'd gotten himself into, all because he wasn't capable of self-reliance.

"Who are you?" the captain shouted in response.

It was the question Drogo feared. That strange conversation from one side of the valley to the other was assuming the tone of an interrogation based on rank. It was an inauspicious beginning since the captain was most likely, if not certainly, stationed at the Fortezza. All the same, a response was necessary.

"Lieutenant Drogo!" Giovanni introduced himself with another shout.

The captain didn't know him nor in all probability could he grasp the name at that distance. But he seemed to be satisfied since he resumed his journey, signaling he understood, as if to say they would soon meet again. After half an hour, in fact, at a pass in the gorge, a bridge appeared. The two paths merged into one.

The men met at the bridge. The captain, remaining on horseback, approached Drogo and held out his hand. He was about forty, perhaps older, judging from his thin, patrician face. His uniform was coarsely cut but correct in every way. He introduced himself: "Captain Ortiz."

When they shook hands, Drogo felt he had finally entered the world of the Fortezza. That was the first bond and from it would issue innumerable other bonds of every variety—within which he would be confined.

The captain resumed the journey without another word. Drogo followed at his side, a bit behind out of respect for rank, while expecting some unpleasant allusion to the embarrassing conversation they'd just had. But the captain was silent. Perhaps he had no desire to speak or perhaps he was shy and didn't know how to begin. Given the steep road and hot sun, the two horses proceeded slowly.

At length Captain Ortiz said, "I didn't catch your name at that distance a little while ago. Was it Droso I heard?"

Giovanni replied, "Drogo, with a 'g.' Giovanni Drogo. But actually, captain sir, I'm the one who should apologize for shouting." Growing flustered, he added, "I didn't see your rank across the valley."

"Right. It wasn't easy to see," admitted Ortiz, choosing to avoid any contradiction. Then he laughed.

They rode a bit farther, both somewhat embarrassed. Ortiz said, "So where are you headed?"

"Fortezza Bastiani. Isn't this the road?"

"Right. This is it."

They fell silent. It was hot. Mountains were everywhere, gigantic mountains, grassy, wild.

Ortiz said, "Then you're coming to the Fortezza? Perhaps with some communication?"

"No, sir. I'm going to take up my commission. I've been assigned there."

"Assigned to the staff?"

"I believe so. My first appointment."

"Then certainly to the staff. Well well, then. I believe I owe you my congratulations."

"Thank you, captain sir."

They rode in silence for a little while. Giovanni was parched. A wooden canteen hung from the captain's saddle and he heard the water sloshing inside.

Ortiz asked, "For two years?"

"Pardon me, captain, two years?"

"For two years, I say, the usual two-year tour—isn't that right?"

"I don't know. I haven't been told how long."

"Oh, it's always two years for you newly appointed lieutenants, two years and then you leave."

"Is two years the rule for everyone?"

"Yes. For determining seniority, of course, the two years count as four. That's really the important thing. Otherwise nobody would request the appointment. If the Fortezza means getting a head start on a career, you can get used to it. Right?"

Drogo had never heard any of this talk but he didn't want to seem stupid. He tried a vague remark: "Certainly. For many men."

Ortiz didn't dwell on the topic; he seemed not to be interested in it. But now that the ice was broken, Giovanni ventured to ask, "Is seniority double for everyone at the Fortezza?"

"Who do you mean by 'everyone'?"

"The other officers."

Ortiz sniggered. "Everyone indeed! Of course not! Only the junior officers, naturally. Otherwise who would apply to go there?"

Drogo said, "I didn't apply."

"You didn't?"

"No, sir. I learned I was assigned to the Fortezza two days ago."

"Right. That's certainly strange."

They were quiet again. Each of them appeared to be thinking of something else. Then Ortiz said, "Unless—"

Giovanni was roused. "You were saying, captain sir?"

"I was saying: unless no other applications had been made, in which case they assigned the post to you, officially."

"That may be, captain sir."

"Right. That must be it, no doubt."

Drogo gazed at the horses' shadows etched sharply in the dusty road, their heads nodding yes at every step. He heard their hooves beating the ground and the buzz of a bluebottle. But nothing else. The end of the road wasn't visible. Every once in a while, at a bend in the valley, you could make out the road zigzagging upward, very high, cut into the steep mountainside. They would reach a bend, lift their eyes, and there stood the road, ever stretching before them, rising higher and higher.

Drogo said, "Pardon me, captain sir . . . "

"Yes, continue."

"Is there a long way to go?"

"Not very long, perhaps two and a half hours, possibly three at this pace. We might actually get there by noon."

They fell silent for a piece. The horses were drenched with sweat. The captain's was exhausted, dragging its hooves.

Ortiz said, "You come from the Royal Academy, no?"

"Yes, sir."

"Right. Is Colonel Magnus still there?"

"I don't think so. I don't recognize the name."

The valley now narrowed, closing off the road to sunlight. Each side occasionally opened into dark gorges from which icy blasts would descend. When they reached the top of a gorge, the steep, conical mountains could be glimpsed. The mountains seemed so high that you might say two or three days weren't enough to reach the summit.

Ortiz said, "Tell me, lieutenant. Is Major Bosco still there? Does he still run the gunnery school?"

"No sir, I don't think so. That's Zimmerman, Major Zimmerman."

"Right, Zimmerman. I've heard the name. The thing is, many years have passed since I was there. Everybody must be new at this point."

They were both absorbed in thought. The road issued into sunlight again and mountains followed upon mountains, increasingly more precipitous, with sheer rock walls.

Drogo said, "I saw it last night from afar."

"What? The Fortezza?"

"Yes." He paused and then, to be polite, he said, "It must be truly impressive. It seemed immense to me."

"The Fortezza impressive? No, no, it's one of the smallest, a very old construction. From a distance it creates a certain effect."

After a moment of silence he added: "Extremely old, completely outdated."

"But it's one of the principal strongholds, isn't it?"

"No, no, it's a second-rate fort," replied Ortiz. He seemed to take pleasure in disparaging it, although with a peculiar tone, like a father who amuses himself by indicating his son's defects, confident they'll always turn out to be ridiculous when compared with his boundless merits.

"It's a tract of dead frontier," Ortiz added. "Nothing has ever changed. It's been the same for a century."

"What do you mean by 'dead'?"

"A frontier that gives no cause for alarm. Before it lies a vast desert."

"A desert?"

"Right. A desert, stones and sunblasted earth. They call it the Tartar desert."

Drogo asked: "Why 'the Tartar'? Do the Tartars exist?"

"In antiquity, I believe. But they're no more than legend. No one has ever crossed the desert, not even in wars past."

"So the Fortezza has never served any purpose?"

"None at all," said the captain.

As the road continued to rise higher, the trees ended and only sparse shrubbery persisted here and there. What remained was scorched fields, rocks, landslides of red earth.

"Pardon me, captain sir, but are there any villages nearby?"

"Nearby, no. There's San Rocco, but that must be thirty kilometers away."

"There's not much in the way of diversion then, I suppose."

"Right. Not much at all."

The air had turned cooler, and the mountains were rounding off, anticipating the final ridges.

"Don't you get bored there, captain sir?" asked Giovanni in a familiar tone, laughing, as if to say he wouldn't mind it anyway.

"One gets used to it," Ortiz replied. Then he added with an implicit reproach: "I've been there for nearly eighteen years. No, I'm mistaken: a full eighteen."

"Eighteen years?" said Giovanni, impressed.

"Eighteen," the captain confirmed.

A flock of ravens passed very close to the two officers and plunged into the funnel of the valley.

"Ravens," said the captain.

Giovanni didn't respond. He was thinking of the life that awaited him. He felt alien to that world, its solitude, the mountains. He asked, "Do any of the newly appointed officers remain there?"

"Not many nowadays," replied Ortiz, almost regretting he had disparaged the Fortezza, realizing the other man was now going a bit too far. "Almost no one, in fact. Nowadays everybody wants a distinguished garrison. Fortezza Bastiani was once an honor. Now it's virtually a punishment."

Giovanni fell silent but the captain persisted: "It's a frontier garrison, after all. Generally speaking, you'll find some first-rate troops there. But a frontier post is no more and no less than a frontier post. Right."

Drogo said nothing, suddenly feeling depressed. The horizon had broadened. In the distance appeared curious silhouettes of rough-hewn mountains, sharp cliffs that overlapped in the sky.

"Nowadays the thinking is different, even in the army," continued Ortiz. "Fortezza Bastiani was once a great honor. They now call it a dead frontier. They don't understand a frontier is always a frontier and you never know what will happen."

A stream crossed the road. They stopped to let the horses drink. After they dismounted, they strolled around a bit to stretch their legs.

Ortiz said, "You know what's really first-rate?" And he burst into a laugh.

"What, captain sir?"

"Right. The cooking. You'll see how they eat at the Fortezza. This explains the frequency of the inspections. It gets a general once-over every fifteen days."

Drogo laughed out of politeness. He couldn't determine whether Ortiz was an idiot or hiding something or just holding forth like that, so irresponsibly.

"Wonderful," said Giovanni. "I'm hungry!"

"Not much farther to go now. See that mound with a spatter of gravel? We're just behind it."

Resuming the journey, the two officers crossed the mound spattered with gravel and emerged on the edge of a plateau with a slight climb. The Fortezza loomed before them, a few hundred meters away.

It seemed quite small, compared with the view Drogo had the night before. From the central fort, which essentially resembled a barracks with few windows, two low crenellated walls branched out, linking it to lateral redoubts, two to a side. The walls thus formed a weak barricade for the entire pass, which was about five hundred meters wide and closed off at the sides by high, precipitous cliffs.

On the right, just beneath the face of the mountain, the plateau sank into a kind of saddle. Through it ran the ancient road of the pass, which ended at the walls.

The fort was quiet, immersed in the full light of the noon sun, devoid of shadow. The walls (the facade wasn't visible since it was positioned to the north) stretched bare and yellowish. A chimney emitted pale smoke. All along the borders of the central building, the walls, and the redoubts, dozens of sentries could be spotted, rifles propped on their shoulders, methodically walking back and forth, each defining a short space. Like a pendulum in motion, they beat out the passage of time without breaking the spell of immense solitude.

The mountains to the right and left extended as far as the eye could see in rugged chains, apparently inaccessible. They too possessed a yellow, sunblasted color, at least at that hour.

Instinctively Giovanni Drogo halted his horse. Slowly turning his eyes, he stared at the dark walls without managing to decipher their meaning. He thought of a prison; he thought of an abandoned palace. Over the fort a light gust of wind rippled a flag that had earlier hung limp, indistinguishable from the flagpole. A faint echo of a bugle could be heard. The sentries paced slowly. On the square before the entry gate three or four men (distance made it impossible to tell if they were soldiers) loaded sacks onto a cart. Everything stagnated, however, in a mysterious lethargy.

Captain Ortiz had also stopped to observe the building.

"There it is," he said, even though the remark was entirely unnecessary.

Drogo thought, Now he's going to ask what it looks like to me. The idea galled him. But the captain was silent.

Fortezza Bastiani was neither imposing, with its low walls, nor beautiful in any way. Its towers and ramparts weren't picturesque. Absolutely nothing alleviated its starkness or recalled the sweet things of life. Yet Drogo gazed at it, hypnotized, as on the previous night from the base of the gorge. And an inexplicable ardor penetrated his heart.

What lay beyond? Beyond that inhospitable edifice, beyond the merlons, casemates, and powder magazines that cut off the line of sight? What world might open there? How would the kingdom of the north look, the stony desert that no one had ever crossed? The map—Drogo vaguely remembered—demarcated a vast area beyond the border with very few names. Yet from the highest point of the fortress could you at least see a few villages, fields, a house, or just the desolation of an uninhabited wasteland?

He suddenly felt alone. And his soldierly boldness, so casual until that moment—as long as his military experience continued serenely, with the comforts of home, cheery friends always at his side, brief encounters in nocturnal gardens—all at once his self-assurance had failed him. The Fortezza seemed like one of those unfamiliar worlds where he never seriously thought he could belong, not because they appeared loathsome to him, but because they were infinitely remote from his accustomed life. It was a much more demanding world, lacking any grandeur except what was afforded by its geometric laws.

Oh, if only he could turn back! If only he could stop before the threshold of the Fortezza and head back down to the plain, to his city, to his old habits. This was Drogo's first thought, and whether such weakness were shameful for a soldier didn't matter. He was prepared to own it, if need be, provided they allowed him to leave immediately. But a dense cloud rose white over the battlements from the invisible northern horizon, and beneath the perpendicular sun the sentries paced back and forth like automatons, imperturbable. Drogo's horse neighed. Then the tremendous silence returned.

Giovanni finally turned his eyes away from the Fortezza and looked at the captain by his side, hoping for a friendly word. Ortiz too had remained motionless, staring intently at the yellow walls. Yes, he who had lived there for eighteen years was mulling over them, almost bewitched, as if he were eyeing something portentous. He seemed never to tire of that contemplation. A faint smile, a mixture of joy and sadness, slowly lit up his face.

3

As soon as Drogo arrived he reported to Major Matti, the adjutant major first class. The lieutenant on guard duty, a confident and cordial young man by the name of Carlo Morel, accompanied him through the heart of the Fortezza. From the entry gate—where a large, deserted courtyard could be glimpsed—they started down a wide corridor, the end of which was imperceptible. The ceiling vanished in shadow. At regular intervals a thin ray of light entered the narrow embrasures.

Only on the floor above did they encounter a soldier who was carrying a bundle of papers. The bare, damp walls, the silence, the dismal lights—everyone inside that space seemed to have forgotten that somewhere in the world existed flowers, laughing women, cheerful, welcoming homes. Everything inside that space constituted a renunciation. But for whom? For what mysterious good? They were now proceeding to the third floor along a corridor that was exactly the same as the first one. Beyond the walls the distant echo of laughter could be heard. But this seemed improbable to Drogo.

Major Matti was corpulent. He smiled with excessive geniality. His office was huge, even his desk was immense, and it was covered with orderly stacks of papers. There was a color portrait of the king. The major's saber hung from a special wooden peg.

Drogo stood at attention, presented his personal documents, and began to explain that he hadn't requested to be assigned to the Fortezza (he was determined to get himself transferred as soon as possible). Matti, however, interrupted him.

"I knew your father years ago, lieutenant. An exemplary gentleman.

Of course you will bring honor to his memory. Presiding judge of the Supreme Court, if I am not mistaken?"

"No, major sir," said Drogo. "My father was a doctor."

"Ah yes, a doctor, my word, I was confused, a doctor, certainly." Matti seemed embarrassed for a moment and Drogo noted how, in repeatedly lifting his left hand to his collar, he tried to conceal a round spot of grease, evidently fresh, on the breast of his uniform.

The major resumed at once: "It pleases me to see you up here. Do you know what His Majesty Pietro III has said? 'Fortezza Bastiani stands guard over my crown.' And I shall add that it is a great honor to be assigned this responsibility. Are you not of the same persuasion, lieutenant?"

He said these things mechanically, like a formula he had learned years ago and needed to brandish on particular occasions.

"Precisely, major," replied Giovanni. "You're perfectly right. But I confess to having been taken by surprise. I have family in the city. I would prefer, if possible, to stay—"

"Ah, but do you really want to leave us before—one might say—you have even arrived? I am disappointed, I confess, very disappointed."

"It isn't a question of wanting. I wouldn't dare disagree. I mean—"

"I understand," the major sighed, as if he were hearing an old story and could sympathize. "I understand: you imagined the Fortezza would be different, and now you're a bit frightened. But tell me honestly: How can you possibly judge—honestly—if you've just arrived a few minutes ago?"

Drogo said, "Major sir, I have absolutely nothing against the Fortezza. I would just prefer to stay in the city, or at least close by. Do you see what I mean? I speak in confidence. I know you understand these things. I trust in your kindness."

"But of course! Of course!" exclaimed Matti with a chuckle. "That's precisely why we're here! We don't want anyone to remain unwillingly, not even the lowest-ranking sentry. I am just disappointed. You seem to be such a capable young man."

The major fell silent for a moment as if he were pondering the best solution. At this point, Drogo turned his head slightly to the left and lifted his eyes to the window, which opened onto the inner courtyard. He could see the wall opposite, pale yellow and sunbeaten, like the others, dotted with the black rectangles of windows. He also saw a dial indicating two o'clock, and on top of the battlement a sentry walked back and forth, a rifle on his shoulder. But above the edge of the building, amid the blaze of afternoon, rose a distant craggy summit. Only the extreme tip could be seen and in itself it didn't amount to anything extraordinary. For Giovanni Drogo, however, it represented the first visible call of the north country, the legendary kingdom that threatened the Fortezza. And what of the rest? A somnolent light, originating from that region, glimmered through a slowly shifting trail of fog. The major resumed speaking:

"Tell me," he asked Drogo. "Would you like to return immediately? Or would you mind waiting a few months? For us, I repeat, it makes no difference." Then he added to avoid seeming uncivil: "From an official point of view, of course."

"Since I must return," said Giovanni, happily amazed by the absence of any difficulty, "I feel the best thing would be to do it straight off."

"Right you are! Agreed," the major reassured him. "But now I should point out: If you wish to depart immediately, the best thing would be to go on sick roll. You visit the infirmary for a couple days' observation and the doctor gives you a certificate. Many men, after all, can't withstand this altitude."

"Is it really necessary to go on sick roll?" asked Drogo, who wasn't fond of such charades.

"It isn't necessary but it does simplify everything. If you don't take that path, you would have to request a transfer in writing. The request would need to be sent to the Supreme Command, the Supreme Command would need to respond, and it would take at least two weeks. Above all, the colonel would need to get involved, and this is what I would prefer to avoid. He really doesn't like these things. They distress him—that's his word—they distress him as if a wrong had been done to his Fortezza. Look: if I were in your shoes, to be perfectly frank, I would prefer to avoid—"

"Pardon me, major sir," Drogo protested. "I wasn't aware of this situation. If leaving might be bad for me, then it's a different matter."

"Don't even dream of that, lieutenant. You haven't understood me. Either way your career won't suffer. It's only a question—how shall I put it?—of nuance. As I mentioned, of course, the matter doesn't please the colonel. But if you've already made up your mind—"

"No, no," interrupted Drogo, "if things are as you say, perhaps the medical certificate is better."

"Unless—" Matti said with an ingratiating smile, breaking off his sentence at the start.

"Unless what?"

"Unless you resign yourself to stay here four months, which would be the best solution."

"Four months?" asked Drogo, already quite disappointed after the prospect of leaving immediately.

"Four months," Matti confirmed. "The procedure would be much more routine. Let me explain: Twice a year everyone undergoes a medical exam. It's an official requirement. The next exam occurs in four months. In my view, that's your best opportunity. The exam result won't bode well, as you wish. I myself will ensure it. You needn't worry at all.

"Apart from that," the major continued after a pause, "four months are four months and they are sufficient for a personal report. You can be certain the colonel will write it for you. He knows how valuable it can be for your career. But let's be perfectly plain: this is merely my advice; you are absolutely free—"

"Yes, sir," said Drogo. "I understand completely."

"The service here is not laborious," the major emphasized. "Almost all of it is guard duty. And the New Redoubt, which is somewhat more demanding, certainly won't be entrusted to you at the start. No hard work, never fear. If anything, you'll be bored."

Drogo was hardly listening to Matti's explanations. He was strangely attracted to the window square with that peak protruding above the facing wall. A vague feeling he couldn't decipher was worming itself into his psyche. Perhaps it was something stupid, or absurd, a sense-less suggestion.

At the same time, he felt rather cheerful. He was still concerned about leaving but gone was his previous anxiety. He was practically ashamed of the apprehension he experienced on his arrival. Did he really fail to measure up to everyone else? An immediate departure, he now thought, could be equivalent to a confession of inferiority. Thus his self-respect struggled against his desire for his old, familiar life.

"Major," said Drogo, "I thank you for your advice but allow me to think about it until tomorrow."

"Very well," Matti said with obvious satisfaction. "And this evening? Would you like to make an appearance before the colonel in the officers' mess? Or would you prefer to leave the matter unresolved?"

"Can't say for sure," replied Giovanni. "But I do think staying hidden is pointless, especially if I have to be here four months."

"Certainly," the major said. "It'll buck you up. You'll find them amiable, all first-rate officers."

Matti smiled and Drogo understood that the moment had come for him to leave. But first he asked in an apparently calm voice:

"Major, can I get a look northward, at what lies beyond the walls?"

"Beyond the walls? I didn't know you were interested in scenery," replied the major.

"Only a glance, major, just to satisfy my curiosity. I've heard talk about a desert and I've never seen a desert."

"It isn't worth the effort, lieutenant. A drab landscape, utterly destitute of beauty. Take my word; don't give it another thought."

"I won't insist, major," said Drogo. "I didn't think there would be a problem."

Major Matti joined the tips of his pudgy fingers as if he were praying.

"You have asked me," he said, "for the single solitary thing I cannot grant you. Only soldiers on duty have access to the walls and guardrooms. You need to know the password."

"No exception is made, not even for an officer?"

"Not even for an officer. Oh, I know what you're thinking: you urban types find these minutiae ridiculous. The password isn't such a big secret down there. Here, however, it's a different matter."

"Pardon my insistence, major sir—"

"Speak, lieutenant, go ahead."

"I wanted to say: Isn't there even an embrasure, a window, where you can look?"

"Only one. In the colonel's office. No one, unfortunately, thought of a belvedere for the curious. But it isn't worth the effort, I repeat, a worthless landscape. You'll get fed up with that view if you decide to stay."

"Thank you, major. Are you finished with me, sir?" He stood at attention and saluted.

Matti gave a friendly wave with his hand.

"Goodbye, lieutenant. Don't give the view a second thought. It's a worthless landscape, I guarantee you, nonsensical."

That very evening, however, after Lieutenant Morel got off guard duty, he secretly led Drogo along the top of the walls so he could see.

An extremely long corridor lit by sporadic lanterns stretched the entire length of the walls from one end of the pass to the other. A door appeared every so often—depots, workshops, guardrooms. They walked approximately one hundred and fifty meters until they reached the entrance to the third redoubt. An armed sentry stood in the doorway. Morel asked to speak to Lieutenant Grotta, who commanded the watch.

Thus, despite the regulations, they were able to enter. Giovanni found himself in a narrow vestibule. On one wall, beneath a lamp, hung a roster listing the names of the soldiers on duty.

"Come this way," said Morel to Drogo. "We have to act quickly."

Drogo followed him up a narrow staircase that led into the open air on the battlements of the redoubt. To the sentry who crossed that space Lieutenant Morel gestured as if to say formalities were unnecessary.

Giovanni suddenly found himself looking out from the merlons that ran along the perimeter: before him, awash in the light of sunset, the valley fell precipitously. The secrets of the north lay open to his eyes.

As Drogo stared, a faint pallor overtook his stony face. The nearby sentry had stopped and a limitless silence seemed to descend amid the haloes of dusk. Then, without shifting his gaze, Drogo asked:

"And behind? What is it like behind those rocks? Is it like this all the way to the end?"

"I've never seen it," replied Morel. "You'd need to go to the New Redoubt, that one down below, on top of the cone-shaped rock. From there you can see the whole plain that stretches before it. They say—" And here he fell silent.

"They say? What do they say?" Drogo asked. An unusual agitation trembled in his voice.

"They say it's a kind of desert consisting entirely of stones, white stones. They say it looks like snow."

"Stones? That's all?"

"So they say, and some marshy ground."

"But all the way to the end? Can't you see anything to the north?"

"Mists usually cover the horizon," said Morel, who had lost the cordial exuberance he displayed before. "The mists from the north obstruct visibility."

"Mists!" exclaimed Drogo, incredulous. "They can't be permanent. On some days the horizon must be clear."

"Almost never, not even in winter. But there are those who claim to have seen."

"Claim? To have seen what?"

"They were dreaming; that's all. You know you can't take soldiers at their word. One says one thing; another says something else. Some say they've seen white towers; others say there's a volcano spewing smoke and that's where the mists originate. Even Ortiz, the captain, swears he saw something, five years ago at this point. To hear him tell it, there's a long black stain, which must be forests."

They were quiet. Where had Drogo seen that world before? Had he perhaps experienced it in a dream? Or had he constructed it by reading some ancient fairy tale? He seemed to recognize it—the crumbling low cliffs, the torturous valley lacking plants or greenery, those crooked ravines, and finally that triangle of desolate plain which the facing rocks could not conceal. The most profound echoes were reawakened in his mind but he failed to grasp them.

Drogo stared at the northern world, the wasteland that no man, according to legend, had ever crossed. No enemies had ever advanced from there, no battle had ever been fought, nothing had ever happened.

"And so?" asked Morel, searching for a jovial tone. "Do you like it?"

"Can't say." This was the only response Drogo could manage. Confused desires swirled inside him, along with senseless fears.

The sound of a bugle could be heard, a muffled sound, from some indeterminate place.

"You better go now," Morel advised. But Giovanni seemed not to hear, absorbed as he was in ransacking his thoughts for something. The evening light grew dim and the wind, revived by the shadows, slipped along the geometric architecture of the Fortezza. The sentry warmed himself by resuming his patrol, glancing periodically at Giovanni Drogo, who was unknown to him.

"You better go now," Morel repeated, grabbing his colleague by an arm.

4

DROGO had often been alone, occasionally as a child, lost in the countryside, at other moments in the city at night, in streets rife with crime, and even that first night, when he slept by the road. But he was now experiencing something quite different, since the excitement of the journey had ended and his new colleagues were already asleep. He was sitting in his room, beneath the lamplight, on the edge of the bed, sad and forlorn. Now he truly understood the nature of solitude (the room wasn't ugly, all paneled in wood, with a huge bed, a table, an uncomfortable couch, a wardrobe). Everyone had been kind to him; in the mess they had opened a bottle in his honor. But now they couldn't care less about him; they had completely forgotten about him (over the bed hung a wooden crucifix, on the opposite wall an old print with a long caption, only the first words of which were legible: *Humanissimi Viri Francisci Angloisi virtutibus*). No one for the duration of the entire night would come to greet him; no one in the whole Fortezza would think of him. And not only in the Fortezza. Probably in the whole world as well not a soul would think about Drogo. Each person has his own concerns; each person can barely fend for himself. Even mamma, even she was likely to be preoccupied with other things at this moment. He wasn't her only child. All day she had thought about Giovanni; now the others would get their chance. It was more than fair, admitted Giovanni Drogo without a trace of reproach. But still he was sitting on the edge of a bed in a room at the Fortezza (he now noticed a life-size saber, carved in the wall panel, painted with extraordinary patience—it might even seem real at first sight—the meticulous work of some officer, who knows how many years ago). His head was bowed slightly, his back hunched, his eyes unfocused and dull. And he felt alone as never before in his life.

Here Drogo stood with effort, opened the window, looked outside. The window gave onto the courtyard; nothing else was visible. Since he was looking southward, Giovanni sought in vain to distinguish, in the night, the mountains he had crossed to reach the Fortezza. They turned out to be lower, hidden by the facing wall.

Only three windows were lit but they belonged to the same side of the building as his, so he couldn't see inside them. The light they cast was imprinted on the opposite wall, enlarged. In one of them a shadow was fidgeting: perhaps an officer was undressing.

He closed the window, undressed, got into bed, and continued to think for a few minutes, staring at the ceiling, which was also paneled in wood. He had forgotten to bring something to read but that evening it didn't bother him, since he felt very sleepy. He extinguished the lamp. The bright rectangle of the window gradually emerged from the darkness. Drogo saw the stars shine.

He felt as if a sudden lethargy were dragging him into sleep. But he was much too aware of it. A confused mass of images, virtually a dream, passed before him; they even began to form a narrative. After a few moments, however, he realized he was still awake.

More awake than before, since the magnitude of the silence struck him. A coughing fit arrived from far away (was it real then?). Close by, a sluggish drip of water traveled through the walls. A tiny green star on its nocturnal journey (lying still, he spotted it) approached the upper edge of the window; in a short while it would disappear. It gleamed for an instant exactly on the black frame, then vanished. Drogo wanted to keep following it a little longer, bending his head forward. At that point he heard another drip, like the sound of an object plopping in water. Would it be repeated? He lay in wait for the sound—noise from cellars, swamps, abandoned houses. Minutes passed at a snail's pace. Absolute silence, finally, seemed to be the uncontested lord of the Fortezza. And again senseless images of a distant life bore down upon Drogo.

Plop! That odious sound again. He sat up. The noise was repetitive. The last drips hadn't been smaller than the first ones; the dripping wasn't tailing off. How could he possibly sleep? Drogo recalled that a cord hung at the side of the bed, perhaps for a bell. He gave it a tug, the cord yielded, and a brief ringing, almost imperceptible, responded in a remote labyrinth of the building. How stupid, Drogo now thought, to call someone for such a petty reason. Who would come at this hour?

After a short while, steps resounded in the corridor outside. They grew closer and someone knocked at the door. "Come in!" said Drogo. A soldier appeared, holding a lantern. "How can I help, lieutenant sir?"

"It's impossible to get any damn sleep here!" shouted Drogo, flying into a cold-blooded rage. "What is that abominable noise? Some leaking pipe? You had better make it stop. I can't possibly get any sleep. Just put a rag under it."

"It's the cistern, lieutenant sir." The soldier replied immediately, as if he were familiar with the matter. "Nothing can be done."

"The cistern?"

"Yes, sir." The soldier explained: "It's where water is stored, right behind that wall. Everybody complains but nothing can be done. This isn't the only place you can hear it. Even Captain Fonzaso shouts every so often but nothing can be done."

"Go on, then, leave me," said Drogo. The door closed. The steps grew distant. The silence unfolded anew and the stars shone in the window. Giovanni's thoughts now turned to the sentries who a few meters away were walking like automatons back and forth without a moment's rest. Scores of men were awake while he was lying in bed, while everything seemed immersed in sleep. Scores, thought Drogo—but for whom, for what? In that fort military formalism had created an insane masterpiece. Hundreds of men to guard a mountain pass that no one would cross. Leave, leave as soon as possible, thought Giovanni, break free of that ambience, of that foggy enigma. Oh, the virtues of home! At this hour, mamma would certainly be sleeping, the lights all put out—unless he lingered in her thoughts for a moment, which was indeed more than likely. He knew her well, the smallest thing might make her anxious, and at night she would toss and turn in her bed without finding any rest.

Again the cistern dripped. Again a star crossed the window frame, and its light continued to reach the world, the battlements of the Fortezza, the sentries' febrile eyes. But not Giovanni Drogo, who was awaiting sleep, now tormented by sinister thoughts.

What if Matti's piddling distinctions were nothing but a pretense? What if in reality they wouldn't let him leave after four months? What if they prevented him from seeing the city again with sophistical pretexts based on regulations? What if he were forced to remain there for years on end, wasting his youth in that room, on that solitary bed? What absurd hypotheses, Drogo said to himself, realizing their foolishness. Yet he couldn't drive them away, for they quickly returned to test him, protected by the solitude of night.

Thus he felt as if an obscure conspiracy were growing around him, seeking to detain him. It probably had nothing to do with Matti. Neither Matti, nor the colonel, nor any other officer had the slightest interest in him, and whether he remained or departed was a matter of utter indifference to them. Nonetheless, an unfamiliar force was militating against his return to the city, perhaps originating in his very soul yet beyond his consciousness.

Then he saw an atrium, a horse on a white road, he heard his name called, and sleep seized him.

5

Two nights later Giovanni Drogo took his first turn of duty at the third redoubt. At six in the afternoon seven guard units assembled in the courtyard: three for the fort, four for the lateral redoubts. The eighth, stationed at the New Redoubt, had set out beforehand because they had some distance to cover.

Sergeant Major Tronk, a fixture at the Fortezza, led twenty-eight men to the third redoubt, plus the bugler, who made twenty-nine. They were all from the second company, under Captain Ortiz, to whom Giovanni had been assigned. Drogo assumed command and drew his sword.

The seven guard units standing at attention were drawn up in a perfect line, and from the window, according to tradition, the commanding colonel examined them. On the yellow earth of the courtyard they formed a black pattern, beautiful to see.

The windswept sky glowed on the walls, which were cut diagonally by the last rays of sunlight. A September evening. The vice commander, Lieutenant Colonel Nicolosi, issued from the main entrance of the command, limping from an old wound, and leaned on his sword. That day the huge Captain Monti was on duty for the inspection. His gruff voice gave the order and all together, positively together, the soldiers presented their weapons with a powerful metallic roar. A vast silence ensued.

Then, one by one, the buglers of the seven units sounded the usual calls. They played the famous silver bugles of Fortezza Bastiani draped with cords of red and gold silk and a noble coat of arms. Their pure tone was dispersed through the sky, vibrating the motionless barrier of bayonets with a faint bell-like resonance. The soldiers stood still as statues; their faces were impassive in military fashion. No, they were certainly not preparing for the monotonous turns of guard duty. Their heroic demeanor rather suggested they were heading to face the enemy.

The final call remained suspended in the air, repeated by the distant walls. The bayonets glittered a moment longer, shiny against the deep sky, whereafter they were engulfed within the ranks, simultaneously extinguished. The colonel had disappeared from the window. The tread of the seven units echoed through the labyrinths of the Fortezza, radiating toward their particular posts.

An hour later Giovanni Drogo stood on the rampart of the third redoubt in the same spot where the night before he had gazed toward the north. Yesterday he had come to gawk like a traveler in transit. Now, however, he was in charge: for twenty-four hours the entire redoubt and a hundred meters of wall fell under his sole authority. Below him, inside the casemate, four gunners were tending to the two cannons aimed at the base of the valley. Three sentries were dividing up the perimeter of the redoubt; another four were spaced out along the wall toward the right, twenty-five meters apart.

The changing of the guard had occurred with meticulous precision under the eyes of Sergeant Major Tronk, who was an expert in regulations. Tronk had been at the Fortezza for twenty-two years and at this point he would stay put even when he was entitled to a furlough. No one knew every corner of the fortification as well as he did. Often at night officers would encounter him carrying out his inspection in pitch darkness without even the dimmest lamp. When he was on duty, the sentries wouldn't abandon their rifles for an instant or lean against the walls, and they would studiously avoid stopping since breaks were granted only as an exception. Tronk wouldn't sleep for the entire night. Instead he made the rounds noiselessly, giving the sentries a start. "Who goes there?" they asked, raising their rifles. "Grotta," answered the sergeant major. "Gregorio," they returned.

In practice officers on guard duty, whether commissioned or non-commissioned, roamed around their own section of the walls without ceremony. The soldiers knew them by sight and the exchange of passwords would've seemed ridiculous. Only with Tronk did the soldiers follow the procedure to the letter.

He was short and thin, his face like a frail old man's, his head shaven. He said very little, even with colleagues, and in general he preferred to spend his free time alone, studying music. That was his obsession, so much so that the bandmaster, Marshal Espina, may have been his only friend. He possessed a splendid accordion but he almost never played it, although legend holds he could've played admirably. He studied harmony and they said he had written diverse military marches. But no one knew anything definite about him.

When he was on duty, there was never any risk he would start whistling as he habitually did when he was off duty. For the most part he would wander around the battlements, scrutinizing the deep valley to the north in search of some unknown thing. Now he was at Drogo's side, pointing out the mule track that led to the New Redoubt along steep ridges.

"Here's the guard that just came off duty," said Tronk, waving his right index finger, although Drogo was unable to discern it in the dim dusk light. The sergeant major shook his head.

"What is it?" Drogo asked.

"It just isn't right," replied Tronk. "I've told them over and over. It's crazy."

"What happened?"

"It isn't right," repeated Tronk. "The changing of the guard should be done first at the New Redoubt. But the colonel doesn't want that."

Giovanni looked at him, amazed. Could it be that Tronk was allowing himself to criticize the colonel?

"The colonel"—the sergeant major continued with profound seriousness and conviction, certainly not in an effort to correct his last words—"the colonel is perfectly right from his point of view. No one, however, has explained the danger to him."

"The danger?" Drogo asked. What danger could there possibly be in traveling from the Fortezza to the New Redoubt by that effortless path in such a deserted area?

"The danger," repeated Tronk. "Someday something is going to happen in this darkness."

"So what should be done?" Drogo asked to be polite. This whole rigmarole really didn't interest him.

"Once upon a time," the sergeant major said, quite pleased with the opportunity to flaunt his expertise, "the guard at the New Redoubt would be changed two hours before the one at the Fortezza. It was always done during the daylight hours, even in winter, and the business with the password was simplified. It was needed to enter the redoubt and a new one was needed for the day's guard and the return to the Fortezza. Two were sufficient. When the off-duty guard was on its way back to the Fortezza, the new guard wasn't yet in place here so the password was still valid."

"Right. I understand," said Drogo, abandoning the effort to follow him.

"But then," Tronk related, "they got scared. It's rash, they said, to let so many soldiers circulate outside the walls when they know the password. You can never know what will happen, they said. One solider in a group of fifty is more likely to turn traitor than a single officer."

"Right," agreed Drogo.

"So they decided that only the commanding officer should know the password. The guard now sets out from the Fortezza three quarters of an hour before the change. Let's take today. The change is scheduled for six o'clock. The guard for the New Redoubt left here at quarter past five and arrived there at exactly six. A password isn't needed to leave the Fortezza because the soldiers form a detachment. To enter the redoubt they needed yesterday's password and only the officer knew it. When the change is completed at the redoubt, today's password goes into effect and again only the officer knows it. It lasts twenty-four hours, until the new guard comes to make the change. Tomorrow evening, then, when the soldiers return to the Fortezza (they should arrive by quarter past six since the journey back is less onerous), the password is again changed. So a third password is needed. The officer must know three: one for the outward journey, one for the guard duty, and one for the return. All these complications exist to keep the soldiers in transit from knowing.

"But here's what I think," he continued without worrying whether Drogo was paying attention. "If only the officer knows the password, and he—let's suppose—gets sick on the road, what do the soldiers do? They can't force him to give it up. They can't go back where they came from because the password has already been changed there. Has anyone thought about this? And if secrecy is the object, don't they realize it makes three passwords necessary instead of two and the third to get back into the Fortezza the next day goes into effect more than twenty-four hours before? Whatever happens, they're forced to keep to it; otherwise the guard can't get back in."

"But won't they be recognized at the gate?" objected Drogo. "Surely they'll be able to see it's the guard returning from their post!"

Tronk responded with a look of superiority. "This is impossible, lieutenant. The Fortezza has its rules. No one, no matter who he is, can enter from the north without the password."

"But then," Drogo said, irritated by this absurd rigidity, "wouldn't it be simpler to create a special password for the New Redoubt? The change is made earlier and the password to reenter is assigned only to the officer. The soldiers would know nothing."

"No doubt," said the noncommissioned officer, nearly triumphant, as if he had headed off the objection at the pass, "it might seem like the best solution. But the regulation would need to be changed and that requires a law. The regulation reads"—he adopted a pedantic tone—"'The password lasts twenty-four hours from one changing of the guard to the next; a single password is in force at the Fortezza and its dependencies.' It says precisely 'its dependencies.' The passage is clear. There are no two ways about it."

"But once upon a time," said Drogo, who from the beginning had not been attentive, "wasn't the change at the New Redoubt done earlier?"

"Exactly!" exclaimed Tronk. But then he checked himself. "Yes, sir. The current procedure has only been in place for two years. Previously it was much better."

The noncommissioned officer fell silent and Drogo stared at him, horrified. After twenty-two years at the Fortezza, what was left of that soldier? Did Tronk ever remember that the world contained millions of men who were like him but didn't wear a uniform, who freely wandered through cities and at night could, at their pleasure, go to bed or the osteria or the theater? No. A mere glance at him was enough to make you comprehend: Tronk had forgotten about other men; for him nothing existed but the Fortezza and its odious regulations. Tronk no longer remembered how the sweet voices of young women sound or how gardens are laid out or what a river is like or trees—he remembered nothing but the scrawny, sporadic bushes scattered around the Fortezza. Tronk looked toward the north, certainly, but not with Drogo's sensibility. His eyes were fixed on the path to the New Redoubt, on the moat and the counterscarp, and he scrutinized every possible approach but not the savage cliffs or that triangle of mysterious plain and certainly not the white clouds that sailed through the sky as night fell.

With darkness descending the desire to flee once again took possession of Drogo. Why—he upbraided himself—didn't he leave immediately? Why had he yielded to Matti's mellifluous diplomacy? Now he had to wait for four months to elapse, one hundred and twenty interminable days, half of which would be spent on the walls, doing guard duty. He felt as if he were among men of another race, in a strange land, a hard, ungrateful world. He gathered his wits about himself and recognized Tronk, who was standing motionless, observing the sentries.

6

Night had now fallen. Drogo sat in his bare room in the redoubt. He had requested that paper, ink, and pen be brought to him. He would write.

"Cara mamma," he began, and at once he felt as if he were a child again. Alone, in the lamplight, unseen by anyone, in the heart of the strange Fortezza, far from home, from all the good, familiar things, he felt consoled that at least he could open his heart completely.

Of course, with the others, with fellow officers, he had to act like a man, had to laugh with them and tell cocksure tales of the military and of women. To whom could he tell the truth, if not his mother? Besides, Drogo's truth that evening wasn't the truth of the consummate soldier. It probably wasn't worthy of the austere Fortezza, and his colleagues would've laughed. His truth was the exhaustion from a journey, the oppression of gloomy walls, and the feeling of being utterly alone.

"I arrived worn out after two days' travel"—he would have written—"and after I arrived, I learned that if I wanted, I could return to the city. The Fortezza is melancholy. It has no nearby villages, no entertainment to speak of, no joy." This is what he would have written.

But Drogo remembered his mother. At that hour she would be thinking precisely of him and she would take comfort in the idea that her son was spending the night pleasurably with congenial friends, possibly even in polite company. She would certainly believe he was satisfied and happy.

"Cara mamma," his hand wrote. "I arrived the day before yesterday after an excellent journey. The Fortezza is magnificent—" Oh, if only

34

he could make her understand the dreariness of those walls, the vague atmosphere of punishment and exile, the alien, absurd men. Instead he wrote, "The officers here gave me a warm welcome. Even the adjutant major has been very kind, from the beginning, and he left me completely free to return to the city if I wanted. Still, I—"

At that moment, perhaps, mamma was walking around his abandoned room, opening a drawer, tidying up his old clothes, his books, his desk. She had already put them in order so many times but the task enabled her to recover his living presence a bit, as if he would be getting home, as usual, before dinner. He felt as if he could hear the recognizable sound of her soft, restless steps, which were always expressive of worry about someone. Did he really have the heart to disappoint her? If he were near her, in the same room, and they were huddled together beneath a familiar lamp, then Giovanni would tell her everything and she wouldn't have enough time to get sad because he was beside her and the painfulness was now past. But from this distance? By letter? Sitting next to her, before the fireplace, in the reassuring peace of the old house, he would've spoken of Major Matti and his insidious cajolery, of Tronk's obsessions! He would've told her how he stupidly agreed to stay another four months and probably they both would've laughed about it. But how could he say this from so far away?

"Still, I thought it best," wrote Drogo, "for me and for my career to stay here for a while. The company is quite pleasant and the service easy, not at all laborious." And what about his room, the noise from the cistern, the encounter with Captain Ortiz, the desolate land to the north? Did he have to explain to her the iron regulations that governed the guard and the bare redoubt where he found himself? No, not even with his mother could he be candid; not even to her could he confess the obscure fear that left him no peace.

In his home, in the city, the clocks would now be striking ten, one after another, in different voices, and their sounds would faintly clink the glasses in the credenzas. From the kitchen would arrive an echo of laughter and from another part of the street a melody played on a piano. From the place where he was sitting, through an extremely narrow window, virtually a slit, Drogo could cast a glance toward the northern valley, that sad land. Yet now nothing but darkness could be seen. The pen squeaked a little. Even though night had triumphed, the wind began to blow through the battlements, bearing unfamiliar messages. Even though dense shadows had accumulated inside the redoubt and the air was damp and noisome, "In general," wrote Giovanni Drogo, "I am quite happy and doing well."

From nine at night till dawn a bell rang every half hour in the fourth redoubt at the far right corner of the pass where the walls stopped. A little bell rang and at once the last sentry called out to his closest colleague. From here to the next soldier and then onward to the opposite end of the walls, from one redoubt to the next, through the fort and again along the ramparts, the call made the rounds during the night. "Stay alert! Stay alert!" The sentries didn't put any enthusiasm in the shout; they repeated it mechanically in strange tones of voice.

Stretched out on the cot, still dressed, invaded by an increasing lethargy, Giovanni Drogo heard that shout arrive at intervals from afar. Only "err . . . err . . . err" would reach him. It would grow louder and louder, pass above him with maximum intensity, and recede on the other side, gradually diminishing into nothing. After a couple of minutes it would return, sent out again as a countercheck from the first redoubt on the left. Drogo heard it approach at a slow, even pace: "err . . . err . . . err." Only when it was above him, repeated by his own sentries, did he manage to distinguish the words. But soon the "Stay alert!" was conflated into a kind of dirge that finally died at the last sentry, against the foot of the cliffs.

Four times Giovanni heard the shout arrive and travel back down the battlements to the point where it had originated. The fifth time it reached Drogo's consciousness as a faint echo that provoked a brief tremor in him. He was aware that sleeping wasn't a good thing for the officer of the guard. The regulations permitted it only if the officer didn't undress. Yet in a gesture of elegant hauteur almost all the young officers at the Fortezza stayed awake the entire night, reading, smoking cigars, indulging in unauthorized visits to each other, and playing cards. Tronk, with whom Giovanni had first made inquiries, led him to understand that staying awake was normal procedure.

Stretched out on the cot, however, outside the glow of the oil lamp, fantasizing about his own life, Giovanni Drogo was suddenly seized by sleep. Meanwhile that very night—if only he had known, he might have lost the desire to sleep—the irreparable flight of time was beginning for him.

Until then he had advanced through the carefree period of early youth, a journey that to a child seems infinite, where years pass slowly with such a light step that no one notices their conclusion. You walk placidly, surveying what lies about you with curiosity. No need to hurry. No one presses behind you; no one expects you. Even friends proceed without thinking, stopping often to joke. From houses, in doorways, adults deal out benign greetings, pointing to the horizon with knowing smiles. Thus your heart begins to beat with desires, both heroic and tender. You savor the foretaste of the marvelous things that lie in wait farther ahead. You still don't see them but you're certain, absolutely certain, that one day you shall reach them.

Still far away? No, you need only cross that river down below and pass beyond those green hills. Or have you, by chance, arrived already? Weren't you searching for these trees, these fields, this white house? For several moments you feel the answer is yes and you'd like to stop here. Then you hear the best is yet to come and you resume the journey, unfaltering.

And so the walk continues in hopeful expectation. The days are long and tranquil. The sun blazes high in the sky and seems to lack the will to set.

But at a certain point, almost instinctively, you turn around and see that a gate has been bolted behind you, closing off the way back. You feel something has changed. The sun no longer seems motionless; it's rather moving rapidly, much to your dismay, leaving you hardly any time to watch it plummet toward the edge of the horizon. You notice the clouds no longer lag in the azure gulfs of the sky but fly in such haste they're heaped on top of each other. You grasp the passage of time and the inevitable end of the journey.

At a certain point they close a heavy gate behind us and lock it with lightning speed, leaving no time to turn back. Giovanni Drogo, however, was now sleeping, unaware, and smiling like a baby.

Days will pass before Drogo comprehends what has happened. He will then experience an awakening. As he gets his bearings, he will be incredulous, at which point he will hear the clamor of footsteps approaching from behind and see the people who have awakened before him, running breathlessly and overtaking him in an effort to arrive sooner. He will hear the beat of time greedily measuring out life. Now the smiling figures that used to appear at windows will be replaced by motionless, indifferent faces. And if he should ask how much of the journey remains, they will still point to the horizon, although not kindly or with pleasure. Meanwhile friends will be lost to sight. Somebody falls behind exhausted, another has bolted ahead, and soon he is no more than a tiny speck on the horizon.

After that river—people will say—another ten kilometers before you get there. But it never ends. The days become shorter and shorter, fellow travelers more rare, and at windows stand pale, apathetic figures shaking their heads.

Until Drogo is left completely alone and the horizon becomes a strip of boundless sea, motionless and leaden. He is weary. The houses lining the street have almost all their windows shut and the few people he encounters respond to him with a disconsolate gesture: the good lies far behind, very far behind, and he passed it without realizing. Ah, too late to turn back. Behind him swells the roar of the multitude in pursuit, driven by the same illusion but still invisible on the empty white road.

Giovanni Drogo is sleeping inside the third redoubt. He dreams and smiles. For the last time that night he is visited by the sweet images of a world that is utterly happy. He would feel different if he could see himself and how he will be one day, there, where the road ends, standing on the shore of the leaden sea, beneath a gray, uniform sky, and around him not a house or man or tree, not even a blade of grass. And thus it has been from time immemorial.

7

Lieutenant Drogo's clothes locker finally arrived from the city. Among his things was a brand-new cloak of extraordinary elegance. Drogo draped it around his shoulders and examined himself meticulously in the small mirror in his room. The cloak seemed a living connection to his world. He delighted in the thought that it would catch everyone's eye, so sumptuous was the fabric, so dignified its flowing folds.

In his view, he shouldn't waste it on service at the fort, during nights of guard duty, amid damp walls. It was also an ill omen to wear it up there for the first time, as if admitting he wouldn't have better occasions. Still, he didn't like the idea of not showing it off, and although the weather wasn't cold, he wanted at least to wear it on his way to the regiment tailor, where he would buy another, ordinary cloak.

So he left his room and started up the stairs, observing the elegance of his shadow wherever light permitted. But as he descended into the heart of the Fortezza, the cloak seemed somehow to lose its initial magnificence. Drogo also noticed he wasn't able to wear it naturally; it seemed strange, like something designed to attract attention.

So he took pleasure in the fact that stairs and corridors were nearly deserted. He finally encountered a captain who responded to his salute without a glance that was longer than necessary. Not even the occasional soldiers turned their eyes to observe him.

He climbed down a narrow spiral staircase cut into the body of a wall and his steps resounded above and below as if other people were present. The precious skirts of the cloak swayed, flapping against the white mold on the walls.

Thus Drogo reached the underground passageways in the fort. The workshop of the tailor Prosdocimo was in fact located in a cellar. On good days a glimmer of light would stream down through a tiny slit at ground level. That evening, however, lamps had already been lit.

"Buona sera, lieutenant sir," said Prosdocimo, the regiment tailor, as soon as he saw Drogo enter. In the large room only a few small features were lit: a table where a frail old man was writing, the bench where three young assistants labored. All around scores of uniforms, overcoats, and cloaks dangled limp with the sinister abandon of hanged men.

"Buona sera," Drogo replied. "I would like a cloak, not very expensive, something that would last four months."

"Let me see," said the tailor with a smile of suspicious curiosity, grasping the hem of Drogo's cloak and drawing it toward the light. His rank was marshal but his skill as a tailor seemed to grant him a certain ironic familiarity with superiors. "Beautiful fabric, beautiful." He gave the cloak a craftsman's once-over. "You must've paid through the nose for it, I imagine. Down there in the city they don't play around." He shook his head so that his ruddy cheeks quivered. "It's a shame, though—"

"What's a shame?"

"The collar is so low. It isn't very military."

"This is the way it's worn now," Drogo said with superiority.

"The low collar might be fashionable," said the tailor, "but for us military men fashion doesn't matter. It has to be regulation and the regulation states that 'the collar of the cloak must be close-fitting to the neck, shaped like a belt, seven centimeters high.' Perhaps, lieutenant, seeing me in this hole, you think I'm some catchpenny tailor."

"Why?" said Drogo. "Just the opposite, in fact."

"You, sir, probably think I'm second-rate. However, many officers appreciate me, even in the city, including officers of distinction. I am up here in an ab-so-lute-ly pro-vi-sion-al capacity." He syllabified the two keywords so as to underscore their considerable importance.

Drogo didn't know what to say.

"I expect to leave any day now," continued Prosdocimo. "If it weren't for the colonel, who doesn't want to let me go… What do you people think is so funny?"

In the dim light, in fact, you could hear the muffled laughter of the three assistants. They had bowed their heads, exaggerating their application to their work. The old man continued to write, keeping to himself.

"What is there to laugh about?" Prosdocimo asked again. "You lads are a bit too flippant. One of these days you'll wise up."

"Indeed," said Drogo. "What is there to laugh about?"

"They're dunces," said the tailor. "Best not pay them any mind."

At that moment you could hear footsteps coming down the staircase. A soldier appeared. Prosdocimo was summoned upstairs by the marshal who oversaw the clothing depot. "Excuse me, lieutenant," the tailor said. "It's a matter of duty. I'll return shortly." And he followed the soldier upstairs.

Drogo sat down, prepared to wait. The three assistants, seeing their master had gone, stopped working. The old man finally lifted his eyes from his papers, rose to his feet, and limped toward Giovanni.

"Did you hear him?" he asked in a strange accent, gesturing to indicate the tailor who had left. "Did you hear him, lieutenant? Do you know how many years he has been here at the Fortezza?"

"No, I wouldn't know."

"Fifteen years, sir, fifteen damn years, and he keeps telling the same old story: 'I am here in a provisional capacity; any day now I expect—'"

Someone mumbled at the assistants' table. That story must be the usual target of their scorn. The old man didn't pay the least attention.

"But he'll never budge. He, the colonel, and many others will stay here till they give up the ghost. It's a sort of illness. You better watch out, lieutenant. You're new; you just turned up. Watch out while you've still got time."

"Watch out for what?"

"Better leave as soon as you can. Don't let their obsession take hold of you."

"I'm only here four months," Drogo said. "I don't have the slightest intention of staying."

The old man said, "Watch out regardless, lieutenant. It all started with Colonel Filimore. 'Great things are about to happen,' he began to say—I remember very clearly. It was eighteen years ago. He would just say 'things.' That was his word for it. He'd gotten it into his head that the Fortezza was extremely important, much more important than all the other forts, and no one in the city understood anything."

He spoke so slowly that silence had enough time to creep in between each word.

"He'd gotten it into his head that the Fortezza was extremely important, that something had to happen."

Drogo smiled. "What would happen? Do you mean a war?"

"Who knows? Maybe even a war."

"A war coming from the desert?"

"Most likely from the desert," confirmed the old man.

"But who? Who would come?"

"How do I know? No one is coming; that's for sure. But the commanding officer has studied the maps and he believes the Tartars are out there, a remnant of the old army roving all over the place."

You could hear the idiotic snickers of the three assistants in the shadows.

"And they are still here, waiting," continued the old man. "Look at the colonel, Captain Stizione, Captain Ortiz, the lieutenant colonel. Year after year something has to happen. It's always the same, until they're pensioned off." He paused and bent his head to one side as if to listen. "I thought I heard footsteps," he said. But none could be heard.

"I didn't hear a thing," said Drogo.

"Prosdocimo too," said the old man. "He's a simple marshal, the regiment tailor, but he's gone along with them. He's waiting too and it's been fifteen years already. But you aren't convinced, lieutenant; I see it. You say nothing and think it's all nonsense." Then he added as if he were pleading: "Watch out, I'm telling you. You'll let them sway you and you'll wind up staying too. I can see it in your eyes."

Drogo was silent. To confide in such a poor devil, he felt, was unworthy of an officer.

"But what about you?" he said. "What do you do?"

"Me?" the old man said. "I'm his brother. I'm here to work with him."

"His brother? His older brother?"

"That's right," the old man smiled. "Older brother. I too served in the military once. Then I broke a leg. Now I'm reduced to this."

In the subterranean silence Drogo heard the beat of his own heart, which had started to pound. So this old man holed up in the cellar doing accounts, this obscure, humble creature—was he too awaiting a heroic destiny? Giovanni stared into his eyes and the other man briefly shook his head with bitter mournfulness as if to signify, There's really no cure, we're done, and we'll never get better again.

Perhaps because a door was opened at some point on the stairs, you could now hear distant human voices of indeterminate origin, filtered by the walls. Every so often they stopped, leaving a void, but a little later they surfaced again, coming and going as if the Fortezza were slowly breathing.

Now Drogo finally understood. He stared at the myriad shadows of the hanging uniforms as they trembled in the flickering lamps and he thought about how at that very moment the colonel had, in the secrecy of his office, opened the window that faced northward. He was certain: at such an hour, so sad in the autumnal darkness, the commanding officer of the Fortezza was gazing toward the north, toward the black abyss of the valley.

From the northern desert would arrive their fortune, the occasion of their exploits, the miraculous hour that befalls everyone at least once. Because of this vague eventuality, which grew increasingly uncertain with time, grown men wasted the best part of their lives there.

They hadn't adapted to ordinary existence, the joys that people usually experience, the unexceptional fate. They were living side by side with the same hope, although without ever mentioning it, because they didn't realize what they shared or simply because they were soldiers who possessed the wary reserve that characterizes the military sensibility.

Perhaps Tronk too, most likely. Tronk pursued rules and regulations as well as rigorous discipline, taking pride in scrupulous responsibility, and he deluded himself that all this would suffice. But if he were told: Your entire life will be the same, utterly the same, till the very last moment, even he would be roused. Impossible, he would respond. Something else must come to pass, something truly worthy, enabling him to say, Now, even if I lie at death's door, I can rest.

Drogo had grasped their transparent secret. And he was relieved to think he stood apart from it, the uncontaminated onlooker. Within four months—thank God—he would leave them behind forever. The dark appeal of the old fort had ridiculously dissipated. Or so he thought. But why did the old man keep staring at him with that ambiguous expression? Why did Drogo feel the desire to whistle, drink wine, stroll out into the open air? Did he feel the need, perhaps, to demonstrate to himself that he was truly free, truly without worry?

8

HERE ARE Drogo's new friends: the lieutenants Carlo Morel, Pietro Angustina, Francesco Grotta, Max Lagorio. They are sitting with him in the mess hall in the dead of night. Only one orderly remains, leaning against the frame of a distant door, along with the portraits of bygone colonels aligned on the surrounding walls, immersed in shadow. Eight bottles stand black against the tablecloth in the disorder of the finished dinner.

They are all somewhat worked up, partly by the wine, partly by the night. Whenever their voices fall silent, you can hear the rain outside.

They are honoring Count Max Lagorio, who departs the following day after two years at the Fortezza.

"Angustina," Lagorio said, "if you come as well, I'll wait for you." His tone was joking, as usual, but he was obviously being sincere.

Angustina had also finished a two-year stint but he didn't want to leave. Pale, he sat with his perennial air of detachment as if he couldn't care less about them, as if he were there by pure chance.

"Angustina," repeated Lagorio on the brink of drunkenness, nearly shouting, "if you come as well, I'll wait for you. I would fain wait three days."

Without responding Lieutenant Angustina assumed a faint smile of tolerance. His blue uniform, faded by the sun, stood out among the others because of an indefinably shabby elegance.

Lagorio turned to the others—to Morel, Grotta, Drogo. "You too must tell him," he said, placing his right hand on Angustina's shoulder. "The city would do him good."

"Do me good?" asked Angustina as if his curiosity were piqued.

"Look: you would feel better in the city. Everybody would, in my view."

"I feel just fine," said Angustina sharply. "I don't need any looking after."

"I didn't say you did. I said the city would do you good."

As Lagorio spoke, you could hear the rain falling outside in the courtyard. Angustina smoothed his moustache with two fingers. He was visibly bored.

Lagorio resumed: "You're not thinking about your mother, your family. Imagine when your mamma—"

"My mother will know how to adapt," interjected Angustina with an undertone of bitterness.

Lagorio sensed it and changed the subject. "Say, Angustina, suppose you turn up at Claudina's place the day after tomorrow? She hasn't seen you in two years."

"Claudina," said Angustina blankly. "Who's Claudina? I don't remember her."

"You don't remember her?! You couldn't talk about anything else tonight. That's a fact. It doesn't take much to figure out—does it? You were seen together every day."

"Ah," said Angustina to be polite, "now I remember: Claudina. No way! She won't even remember I exist."

"Come off it," protested Grotta. "Everybody knows women go crazy for you. Don't play modest!" Angustina stared at him without batting an eye, clearly taken aback by such banality.

They were quiet. Outside, in the night, under the autumnal rain, the sentries paced. The water was bucketing down on the terraces, gurgling in the gutters, streaming down the walls. Outside the night was deep. Angustina suffered a brief bout of coughing. It seemed strange that such a refined young man could make a sound so disagreeable. Yet he coughed with a calculated restraint, lowering his head each time as if to indicate that he couldn't prevent it, that fundamentally it didn't belong to him, but out of politeness he had to put up with it. Thus he transformed the cough into a kind of whimsical affectation, worthy of being imitated.

All the same, an awkward silence had descended upon them and Drogo felt the need to break it.

"Say, Lagorio," he asked, "what time do you depart tomorrow?"

"Around ten, I believe. I wanted to set out earlier but I still have to take my leave of the colonel."

"The colonel rises at five, summer or winter. He'll make sure you don't waste any time."

Lagorio laughed. "But I don't wake at five. And on my last morning I want to move at my own speed. No one will be hounding me."

"So you'll arrive the day after tomorrow," noted Morel enviously.

Lagorio said, "I feel like it really can't be possible, I swear."

"What can't be possible?"

"Being in the city in two days—and happily ever after."

Angustina was pale. At this point, he was no longer smoothing his moustache but staring at the shadow before him. The room was burdened with the feelings evoked by night, when fears seep through decrepit walls and unhappiness turns sweet, when the soul proudly beats its wings over sleeping humanity. The colonels' glassy eyes in the grand portraits expressed heroic portents. Outside the rain persisted.

"Can you imagine?" Lagorio asked Angustina mercilessly. "The day after tomorrow evening, at this hour, I'll most likely be at Consalvi's. Great milieu, music, beautiful women," he said, repeating an old jest.

"Well, isn't that the cat's meow?" responded Angustina scornfully.

"Or else," Lagorio continued with the best of intentions, trying to persuade his friend, "maybe it's better if I go to Tron's, your uncle's. The people there are so simpatico and they 'act like the upper crust,' as Giacomo would say."

"That just tops everything," said Angustina.

"Anyhow," Lagorio said, "the day after tomorrow I shall be amusing myself and you'll be on duty. I'll be out strolling through the city and you'll be standing muster before the captain. 'Nothing to report; the sentry Martini has fallen ill.' At two o'clock the sergeant will wake you: 'Lieutenant sir, time for inspection.' He'll wake you at two, you can bet on it, and at the very same hour I'll no doubt be in bed with Rosaria."

Such were Lagorio's cruelties, at once fatuous and unthinking. Everyone had grown accustomed to them. But behind his words his companions perceived the image of the distant city with its mansions and immense churches, airy domes, romantic paths along the river. At that hour, they were thinking, a fine mist must have materialized and the lamps were casting a tenuous, yellowish light. At that hour shadowy couples sauntered down solitary streets and you could hear coachmen shouting before the illumined glass facade of the opera, echoes of violins and laughter, women's voices in the dark portals of wealthy homes, as windows glowed at incredible heights amid labyrinthine roofs. It was the city made fascinating by their youthful dreams, by its still-unknown adventures.

Everyone was now watching Angustina on the sly, his face heavy with unconfessed weariness. They realized they weren't there to celebrate Lagorio's departure. In reality they were bidding farewell to Angustina because he alone would stay behind. One by one, after Lagorio, they would take turns leaving—Grotta, Morel, and earlier still Giovanni Drogo, who scarcely had four months to do. Angustina, however, would stay behind. Although they couldn't understand why, they were certain of it. They vaguely sensed that on this occasion as well he was goose-stepping in line with his ambitious aspirations. But they could no longer envy it. It seemed, after all, like an absurd obsession.

So why does Angustina, that damn snob, keep on smiling? Why doesn't he rush to pack his bags, sick as he is, and prepare to leave? Why does he rather stare at the shadow before him? What is he thinking? What secret pride detains him at the Fortezza? Has he too been felled by it, then? Look at him, Lagorio, you who are his friend; look at him carefully while time remains. See that his face burns into your brain exactly as it appears tonight—thin nose, blank stare, disagreeable smile. Perhaps one day you'll understand why he didn't want to follow you and you'll know what was barricaded behind his steely brow.

Lagorio left the next morning. His two horses were waiting for him with the orderly at the gate of the Fortezza. The sky was overcast but rain wasn't falling.

Lagorio wore a cheerful expression on his face. He had exited his room without even bestowing a glance on it, and when he reached the open air he didn't turn back to look at the Fortezza. The walls towered over him, dark and severe. The sentry stood motionless at the gate. Not a living soul appeared in the vast expanse that stood before him. The rhythmic sound of hammering issued from a shed built against the fort.

Angustina had come to see off his friend. He stroked the horse. "Still a superb animal," he said. Lagorio was leaving, heading down to their city, to the easy, happy life. Angustina was staying, however. His impenetrable eyes watched his friend, who was busying himself around the animals. He was barely able to smile.

"Leaving seems so unimaginable to me," said Lagorio. "The Fortezza was my obsession."

"Go visit my family when you get there," Angustina said without paying him any attention. "Tell my mother I'm well."

"Don't worry," replied Lagorio. After a pause he added: "You know I'm sorry about last night, don't you? We're quite different. I've never really understood how you think. You seem obsessive. I don't know; perhaps you're right."

"I didn't give it a thought," Angustina said, placing his right hand on the horse's flank and looking at the ground. "I certainly didn't get angry."

They were different men who loved different things, divergent in intelligence and culture. Seeing them always together was a source of astonishment, so pronounced was Angustina's self-importance. Still, they were friends. Of all the soldiers at the fort only Lagorio instinctively understood him; only he felt sorry for his friend, so much so he was almost ashamed to leave in his presence, as if he were causing an ugly scene. He couldn't make up his mind.

"If you see Claudina," Angustina said, his voice still impassive, "say hello . . . Actually, don't; it's better if you say nothing."

"But if I see her, she'll be the one who asks. She knows very well you're here."

Angustina fell silent.

"Well then," said Lagorio, who had finished arranging his saddle-bag with the orderly. "Perhaps it's better if I leave. I don't want to be late. Farewell."

He grasped his friend's hand. Then, with an elegant movement, he vaulted into the saddle.

"Goodbye, Lagorio," Angustina shouted. "Buon viaggio!"

Sitting upright in the saddle, Lagorio looked at him. He wasn't especially intelligent, but an enigmatic voice told him he wouldn't see his friend again.

A prick of the spurs and the horse proceeded. At that point Angustina raised his right hand slightly as if to gesture—to call back his friend, to ask him to wait a moment longer, since he had one last thing to tell him. Lagorio spotted the gesture out the corner of his eye and stopped some twenty meters away. "What is it?" he asked. "Did you want something?"

But Angustina lowered his hand, assuming the indifferent air he had before. "Nothing, nothing," he replied. "Why?"

"Ah, I thought—" said Lagorio, perplexed. As he drew away across the clearing, he was swaying in the saddle.

9

THE TERRACES of the Fortezza were white, just like the southern valley and the desert to the north. Snow entirely covered the battlements, laying a fragile cornice along the merlons, dropping from gutters with soft thuds, occasionally breaking off from the flanks of precipices for no comprehensible reason so that horrific masses thundered in the gorges, emitting clouds of smoke.

The snowfall wasn't the first, but the third or fourth, and it served to indicate that many days had passed. "I feel like I arrived yesterday at the Fortezza," said Drogo, and this was true. It felt like yesterday and yet time had been consumed with the same static rhythm, identical for every man, neither slower for the happy nor quicker for the unfortunate.

Neither slowly nor quickly another three months had passed. Christmas had already melted into the distance and the new year had come, momentarily bringing strange hopes to the men. Giovanni Drogo was preparing to leave. The formality of the medical exam, as Major Matti had promised him, was still necessary, and then he would be able to go. He kept on telling himself that this event would prove joyful, that the life waiting for him in the city would be comfortable, fun, perhaps happy. And yet he wasn't pleased.

On January 10, in the morning, he entered the doctor's office on the top floor of the Fortezza. The doctor's name was Ferdinando Rovina. He was past fifty, his face was flabby yet intelligent, and he carried an air of resigned weariness. Instead of a uniform he wore a long, dark jacket like a magistrate. He was sitting at his desk with various books and papers in front of him. Yet when Drogo rather abruptly entered, he understood immediately that Rovina wasn't doing anything at all. He was sitting motionless, thinking about something or other.

The window gave onto the courtyard from which rose the sound of cadenced footsteps. Evening had already arrived and the change of guard was beginning. From the window you could glimpse part of the facing wall and the extraordinarily serene sky. The two men exchanged greetings and Giovanni soon noticed the doctor was completely familiar with his case.

"Crows build nests, but swallows leave," joked Rovina. From a drawer he pulled out a document with a printed form.

"Perhaps you're not aware, doctor, but I've come here because of an error."

"Everyone, my dear boy, comes here because of an error," said the doctor, alluding pathetically to the situation at the fort. "Some more, some less. Even those who have remained."

Drogo didn't quite understand but he made do with a smile.

"Oh, I'm not blaming you! You young people do the right thing by not rotting away up here," continued Rovina. "There are much better opportunities down in the city. I too think about it sometimes, if only I could—"

"Why?" Drogo interrupted. "Can't you get yourself transferred?"

The doctor threw up his hands as if he'd just heard about some monstrous crime.

"Get myself transferred?" He burst out laughing. "After twenty-five years here? Too late, my boy. I needed to think of that earlier."

Perhaps he would've liked for Drogo to contradict him again, but since the lieutenant was silent, the doctor proceeded with the matter at hand. He invited Giovanni to sit down and made him give his first and last names, which he wrote in the appropriate space on the regulation form.

"Good," he concluded. "You suffer from some heart disorder—correct? Your system cannot withstand this altitude—correct? Shall we put it in these terms?"

"Yes, in those terms," Drogo agreed. "You're the best judge of these things."

"Shall we also prescribe a convalescent leave while we're at it?" said the doctor with a wink.

"Thank you," said Drogo, "but I wouldn't want to go too far."

"As you wish. No leave. I didn't have such scruples at your age."

Instead of sitting, Giovanni had approached the window. Every so often he glanced down at the soldiers lined up in the white snow. The sun had just set; a blue shadow had diffused within the walls.

"More than half of you people want to leave after three, four months," continued the doctor with a peculiar sadness. He too was now enveloped in shadow, raising the question of how he could see to write. "I'd do the same, if I could turn back the clock. But what's the use now?"

Drogo listened without interest, intent as he was on gazing out the window. Then he seemed to see the yellowish walls of the courtyard rise very high toward the crystalline sky, and above them, higher still, stood solitary towers, slanted ramparts crowned with snow, airy battlements and fortifications, none of which he had ever noticed before. A bright light from the west was still emblazing them, so that they shone mysteriously with an impenetrable life. Never had Drogo realized that the Fortezza might be so complicated and immense. At an almost incredible height he saw a window (or an embrasure?) opening onto the valley. Up there must be men he didn't know, perhaps some officers like him, with whom he could strike up a friendship. He saw the geometric shadows of abysses between one bastion and the next, narrow bridges suspended between roofs, strange barred gates flush against walls, ancient arrow slits that had been blocked up, and long beveled edges curved by years.

Amid lanterns and torches, on the bluish ground of the courtyard, he saw proud soldiers of enormous height unsheathing their bayonets. Against the luminosity of the snow they formed black, motionless lines as if cast in iron. They were extremely handsome, standing stonelike while a bugle started to blare. The sound, amplified by the bright, biting air, penetrated straight to the heart.

"One by one you all have left," murmured Rovina in the shadow. "We'll wind up staying, just us old men. This year—"

The bugle blared down in the courtyard, a pure sound that joined human voice and metal. It throbbed again with a warlike surge. Falling silent it left an inexpressible spell, even in the doctor's office. The silence became such that a long stride could be heard crunching across the frozen snow. The colonel himself had come down to salute the guard. Three blasts of extreme beauty slashed the sky.

"Who are the others?" the doctor continued to recriminate. "Lieutenant Angustina is the only one. Even Morel, I wager, will need to return to the city next year to be treated. Even he, I wager, will wind up getting sick."

"Morel?" Drogo couldn't avoid responding, if only to show he was listening. "Sick?" he asked, since he had caught only the doctor's final word.

"Not really," said Rovina. "A kind of metaphor."

Even through the closed window the colonel's brittle steps could be heard. The bayonets were arrayed in a line, forming so many silver strips in the dusk. Echoes of the bugle arrived from improbable distances, the same sound as before, perhaps, sent back by the maze of walls.

The doctor was silent. Then he stood up and said, "Here is the certificate. I'm going to get the commanding officer's signature." He folded the sheet and slipped it into a file. He removed an overcoat and a fur cap from the clothes stand. "Coming, lieutenant?" he asked. "What in the world are you looking at?"

The guards coming on duty had lowered their weapons and one by one they moved toward various parts of the Fortezza. The cadence of their footsteps on the snow made a dull noise but the music of the fanfares flew skyward. Then the walls, already besieged by night, soared slowly toward the zenith, however implausible this might seem, and from their utmost edge, framed by streaks of snow, white heron-shaped clouds began to break away and navigate through sidereal spaces.

Through Drogo's mind passed the memory of his city, an indistinct image—streets thunderous under the rain, plaster statues, dampness in barracks, dreary bells, faces weary and haggard, endless afternoons, attics dirty with dust.

Here, however, the vast mountain night was advancing, clouds in flight over the Fortezza, miraculous omens. From the north, from the invisible north behind the walls, Drogo felt that his own destiny was pressing.

"Doctor, doctor," said Drogo, nearly stuttering. "I'm fine."

"I know," the doctor replied. "What were you thinking?"

"I'm fine," repeated Drogo as if he didn't recognize his own voice. "I'm fine and I want to stay."

"Stay here? At the Fortezza? You don't want to leave anymore? What has gotten into you?"

"I don't know," said Giovanni. "But I can't leave."

"Oh my," Rovina exclaimed, drawing close to Drogo. "If you're not joking, I swear I'm pleased."

"I'm not joking, no," said Drogo, who was feeling exaltation transform into a strange ache, quite similar to happiness. "Doctor, throw away that certificate."

10

THIS IS how it had to happen. And perhaps it had already been decided a long time ago; namely, on that distant day when Drogo first looked out over the plain with Ortiz and the Fortezza appeared to him in all its imposing noonday splendor.

Drogo has decided to remain, held by desire but not only by that: the heroic conviction wouldn't have been compelling enough. For now he believes he has done something noble and he marvels at it in good faith, discovering he's a better man than he might've thought. Only many months from now, looking back, will he recognize the pitiful things that bind him to the Fortezza.

If bugles had sounded, if war songs had been heard, if disquieting messages had arrived from the north—if this alone had hung in the balance, Drogo would've departed just the same. But he was already instilled with the lethargy of routine, military vanity, the domestic love for quotidian walls. Four months were enough to lure him into the monotonous rhythm of service.

The turn at guard duty, which the first few times seemed an unbearable burden, had become routine for him. He gradually learned the rules, the figures of speech, his superiors' manias, the topography of the redoubts, the sentries' posts, the corners where the wind didn't blow, the language of the bugles. From his mastery of service he derived a special pleasure, appreciating the increasing esteem of the soldiers and the noncommissioned officers. Even Tronk, noticing how serious and conscientious Drogo proved to be, had almost grown fond of him.

Colleagues had become routine. He knew them so well by now that even the subtlest subtext failed to catch him unprepared. For a long time they'd get together in the evening to gab about what was happening in the city, a topic that acquired boundless interest because of the distance. Routine had settled over the mess, which was enjoyable and convenient, over the welcoming fireplace in the officers' quarters, which was lit day and night, and over the thoughtfulness of the orderly, a decent soul named Geronimo who gradually learned Drogo's special preferences.

The excursions Drogo occasionally took with Morel to the least distant village had become routine. They would travel a good two hours by horse through a narrow valley which by this point he had committed to memory. Then they would arrive at an inn where they might actually see some different faces, sumptuous dinners would be prepared, and they would hear the sweet laughter of girls with whom you could make love.

The riotous horse races up and down the clearing behind the Fortezza, bravura competitions with colleagues on free afternoons, and the patient chess games that lasted from evening till the middle of the night, where Drogo was often victorious—these too had become routine. (Captain Ortiz, however, had told him, "It's always like this: the new arrivals always win at the beginning. The same thing happens to everyone. They delude themselves that they're really clever but it's only a question of novelty. The others wind up learning our system too and suddenly one day you can't pull anything off anymore.")

Routine had settled over Drogo's room, the reading he did at night undisturbed, the crack in the ceiling—over his bed—which resembled the head of a Turk, the dripping cistern, which had become a friend over time, the sag his body hollowed out in the mattress, the blankets that felt so inhospitable in the early days but were now meekly welcoming, the movement to extinguish the oil lamp or put a book on the nightstand (at this point, he would instinctively reach the exact distance). He now knew how he had to present himself in the morning, when he would trim his beard in the mirror so the light would shine on his face at the right angle, how to pour water from the pitcher into the basin without spilling it, how to release the rebellious lock of a drawer (by tilting the key down slightly).

Routine had settled over the creak of the door during periods of rain, the spot that moonlight usually hit when it entered the window and its slow migration as the hours passed, the ruckus in the room beneath his every night at precisely one thirty, when the old wound in Lieutenant Colonel Nicolosi's right leg was mysteriously reactivated, interrupting his sleep.

All these things had now become Drogo's and to leave them would have caused him pain. Yet he neither knew nor suspected that his departure would have cost him any effort, or that life at the Fortezza would have swallowed up his days, one after another, all alike, with dizzying speed. Yesterday and the day before were the same; he could no longer tell them apart. Something that happened three days ago or twenty wound up seeming equally remote to him. Thus the flight of time unfolded without his awareness.

For the moment, however, take a look at him, cocky and devil-may-care, on the battlements of the fourth redoubt during a clear, icy night. Because of the cold the sentries kept pacing without pause and their footsteps crunched the frozen snow. A huge moon, immaculately white, illumined the world. The fort, the cliffs, the rocky valley to the north, were flooded with marvelous light. Even the screen of mist that stood stock-still at the northern boundary was shimmering.

Below, inside the redoubt, in the room reserved for the officer on duty, the lamp had remained lit. The flame wavered slightly, causing the shadows to sway. A little while ago Drogo had begun to write a letter. He needed to reply to Maria, the sister of his friend Vescovi, who may one day become his wife. But after two lines he stood up— he really didn't know why—and climbed to the roof to survey the scene.

That was the lowest level of the fortification, corresponding to the deepest cavity of the pass. Located at that point in the rock face was a gate that communicated between the two nations. Its massive, ironclad wings hadn't been opened since a time long forgotten. Every day the guard for the New Redoubt left and entered through a secondary door, covered by a sentry, which was barely the width of a man.

For the first time Drogo joined the watch on the fourth redoubt.

As soon as he walked out into the open air, he gazed at the cliffs looming on the right, completely encrusted in ice and resplendent beneath the moon.

Windy blasts began to drive small white clouds through the sky, stirring Drogo's cloak, his new cloak, which signified so many things to him.

Motionless, he stared at the rocky barriers facing him, the impenetrable distances of the north. The wings of his cloak snapped like a flag, draping him tempestuously. That night Drogo felt he possessed a proud, militaristic beauty, standing on the border of the terrace, his splendid cloak agitated by the wind. Near him Tronk, wrapped in a heavy overcoat, didn't even look like a soldier.

"Tell me, Tronk," asked Giovanni, feigning an attitude of concern. "Is it only my impression or is the moon tonight much wider than usual?"

"I don't believe so, lieutenant sir," Tronk said. "Here at the Fortezza it always gives that impression."

Their voices echoed loudly, as if the air were made of glass. Tronk, seeing the lieutenant had nothing else to say, moved along the border of the terrace, goaded by his perennial need to supervise the watch.

Drogo remained alone, feeling more or less happy. He proudly savored his determination to stay at the Fortezza, the bitter taste of abandoning small but dependable joys for a greater good whose duration was lengthy but uncertain (and perhaps beneath these thoughts could be found the consolation that he would always have time to leave).

A premonition—or was it only hope?—of exploits noble and grand had motivated him to stay there, but it could also be no more than a postponement. Nothing, after all, was jeopardized. So much time still stretched before him. All the good in life seemed to await him. Was there any need to get worked up? Even women, those strange, lovable creatures—he expected them like an inevitable delight, formally promised to him by the natural order of things.

How much time lay before him! Even a single year seemed interminably long and the good years had scarcely begun. They seemed to form an extremely long series, the end of which was impossible to glimpse, a treasure still untouched and so enormous that it could cause boredom. There was no one to tell him, "Beware, Giovanni Drogo!" Life appeared inexhaustible, a tenacious illusion, even though his youth had already begun to fade. Yet Drogo was unacquainted with time. If his youth might last hundreds of years, as with the gods, it would still seem a paltry thing. He, however, had only a simple, normal life at his disposal, a brief human youth, a miserly gift that could be counted on the fingers of two hands and would vanish before he was even aware of it.

How much time lies before me, he thought. And yet there were men—he had heard tell—who at a certain point (strangely enough) started waiting for death. This fact, well known yet utterly absurd, couldn't have had anything to do with him. Drogo smiled as he thought about it. Spurred by the cold, he started to pace.

That section of the wall followed the slope of the pass, forming a complicated, cascading sequence of terraces and platforms. Below him, pitch black against the snow, Drogo saw the successive sentries in the moonlight, their methodical footsteps grating on the frozen surface.

The closest sentry, in an underlying terrace ten meters away, stood motionless, less sensitive to cold than the others, his back propped against a wall. You might have thought he was asleep. Drogo, however, heard him singing a dirge to himself in a deep voice.

It was a succession of words (which Drogo couldn't make out) linked by a monotonous melody, potentially endless. To speak and, worse, to sing on duty were strictly prohibited. Giovanni should have punished him but instead felt pity, thinking of the cold and the solitude of that night. He then started down the short flight of stairs that led to the terrace and coughed to give the soldier a warning.

The sentry turned his head and as soon as he spotted the officer corrected his posture. But he didn't break off the dirge. Drogo was seized by rage: Did these soldiers think they could play him for a fool? He would give the man a taste of something harsh.

The sentry immediately noticed Drogo's threatening manner. Although the recitation of a password, according to silent, long-standing agreement, wasn't practiced among the soldiers and the commander of the guard, the sentry chose to be excessively scrupulous. He raised his rifle and asked in the very peculiar accent adopted at the Fortezza, "Who goes there? Who goes there?"

Drogo abruptly stopped, disoriented. At perhaps less than five meters away, in the limpid moonlight, he saw the soldier's face quite clearly and his mouth was closed. But the dirge wasn't interrupted. Where was the voice coming from?

Mulling over the strange incident yet seeing that the soldier continued to wait, Giovanni mechanically recited the password: "Miracolo." The sentry replied, "Miseria." Then he rested the butt of his rifle on the ground by his right foot and stood at ease.

There ensued an immense silence that transmitted the mumbling of word and song more loudly than before.

Finally Drogo understood and a slow shiver traveled down his back. It was water—that was it—a distant waterfall roaring down from the heights of nearby cliffs. The wind that caused the tall cataract to waver, the mysterious play of echoes, the different sounds of struck stones, gave rise to a human voice that would speak forever—words that described your life. You were always on the brink of understanding them but you never did.

Hence it wasn't the soldier who was singing, not a man sensitive to cold, to punishment, to love, but the hostile mountain. What a sad error, thought Drogo. Perhaps everything is like this: We believe we're in the midst of creatures that resemble us but there's only icy cold, stones that speak a strange language. We're about to greet a friend but our arm falls lifeless, our smile fades, because we realize we're completely alone.

The wind beats against the officer's splendid cloak and even the blue shadow on the snow waves like a flag. The sentry stands motionless. The moon moves ever so slowly yet without losing a single moment, impatient for dawn. And the heart in Giovanni Drogo's chest is beating like the knock on a door.

11

ALMOST two years later Giovanni Drogo was sleeping one night in his room at the Fortezza. Twenty-two months had passed without bringing anything new but he had remained steadfastly waiting, as if life was bound to show him some special leniency. Twenty-two months is a long time, however, and many things can happen. New families might be initiated, children born, and they might even begin to speak. A great house might spring up where previously only a meadow stood. A beautiful woman might age and no one desire her any longer. A disease might erupt, particularly a disease that takes a drawn-out course (while men continue to live unconcerned). It might slowly waste away the body, subside momentarily when health seems in reach, but then resume more intensely, engulfing every last hope. Twenty-two months is time enough for a dead man to be buried and forgotten and for his son to regain the ability to laugh and in the evenings lead girls down avenues past cemetery gates without a second thought.

But Drogo's existence had come to a standstill. That same day had been repeated hundreds of times, identically, although without advancing a single step. The river of time passed over the Fortezza, cracking walls, dragging down dust and fragments of stone, eroding stairs and chains. But over Drogo it passed in vain. It still hadn't managed to snatch him in its flight.

That night too would've been the same as all the others if Drogo hadn't had a dream. He was a child again and found himself before a window at night.

Beyond a deep recess formed by his house he saw the facade of an opulent mansion illuminated by the moon. The attention of the child

Drogo was completely focused on a tall, narrow window crowned by a marble canopy. The moonlight, entering through the panes, struck a table that bore a carpet, a vase, and several ivory statuettes. These few visible objects prompted him to imagine that farther back the darkness would yield to the intimacies of a vast parlor, the first of an interminable series, full of precious things. The entire mansion was sleeping that untroubled, seductive sleep associated with the residences of wealthy, happy people. How delightful, thought Drogo, to be able to enjoy those parlors and wander for hours on end, constantly discovering new treasures.

Between the window where he was stationed and the marvelous mansion—an interval of some twenty meters—fragile apparitions, quite like fairies, began to surge, dragging trains of voile that glistened in the moonlight.

In the dream the presence of such creatures, never seen in the real world, didn't astonish Giovanni. They undulated in the air in slow vortices, insistently grazing the narrow window.

Because of their nature, they seemed logical appurtenances to the mansion. Yet the fact that they didn't pay the least attention to Drogo, never drawing near his house, was mortifying to him. Didn't fairies likewise shrink from ordinary children, attending only to fortunate people who weren't even watching for them, who rather slept indifferently beneath silk canopies?

"Psst, psst," whispered Drogo two or three times, timidly, so as to attract the spirits' attention, although he knew deep in his heart it would prove useless. None of them actually seemed to hear; none approached even as close as a meter from his window.

But here one of those magical creatures seized the sill of the facing window with some sort of arm and discreetly knocked on the pane as if to call someone.

Many moments hadn't passed before a slender figure—how small in contrast to the monumental window—turned up behind the glass. Drogo recognized it as Angustina, who was also a child.

Angustina appeared shockingly pale. He wore a velvet suit with a white lace collar. He didn't seem very pleased with the silent serenade.

Drogo thought his companion would invite him to play with the spirits, if for no other reason than courtesy. But this wasn't the case. Angustina didn't seem to notice him. Not even when Giovanni called out "Angustina! Angustina!" did he turn to look.

With a weary gesture, however, his friend opened the window and bent down toward the spirit hanging from the sill as if they were on familiar terms and he wanted to tell it something. The spirit made a sign, and following the direction of the gesture Drogo turned his eyes to a large square, absolutely deserted, which stretched before the houses. Over this square, about ten meters from the ground, a small procession of other spirits advanced through the air, hauling a sedan chair.

Evidently made of the same essence as the spirits themselves, the sedan chair was overflowing with veils and feathers. Angustina watched it approach with his characteristic expression of detachment and boredom. The chair was obviously coming for him.

The injustice deeply wounded Drogo. Why was everything for Angustina and nothing for him? With someone else he would've borne it patiently but with Angustina, who was always so proud and arrogant! Drogo looked at the other windows to see if someone would eventually take his side. But he couldn't make out anybody.

Finally the sedan chair stopped, swaying just before the window, and in one leap all the spirits huddled around it, forming a pulsating crown. They were reaching out to Angustina, no longer obsequious but with greedy curiosity that bordered on malice. Abandoned to itself, the chair stayed in the air as if suspended by invisible wires.

Suddenly Drogo was emptied of envy, since he understood what was happening. He saw Angustina, standing on the windowsill, his eyes fixed on the sedan chair. Yes, the fairies' messengers had come for him that night, but on what kind of errand? The chair would have to serve for a long journey and it wouldn't return before dawn, or even tomorrow, or the next night, or ever. The parlors in the mansion would wait in vain for the little master. A woman's two hands would cautiously close the window left open by the fugitive, and every other window would be bolted fast to brood over the weeping and desolation in darkness.

The spirits, formerly lovable, hadn't come to play with moonbeams. Nor were they innocent creatures that issued from perfumed gardens. They originated in the abyss.

Other children would have wept and called for their mothers but Angustina wasn't afraid. He chatted calmly with the spirits as if to establish certain procedures that needed to be clarified. Squeezed tight around the window like foam drapery they piled on top of each other, pressing toward the child. He nodded yes as if to say: All right, all right, everything is just dandy. In the end, the spirit who first seized the windowsill, perhaps the leader, made a small, imperious gesture. Angustina, still assuming a bored attitude, climbed down from the window (he seemed to have become as light as a spirit) and sat in the chair like a lord, crossing his legs. The cluster of spirits dissolved into a wave of veils. The fairy carriage moved gently to depart.

A procession assembled. The apparitions made a semicircular maneuver in the recess before the houses, whereafter they rose into the sky in the direction of the moon. In tracing the semicircle the sedan chair passed a few meters from Drogo's window. Waving his arm he tried to shout out a final farewell: "Angustina! Angustina!"

Then the dead friend at last turned his head toward Giovanni, staring at him for a few moments. In that stare Drogo seemed to read a seriousness that was positively excessive for such a little child. But Angustina's face suddenly opened into a smile of complicity, as if Drogo and he could understand many things that were beyond the ken of the spirits—an utmost desire to joke, the last opportunity to show that he, Angustina, had no need of anyone's pity. The episode was prosaic, he seemed to say, and to marvel at it would've been foolish.

As the chair drew him away, Angustina detached his gaze from Drogo and turned to look ahead, in the direction of the procession, with a kind of curiosity that was simultaneously amused and wary. He seemed to be making his first trial with a toy he didn't treasure at all but couldn't reject out of politeness.

So he departed into the night with almost inhuman nobility. He bestowed not one glance on his mansion, not one on the square that lay before it, or on the other houses, or on the city where he lived.

The procession slowly meandered in the sky, rising higher and higher, becoming a confused trail, then a slight tuft of cloud, then nothing.

The window remained open. The moonlight still illumined the table, the vase, the ivory statuettes, which continued to sleep. Inside that house, in another room, stretched out on the bed in trembling candlelight, lay perhaps a small human body devoid of life. The face resembled Angustina's. He must be wearing a velvet suit with a wide lace collar and frozen on his white lips a smile.

12

THE NEXT day Giovanni Drogo commanded the guard at the New Redoubt. This detached fortification, three-quarters of an hour from the Fortezza, sat on top of a conical rock formation that overlooked the Tartar plain. It was the most important garrison, completely isolated and assigned the essential task of sounding the alarm if any threat were approaching.

In the evening Drogo left the Fortezza in command of approximately seventy men. This many soldiers were required to cover the ten sentry posts, not counting two gunners. It was the first time he had set foot beyond the pass; for all practical purposes he had crossed the border.

Giovanni thought about the responsibilities he had undertaken but above all he reflected on his dream about Angustina. This dream had continued to echo in his mind. He felt it must be linked obscurely to future events, although he wasn't particularly superstitious.

They entered the New Redoubt and the sentries were relieved. Then the off-duty guard left. Drogo stood at the border of the terrace to watch them recede down the rocky trail. The Fortezza beyond seemed like a single expanse of wall, a mere wall with nothing behind it. The sentries couldn't be discerned because they were too far away. Only the flag was visible every now and then when wind stirred it.

For the next twenty-four hours Drogo would be the sole commanding officer in the solitary redoubt. Whatever might happen, support couldn't be requested. Even if an enemy arrived, the fort would need to be self-sufficient. For the next twenty-four hours the king himself counted for less than Drogo within those walls.

Waiting for nightfall, Giovanni remained to look at the northern plain. From the Fortezza you could see only a small triangle because of the facing mountains. Now, however, he could observe everything, even to the farthest limits of the horizon, where the lone barrier of fog lingered. The flatland was a kind of desert, paved with rocks, dotted here and there with scrub in the form of low, dusty bushes. To the right, far in the distance, appeared a black strip, which could have been forest. On both flanks stood the rugged chain of mountains. They were very beautiful with immense vertical walls and white peaks from the first autumnal snow. Yet no one looked at them. Everyone— Drogo as well as the soldiers—tended instinctively to look toward the north, toward the desolate plain, devoid of meaning, mysterious.

Whether the cause were the thought of being completely alone in commanding the fort or the sight of the empty wasteland or the memory of the dream of Angustina, Drogo now felt a dull uneasiness growing around him as night unfolded.

It was an October evening. The weather was variable. Splashes of reddish light were strewn here and there on the earth, reflections of unknown origin, progressively swallowed by the lead-colored dusk.

As usual, a kind of poetic energy infiltrated Drogo's mood at sunset. It was the hour of hope. He resumed his meditation on heroic fantasies, so often constructed during long shifts on guard duty and daily perfected with new details. In general he would imagine a desperate battle in which he was engaged with few men against innumerable enemy forces—as if that night the New Redoubt had been besieged by thousands of Tartars. He resisted for many days and almost all his men were dead or wounded. A bullet had hit him as well. The wound was serious, but not extremely so, allowing him to maintain command. And now the cartridges were on the verge of running out. He mounts a sortie at the head of the last squad. A bandage wraps his forehead. At that point reinforcements finally arrive. The enemy disbands and turns in flight. He falls exhausted, gripping a bloody saber. But someone calls, "Lieutenant Drogo, Lieutenant Drogo," shaking his inanimate body in an effort to resuscitate him. Drogo slowly opens his eyes. The king, the king in person, has bent over him to say, Bravo!

It was the hour of hope and he meditated on heroic tales that would probably never come to pass. Nonetheless, they served as a source of encouragement for him. Sometimes he was satisfied with much less, renouncing his status as the sole hero, renouncing the wound, renouncing even the praise from the king. A simple battle would be enough, after all, a single but really serious battle, so that he could charge in full-dress uniform and be capable of smiling as he hurtled toward the hermetic faces of the enemy. A single battle and later perhaps he would be content for the rest of his life.

But that night he didn't find it easy to feel heroic. Darkness had already shrouded the world. The northern plain had been drained of color but it still hadn't grown drowsy, as if something evil were hatching there.

The clock had struck eight and the sky was entirely filled with clouds when Drogo seemed to glimpse a small black spot moving in the plain, slightly to the right, just below the redoubt. My eyes must be tired, he thought. They're tired from keeping watch and I'm seeing spots. The same thing had happened to him on another occasion, when he was a boy and had stayed up at night to study.

He tried to keep his eyelids closed for a few moments. Then he turned toward the objects around him—a bucket that must've been used to clean the terrace, an iron hook on the wall, a stool the previous officer must've had brought there to serve as a seat. Only after several minutes did he again look at the area where he had apparently glimpsed the black spot a little while earlier. It was still there. And it was moving slowly.

"Tronk!" Drogo called in an agitated tone.

"Yes, lieutenant sir!" The voice that answered immediately was so close it made him jump.

"Ah, you're here?" he said and took a breath. "Tronk, I wouldn't like to be mistaken but I think—I think I see something moving down there."

"Yessir," responded Tronk in a manner that accorded with the regulations. "I've been observing it for a few minutes now."

"What?" said Drogo. "You've seen it too? What did you see?"

"Something moving, lieutenant sir."

Drogo felt his blood run cold. Now here we go, he thought, completely forgetting his soldierly fantasies. This just had to happen on my watch. What a mess it's going to create.

"So you've seen it too?" he asked again, absurdly hoping the other man might deny it.

"Yessir," said Tronk. "It must've been ten minutes ago. I went down below to see whether the cannons were cleaned. Then I came up here and saw it."

They both fell silent. Even for Tronk the thing had to be strange, disturbing.

"What do you think it might be, Tronk?"

"I can't say. It's moving too slow."

"Too slow?"

"Yes. I think it could be tufts from canes."

"Tufts? What tufts?"

"There's a canebrake down there at the far end." He pointed toward the right but the gesture was useless because nothing could be seen in the dark. "Canes are topped with black tufts in this season. Sometimes the wind detaches these tufts and since they're light they fly away. They look like little clouds of smoke." He paused, then added: "But this can't be that. They would move faster."

"What could it be then?"

"I don't know," Tronk said. "Men would be peculiar. They'd approach from a different direction. And then it keeps on moving. I don't understand."

"Sound the alarm!" shouted a nearby sentry at that moment. Then another echoed him, then yet another. They too had caught sight of the black spot. From within the redoubt other, off-duty soldiers rushed out. They gathered on the parapet, intrigued and a little frightened.

"Do you see it?" said one soldier. "Right below. Now it stopped."

"It's got to be fog," said another. "Sometimes fog has holes and you can see what's behind it through them. Someone seems to be moving but it's just the holes in the fog."

"Yes, yes, now I see it. But that black thing is always there. It's a black stone. That's what it is."

"What stone do you mean? Don't you see it's still moving? Are you blind?"

"It's a stone, I tell you. I've always seen it, a black stone that looks like a nun."

Someone laughed. "Leave this area. Go back inside immediately," Tronk intervened, anticipating the lieutenant, whose agitation was increased by all those voices. The soldiers reluctantly withdrew to the interior and silence was restored.

"Tronk?" asked Drogo, suddenly unable to decide on his own. "Should we sound the alarm?"

"Sound the alarm to the Fortezza? Are you saying we should fire a shot, lieutenant sir?"

"I really don't know. Do you think there's reason to sound the alarm?"

Tronk shook his head. "I'd wait to get a better look. If we fire a shot, it'll cause a commotion at the Fortezza. And then what if it's nothing?"

"Right," admitted Drogo.

"Besides," Tronk added, "it would violate regulations. The regulations say the alarm should be given only in case of threat. That's the exact wording: 'in case of threat, the appearance of armed forces, and in every case where suspect persons approach at least one hundred meters from the base of the walls.'"

"Right," assented Drogo. "And they're farther than a hundred meters—correct?"

"So say I," agreed Tronk. "And then how can we be certain it's a person?"

"What do you want it to be then? A spirit?" Drogo was slightly irritated.

Tronk didn't answer.

Suspended over the interminable night, Drogo and Tronk stood leaning against the parapet, their eyes fixed on the farthest point where the Tartar plain began. The enigmatic spot appeared to be motionless, as if it were sleeping. Giovanni gradually reverted to the thought that nothing was really there, just a black boulder that resembled a nun, and his eyes had been deceived by a touch of fatigue, nothing more, a foolish hallucination. Now he even felt a trace of obscure bitterness, as when the grave hours of destiny pass close to us without touching and their roar is lost in the distance while we remain alone amid a whirl of dried leaves, lamenting the loss of a terrible yet momentous opportunity.

But then, with the passage of night, the breath of fear rose from the dark valley. With the passage of night Drogo felt small and alone. Tronk was too different from him to be capable of acting as a friend. Oh, if only he were near his friends, even just one of them, then things would be different. He might even have found the will to joke. Waiting for dawn wouldn't be so painful.

Meanwhile strips of fog were forming in the plain—a white archipelago on a black ocean. One island stopped right at the foot of the redoubt, concealing the mysterious object. The air had become humid. Drogo's cloak hung limp and heavy from his shoulders.

What a long night. He had already lost hope it would ever end when the sky began to whiten and icy blasts announced the dawn wasn't far away. At that point sleep surprised him. On his feet, leaning against the parapet, Drogo let his head drop twice and twice he abruptly straightened up. Finally his head sank inert and his eyelids yielded to the weight. The new day was breaking.

He was awakened when someone touched his arm. Surfacing slowly from dreams, he was stunned by the light. A voice, Tronk's voice, said to him, "Lieutenant sir, it's a horse."

Then he recalled his life, the Fortezza, the New Redoubt, the enigma of the black spot. He immediately looked in the distance, keen to know. He felt the cowardly desire to see nothing but stones and shrubs, nothing other than the plain, just as it had always been, solitary and empty.

But the voice repeated to him, "Lieutenant sir, it's a horse." And Drogo made out the implausible thing, motionless at the foot of the cliffs.

It wasn't a large horse, but short and stocky, and curiously beautiful with its thin legs and flowing mane. Its shape was odd but its color was marvelous, a shiny black that left a spot on the landscape.

Where had it come from? Who was its owner? For countless years no creature had ventured into those places—except, perhaps, the occasional crow or snake. Now, however, a horse had appeared, and you could perceive at once that it wasn't wild, but a first-rate animal, a true military horse (apart from the legs, which were a bit too thin).

It was an extraordinary thing, its significance disturbing. Drogo, Tronk, the sentries—as well as the other soldiers at the embrasures on the floor below—couldn't take their eyes off it. That horse broke the rules. It brought back the ancient legends of the north with their Tartars and battles. It filled the entire desert with its illogical presence.

The horse didn't mean a great deal on its own. But you knew other things had to come of it. It wore a saddle that was in good shape, as if it had been mounted a short time ago. Thus it told a story that had been interrupted. What until yesterday was absurd, a ridiculous superstition, could be true. Drogo had the impression he could sense them—the mysterious enemy, the Tartars, lying flat among the bushes, in the fissures of the rocks, motionless and silent, their teeth clenched. They were waiting for darkness to launch their attack. In the meantime others would arrive, a threatening swarm that slowly issued from the mists of the north. They possessed neither music nor song, neither gleaming swords nor beautiful banners. Their weapons were matte so they wouldn't glitter in the sun and their horses were trained not to neigh.

But a pony—this was the immediate thought at the New Redoubt— a pony had escaped the enemy and ran ahead to betray them. They probably hadn't noticed it because the animal had fled from the camp during the night.

Hence the horse had brought a precious message. Yet how much time did they have before the enemy arrived? Drogo couldn't inform the command at the Fortezza until nightfall. By then the Tartars could creep up on them.

Sound the alarm, then? Tronk said no. After all, he said, it was just an ordinary horse. The fact that it reached the foot of the redoubt could mean that it had found itself on its own. Perhaps the owner was a solitary hunter who had imprudently ventured into the desert and died or fell ill. The horse, left alone, had gone in search of safety. He sensed the presence of men from the Fortezza, and he was now expecting them to bring him fodder.

This objection raised serious doubts as to whether an army was approaching. What would have motivated the animal to flee from a camp in a region so inhospitable? Besides, Tronk said, he had heard the Tartars' horses were almost all white. In an old painting that hung in a room at the Fortezza you could see them all mounted on white chargers. This horse, however, was black as coal.

So Drogo, after much indecision, decided to wait till evening. In the meantime the sky had cleared and the sun brightened the landscape, warming the soldiers' spirits. Even Giovanni felt cheered by the bright light. The fantasies about the Tartars lost consistency. Everything returned to normal proportions. The horse was an ordinary horse. You could find a number of explanations for its presence without recourse to enemy incursions. Then, forgetting nocturnal fears, Drogo suddenly felt open to any sort of exploit. He gloried in the premonition that his destiny stood at the gates, a happy fate that would lift him above other men.

He took pleasure in attending to the most minute formalities of guard duty as if to demonstrate to Tronk and the soldiers that the appearance of the horse, although strange and worrisome, hadn't troubled him at all. This he found a most military attitude.

The soldiers, if truth be told, hadn't experienced any fear. They took the horse as an occasion for laughter. To be able to capture it and bring it to the Fortezza as a trophy would've pleased them greatly. One of them actually sought permission from the sergeant major, who limited himself to a glance of reprimand as if to say joking about a matter of duty wasn't allowed.

On the lower floor, however, where two cannons had been installed, one of the gunners had been very shaken by the sight of the horse.

His name was Giuseppe Lazzari, a young fellow who had enlisted not too long ago. He said the horse was his. He recognized it hands down; he couldn't be mistaken. They must've let it escape when the animals had gone out of the Fortezza for watering.

"It's Fiocco, my horse!" he shouted, as if it were truly his property and they had stolen it from him.

Tronk went down below and immediately silenced the shouting. He brusquely demonstrated to Lazzari how the horse couldn't possibly have escaped: in order to cross into the northern valley, it would've had to go past the walls of the Fortezza or climb over the mountains.

Lazzari responded that he heard about a passage, a convenient passage across the cliffs, an old abandoned road that no one remembered anymore. This curious legend, among so many others, did in fact circulate at the Fortezza. But it had to be a tall tale: not a trace of that secret passage had ever been found. Savage mountains that had never been crossed rose to the right and left of the Fortezza for kilometers on end.

But the soldier wasn't persuaded. He chafed at the idea that he had to stay confined inside the redoubt, unable to retrieve his horse, when half an hour's ride would be enough to go and come back.

Meanwhile the hours wore away. The sun continued its journey toward the west and the sentries relieved each other at the designated time. The desert shone more solitary than ever. The pony stood in the same place as before, motionless for the most part, as if it might be sleeping, or it wandered around, searching for a patch of grass. Drogo's gaze searched in the distance but he spotted nothing new, still the same rocky cliffs, shrubs, and mists at the northern border, which would slowly change color as the evening approached.

The new guard relieved the unit on duty. Drogo and his soldiers left the redoubt and headed back down the rocky trail to the Fortezza amid the purple shadows of dusk. As soon as they reached the walls, Drogo said the password for himself and his men and the gate was opened. The guard coming off duty lined up in a small courtyard and Tronk began the roll call. Drogo in turn withdrew to advise the command of the mysterious horse.

As was prescribed, Drogo presented himself to the duty officer and then together they went to look for the colonel. Reporting news to the adjutant major was, as a rule, sufficient. But on this occasion the matter might be serious, and it was essential that time not be wasted.

The rumor had sped like lightning through the Fortezza. Someone in the last guard detail was already muttering about entire squadrons of Tartars camped at the foot of the rocks. The colonel, when he heard, said only, "We should try to capture this horse. If it has a saddle, we might be able to learn where it comes from."

But at this point the effort was futile. While the guard coming off duty was returning to the Fortezza, the soldier Giuseppe Lazzari had managed to hide behind a boulder without attracting anyone's notice. He then descended the rocky trail by himself, reached the pony, and was now leading it back to the Fortezza. He verified, much to his amazement, that the horse wasn't his. But now nothing could be done.

Only when the unit was entering the Fortezza did several friends notice he had disappeared. If Tronk were to learn of it, Lazzari would wind up in prison for at least a couple of months. He had to be saved. So when the sergeant major called the roll and Lazzari's name came up, someone answered "presente" for him.

A few minutes later, when the soldiers had already broken ranks, some recalled that Lazzari didn't know the password. No longer was the issue prison, then, but life. If he turned up at the walls, it could prove fatal: they would shoot at him. Two or three of his supporters went in search of Tronk so that a remedy might be found.

Too late. Holding the black horse by the reins, Lazzari was already close to the walls. And Tronk was making the rounds, summoned back by a vague premonition. Right after the sergeant major had called the roll, an uneasiness came over him. He was unable to establish its cause, but he knew instinctively that something wasn't right. Reviewing the events of the day, he got as far as the return to the Fortezza without finding anything suspect. Then he ran into a kind of stumbling block. Yes, an irregularity must've occurred during roll call, but at that moment, as often happens in these cases, he hadn't noticed it.

A sentry was patrolling right over the entry gate. In the shadow he saw two dark figures approaching over the gravel. They were two hundred meters away. He paid no attention, thinking he was hallucinating. Quite often, when you spend a long time waiting in deserted places, you wind up glimpsing human shapes slipping out from behind bushes and rocks in the full light of day. You have the impression that someone is spying on you, but when you go and look, no one is there.

To distract himself the sentry looked around. He waved to a colleague, another sentry about thirty meters to the right. He adjusted his heavy cap, which pinched his forehead. Then he turned his eyes to the left—and saw Sergeant Major Tronk, unbudging, staring sternly at him.

The sentry got his bearings and again looked ahead. He saw that the two shadows weren't a dream. They were closer now, scarcely seventy meters away: a soldier and a horse, to be exact. At this point, he raised his rifle to his shoulder, cocked it, and stood stiffly in the position he had repeated hundreds of times in training. Then he shouted, "Who goes there? Who goes there?"

Lazzari had been a solider for a short time. He didn't think—even remotely—that he wouldn't be able to get back inside without the password. At most he feared punishment for leaving without permission. But you can't be certain: maybe the colonel would pardon him for retrieving the horse. It was a very beautiful animal, a horse worthy of a general.

About forty meters remained. The horse's shoes resounded on the stones. It was almost completely dark. The distant sound of a bugle could be heard. "Who goes there?" repeated the sentry. "Who goes there?" One more time and then he would have to shoot.

A sudden uneasiness had taken hold of Lazzari at the sentry's first challenge. To be interrogated like that by a friend, now that he found himself personally in a tough spot, seemed so strange to him. But he brightened up at the second "Who goes there?" because he recognized the voice of a friend, someone from the same company. They had given him the nickname Moretto.

"It's me, Lazzari!" he shouted. "Send for the commander of the guard to open up! I've nabbed the horse! Don't let them catch sight of you till they get me inside!"

The sentry didn't move. He stood firm, his rifle raised, trying to delay the third "Who goes there?" as long as possible. Maybe Lazzari would realize the danger on his own and turn back. He could even join up with the guard at the New Redoubt the next day. A few meters away stood Tronk, however, staring at him sternly.

Tronk said not a word. His eyes shifted between the sentry and Lazzari, for whose infraction the officer would probably be punished. What did his stares mean?

Soldier and horse were no more than thirty meters away. To wait longer would have been imprudent. The closer Lazzari came to the gate, the more likely he would be shot.

"Who goes there? Who goes there?" shouted the sentry for the third time. The tone of his voice implied a private warning that ran counter to the regulations. He wanted to say, Turn back while there's time! Do you want to get yourself killed?

Finally Lazzari understood. In a flash he recalled the harsh laws of the Fortezza. He felt lost. But rather than flee he inexplicably dropped the horse's reins and began to advance by himself, imploring in a piercing voice, "It's me, Lazzari! Don't you see me? Moretto, please, it's me! What are you doing with that rifle? Are you crazy, Moretto?"

The sentry, however, was no longer Moretto. He was simply a soldier with a hard face who had raised his rifle and was now taking aim against his friend. He rested the gun against his shoulder while out of the corner of his eye he spied the sergeant major. He was silently begging for a sign to stand down. But Tronk remained motionless, staring at him sternly.

Without turning Lazzari retreated several steps, stumbling on the stones. "It's me, Lazzari!" he shouted. "Don't you see it's me? Don't shoot, Moretto!"

But the sentry was no longer the Moretto who would frankly joke with his colleagues. He was just a sentry at the Fortezza, wearing a uniform made from dark blue cloth with a leather bandolier, absolutely identical to every other sentry in the night, an ordinary sentry who had taken aim and was now pressing the trigger. He felt a roar in his ears and thought he heard Tronk's gruff voice—"Aim well!"—although Tronk hadn't breathed a word.

The rifle emitted a small flash and a tiny cloud of smoke. Initially the shot wasn't so loud, but it was multiplied by echoes. Resonating from wall to wall, it hung in the air for some time, dying away in a distant rumble like thunder.

Now that the sentry had done his duty, he placed the rifle on the ground, leaned out from the parapet, and looked down, hoping he had missed. In the darkness, in fact, he judged that Lazzari hadn't fallen.

No, Lazzari was still on his feet and the horse had drawn close to him. Then, in the silence left by the shot, you heard his voice making such a desperate sound: "Oh, Moretto, you've killed me!"

So Lazzari said as he slowly slumped forward. Tronk, his face impenetrable, still hadn't moved. A warlike confusion spread through the mazes of the Fortezza.

13

Thus began that memorable night, traversed by winds, amid swaying lanterns, unexpected bugle calls, footsteps in passageways beneath parapets. Clouds descending headlong from the north got tangled in rocky peaks, leaving shreds attached. They had no time to stop. Something very important was summoning them.

One shot was enough, a modest discharge from a rifle, and the Fortezza was awakened. For years silence had coincided with constant straining toward the north to hear the voice of impending war—a silence that lasted much too long. Now a rifle had been shot—with its prescribed load of powder and a lead ball of thirty-two grams—and the men looked at each other as if a signal had been given.

On this night, of course, only a few soldiers utter the name that lies in the hearts of all. The officers prefer to suppress it because it constitutes their very hope. Because of the Tartars, they've raised the walls of the Fortezza, wasting substantial portions of their lives there. Because of the Tartars, the sentries patrol day and night like automatons. For some, this hope feeds every morning with new faith; others cherish it, hidden deep within themselves; still others are unaware of whether they even possess it, believing it to be lost. But no one has the courage to speak it. That would seem to make it an ill omen. Above all, that would mean confessing their own most precious thoughts, an act that soldiers find shameful.

For now there's only a dead soldier and a horse of unknown provenance. In the ranks of the guard, at the gate that gives onto the north—the location of the tragedy—a great deal of turmoil has erupted. Tronk too can be found there, although it isn't consistent with the regulations. He's troubled, dwelling on the punishment that awaits him. The responsibility falls on him. He should've stopped Lazzari from slipping away. He should've noticed immediately, when the unit returned, that the soldier hadn't answered during roll call.

Now Major Matti shows up as well, eager to impose his own authority and competence. He wears a strange face that evades understanding; it can even give the impression that he is smiling. Evidently he received a first-rate report about the whole affair and ordered Lieutenant Mentana, who was on duty at that redoubt, to have the soldier's corpse removed.

Mentana is an insignificant officer, the oldest lieutenant at the Fortezza. If he didn't wear a huge diamond ring and play chess well, no one would take any notice of his existence. The precious stone on his ring finger is gigantic, and few players manage to beat him on the chessboard. Yet before Major Matti he literally trembles. In a matter as simple as sending a recovery party for a dead man he loses his head.

Fortunately for him, Major Matti spots Sergeant Major Tronk standing in a corner and calls out, "Tronk, seeing you have nothing to do here, take charge of the squad!"

This he says with the utmost ease, as if Tronk might've been an ordinary noncommissioned officer without any personal connection to the incident. Because Matti is incapable of giving a direct reprimand, he ends up blanching with rage and can't find the words. He prefers the much harsher weapon of inquests, complete with phlegmatic interrogators and written documentation, which succeed in magnifying the slightest failures monstrously and almost always carry severe punishments.

Tronk doesn't bat an eye. He responds, "Yessir," and hurries down to the courtyard immediately behind the entry gate. Soon thereafter a small group exits the Fortezza in the light of lanterns: Tronk at the head, then four soldiers with a stretcher, four additional soldiers— armed as a precaution—and lastly Major Matti himself, wrapped in a faded cloak, dragging his saber across the stones.

They find Lazzari just as he died, facedown on the ground, arms outstretched before him. His rifle, slung over his shoulder, was wedged between two stones when he fell and it stands straight up, butt in the air, a strange thing to see. The soldier injured his hand in his fall and before the body got cold a small amount of blood managed to drip, forming a stain on a white stone. The mysterious horse has disappeared.

Tronk bends over the dead man. He is about to seize him by the shoulders but he suddenly draws back, as if he realized he would be going against the rules. "Pick him up," he orders the soldiers in a low, nasty voice. "But first remove the rifle."

A soldier stoops to unfasten the strap, setting down the lantern on the stones, right next to the dead man. Lazzari didn't have time to close his eyes. The flame casts a pale reflection on the gap between his lids, the white parts.

"Tronk," calls Major Matti, who has remained entirely in shadow.

"Yes, major sir," Tronk answers, standing at attention. The soldiers also stop.

"Where did it happen? Where did he run off?" asks the major, dragging out the words as if he spoke with bored curiosity. "Was it at the spring? Where those boulders are?"

"Yessir, at the boulders," Tronk responds without adding a word.

"And no one saw him when he ran off?"

"No one, sir," says Tronk.

"At the spring, eh? Was it dark?"

"Yessir, quite dark."

Tronk waits a few moments at attention. Then, since Matti is silent, he signals the soldiers to continue. One tries to unfasten the rifle strap but the buckle is difficult and he struggles with it. As the soldier pulls, he feels the weight of the dead body, an enormous weight, like lead.

After the rifle is removed, two soldiers delicately turn over the corpse so it lies faceup. Now his countenance is completely visible. The mouth is closed and inexpressive. Only the eyes, half-opened and motionless, withstanding the lantern light, know of death.

"In the forehead?" asks Matti, who has immediately noticed a kind of small indentation, just above the nose.

"Sir?" says Tronk without comprehending.

"I say: Was he shot in the forehead?" Matti is irritated that he has to repeat himself.

Tronk raises the lantern, fully lighting Lazzari's face. He too sees the small indentation and instinctively stretches out a finger as if to touch. At once, however, he withdraws it, disturbed.

"I believe so, major sir, right here in the middle of the forehead." (But why doesn't he come himself to examine the dead man if he's so interested? Why all these stupid questions?)

The soldiers, noticing Tronk's embarrassment, attend to their work. Two lift the corpse by the shoulders, two by the legs. The head, left to itself, dangles backward horribly. The mouth, although frozen by death, twists as if to open.

"Who fired the shot?" Matti persists, still motionless in the darkness.

But at that moment Tronk isn't following him. Tronk is focused only on the dead man. "Hold up the head," he orders, infuriated, as if he were the dead man. Then he realizes that Matti has spoken and he snaps back to attention.

"Pardon me, major sir. I was—"

"I said," repeats Major Matti, "who fired the shot?" He emphasizes each word, making clear that if he doesn't lose patience, it's entirely due to the dead man.

"What's his name?" Tronk whispers to the soldiers. "Do you know him?"

"Martelli," someone says. "Giovanni Martelli."

"Giovanni Martelli," Tronk responds to Matti.

"Martelli," the major repeats to himself. (That name isn't new to him. It must belong to one of the prizewinners in the shooting competition. Matti himself directs the gunnery school and he remembers the best by name.) "Is he perhaps the one they call Moretto?"

"Yessir," answers Tronk, still standing at attention. "I believe they call him Moretto. You know, major sir, among friends."

Tronk resorts to this explanation as if to excuse Martelli, as if to demonstrate he isn't responsible for them calling him Moretto, it isn't his fault, and there's really no reason to punish him.

But by no means is the major thinking of punishing him; it doesn't even cross his mind. "Ah, Moretto!" he exclaims without concealing a certain satisfaction.

The sergeant major directs a harsh stare at him and understands. Of course, of course, he thinks, give him a prize, the swine, because he did a swell job of killing. A magnificent bull's-eye, right?

A magnificent bull's-eye, undoubtedly. That's exactly what Matti is weighing (and to think that when Moretto fired the shot, night had already fallen. At the top of his game, like all the major's marksmen.)

Right now Tronk hates him. Go ahead, go on, he thinks, say you're pleased. Do you give a damn Lazzari is dead? Shout bravo to your Moretto! Give him a grand commendation!

This is essentially what happens. The major, absolutely calm, congratulates him in a loud voice: "That Moretto doesn't miss," he crows, as if to say, Lazzari was crafty. He thought Moretto's aim wouldn't be true and he would get away with it. Instead Lazzari learned what sort of a shot Moretto was. And Tronk? Probably he too hoped Moretto would miss (and then the whole matter would be settled with a few days in the stockade).

"He certainly doesn't miss," repeats the major, entirely forgetting that he is standing before a dead man. "A crack shot, that Moretto!"

Finally, however, he falls silent and the sergeant major can turn his attention to the way they've placed the corpse on the stretcher. It's already laid out properly. They've thrown a field blanket over the face. Only bare hands can be seen, the coarse hands of a farmworker, which still seem red with life and warm blood.

Tronk nods. The soldiers lift the stretcher. "Can we go, major sir?" he asks.

"Who are you waiting for?" Matti's response is bitter. He is truly astonished to have felt Tronk's hatred and he aims to repay it in spades, adding the disdain of a superior.

"Forward," orders Tronk. He should have said, "Forward march," but he feels that would be virtually a desecration. Only now does he survey the walls of the Fortezza, taking in the sentry on the parapet faintly lit by the reflections from the lanterns. Behind those walls, in the barracks, lie Lazzari's cot and his locker with the things he brought from home: a holy image, two corncobs, a tinderbox, some colored handkerchiefs, four silver buttons for a dress suit. The buttons had belonged to his grandfather; they could never be of any use at the Fortezza.

The pillow may still bear the imprint of his head, exactly as he left it two days ago when he awoke. Then there is probably a small bottle of ink as well—Tronk makes this mental addition, meticulous even in his solitary thoughts—a small bottle of ink and a pen. All this will be put in a parcel and sent to his home with a letter from the colonel. The remaining things, issued by the government, will naturally pass to another soldier, including the change of shirt. But not the handsome uniform or even the rifle: rifle and uniform will be buried with him because such is the time-honored rule of the Fortezza.

14

At the crack of dawn the New Redoubt saw a narrow black band on the northern plain. It was a thin, moving target; it couldn't be a hallucination. It was spotted first by the sentry Andronico, next by the sentry Pietri, followed by Sergeant Batta, who initially burst into laughter, and then even by Lieutenant Maderna, commanding officer of the redoubt.

A narrow black band was advancing from the north across the uninhabited plain. It seemed an absurd portent, although premonitions had been circulating throughout the Fortezza during the night. At approximately six the sentry Andronico issued the first alarm. Something was approaching from the north, a development that had never occurred in recent memory. As the light intensified, the human formation that was forging ahead stood out sharply against the white background of the desert.

Several minutes later the head tailor Prosdocimo, as he had done every morning from time immemorial (motivated at first by sheer hope, then by scruples alone, now almost entirely by habit), climbed to the roof of the Fortezza to take a gander. The guards customarily allowed him to pass. He would look out from the walkway on the battlements, chat a bit with the sergeant on duty, and then descend again to his cellar.

That morning when he looked out he directed his gaze toward the visible triangle of desert—and believed he was dead. He didn't think it could be a dream. Dreams always contain something absurd and confused; you never shake off the vague sensation that everything is untrue, that eventually you'll have to wake up. In dreams things are never limpid and concrete like that desolate plain where ranks of unknown men were gaining ground.

Yet the thing was so strange, identical to some of Prosdocimo's youthful ravings, that he didn't think it could be true. Hence he believed he had died.

He believed he had died and God had pardoned him. He thought he was in the other world, apparently identical to ours, except that beautiful things happen according to just desires, and after desires have been satisfied, you're left with peace of mind, not like down here, where something always poisons even the best days.

Prosdocimo believed he had died, and he didn't budge. He supposed not only that he wasn't obliged to move any longer, since he was deceased, but that an arcane intervention would rouse him. It was rather a sergeant major who respectfully touched his arm.

"Marshal," he said. "What's wrong? Don't you feel well?"

Only then did Prosdocimo begin to comprehend.

Almost as if he were dreaming, just better, mysterious people were descending from the northern kingdom. Time was passing rapidly. Eyes ceased to blink as they fixed on the unusual image. The sun was already shining on the red border of the horizon. Little by little the foreigners were drawing closer, yet with the utmost slowness. Someone said they were on foot and horseback, they were advancing in single file, they were flying a flag. So said someone and others too were under the same illusion—everyone got it into their heads that they had glimpsed foot soldiers and cavalry, the cloth of a standard, a single file, even though in reality they discerned only a narrow black band moving slowly.

"The Tartars," the sentry Andronico dared to say as if it were some brash joke, while his face turned deathly pale. Half an hour later, at the New Redoubt, Lieutenant Maderna ordered a blank shot from a cannon, a warning shot, as was prescribed in case an armed contingent of foreigners was seen approaching.

A cannon hadn't been heard there for many years. The walls sustained a slight tremor. The report broadened into a slow roar, the foreboding sound of destruction among the cliffs. Lieutenant Maderna's eyes turned to the flat profile of the Fortezza, expecting signs of agitation. The cannon shot, however, didn't cause amazement, because the foreigners were advancing precisely over that triangular portion of the plain visible from the central fort. Everyone had already been informed. The news had reached the most peripheral tunnel where the rampart that ran to the left terminated against the rock face. It had reached even the sentry who guarded the underground storeroom for lanterns and masonry equipment and could see nothing, sealed off in a dark cellar. He trembled with impatience for time to hurry, for his shift to end, so that he too might climb up to the walkway to catch a glimpse.

Everything continued as before. The sentries remained at their posts, pacing back and forth in the prescribed space. The clerks copied reports, scratching their pens and dipping them in inkwells with the usual rhythm. Yet unknown men whom you might reasonably presume to be enemies were coming from the north. Men curried animals in the stables. The fireplaces in the kitchens emitted smoke phlegmatically. Three soldiers swept the courtyard. Yet over everything hung an intensely solemn feeling, an immense suspension of thought, as if the momentous hour had arrived and nothing could stop it.

Officers and soldiers breathed the morning air deeply in an effort to feel the vibrancy of youth. The gunners began to prepare the cannons. They joked among themselves as they worked around the guns, treating them like animals that needed to be kept docile, watching them with a certain apprehension. Perhaps, after so long a time, the guns wouldn't be capable of firing; perhaps in the past they hadn't been cleaned with sufficient care and some remedy would need to be found. In a short while everything would be decided. Never had couriers dashed up stairs so fast; never were uniforms so neat, bayonets so shiny, bugle calls so military. The wait hadn't been in vain; the years hadn't been wasted. The old Fortezza would serve some purpose after all.

Now a special bugle sound was anticipated, the signal for the general alarm, which the soldiers had never had the privilege of hearing. The buglers rehearsed the famous signal during placid summer afternoons in their training, conducted outside the Fortezza in a remote ravine (so the sound wouldn't reach the fort and cause any misunderstanding). They rehearsed it more from excessive zeal than anything else (no one imagined it would be of any use). Now they regretted they hadn't practiced it enough. It was an extremely long arpeggio, rising to a very high note. Some of the playing would probably be off.

Only the commanding officer of the Fortezza could order the signal, and everyone's thoughts were fixed on him. The soldiers were already awaiting his arrival to inspect the walls from end to end. They already saw him advancing with a proud smile, staring everyone straight in the eyes. It had to be a good day for him. Hadn't he spent his life looking forward to this opportunity?

Colonel Filimore, however, remained in his office. From the window he looked toward the north at the small triangle of empty plain that the cliffs didn't hide. He saw a series of black points moving like ants, precisely in his direction, toward the Fortezza. They truly seemed to be soldiers.

Every so often some officer or another would enter, whether Lieutenant Colonel Nicolosi or the orderly captain or officers on duty. Waiting impatiently for the colonel's orders, they entered on various pretexts and announced insignificant news: another carriage of provisions had arrived from the city; the task of repairing the oven would be started that morning; about ten soldiers were coming off furlough; a telescope had been assembled on the terrace of the central fort, should the colonel ever wish to take advantage of it.

They reported their news and saluted, clicking their heels. They didn't understand why the colonel stood there mute, failing to issue the commands they all expected for certain. He still hadn't reinforced the guards or doubled the ammunition supply for each soldier or decided to sound the signal for the general alarm.

He seemed to have succumbed to some mysterious lethargy so that, neither sad nor happy, he was coldly observing the foreigners' approach as if it had nothing to do with him.

It was, furthermore, a splendid October day. The sun was clear, the air buoyant—the most desirable weather for a battle. The wind stirred the flag raised over the roof of the fort. The yellow earth of the courtyard glistened, and the soldiers who crossed it left precisely etched shadows. A beautiful morning, colonel sir.

But the commandant left no doubt that he preferred to remain alone. When the office had been vacated, he moved from the desk to the window, from the window to the desk, unable to choose between them. He would smooth his gray moustache for no reason and heave long sighs which were exclusively physical, as happens with the elderly.

At this point, the black band of foreigners could no longer be perceived on the small triangle of plain visible from the window, a sign they had traveled past it and were increasingly close to the border. In three or four hours they would be at the foot of the mountains.

The colonel, however, pointlessly kept cleaning the lenses of his spectacles with a handkerchief. He leafed through the files stacked on the table: the orderly log, which needed to be signed; a request for leave; the daily report from the medical officer; a bill of lading from the saddlery.

Why are you waiting, colonel? The sun is already high. Even Major Matti, who entered the office a little while ago, doesn't conceal a certain apprehensiveness—he who never believes anything. At least show yourself to the sentries; take a turn on the walls. According to Captain Forze, who has gone to inspect the New Redoubt, the foreigners can now be distinguished individually. They turn out to be armed: they're carrying rifles on their shoulders. There's no time to waste.

But Filimore wants to wait. Those foreigners are soldiers, he doesn't deny. But how many are there? Someone said two hundred, someone else two hundred and fifty. They also pointed out to him that if this is the vanguard, the main force will be at least two thousand men. Yet that force has yet to be seen. It might not even exist.

The main force has yet to be seen, colonel, only because of the mists from the north. This morning the mists were far advanced; the northerly wind has pushed them downward so they cover a vast area of the plain. Those two hundred men would be meaningless if a strong army weren't descending behind them. The others will certainly show up before noon. A sentry says, in fact, that a little while ago he saw something moving at the edge of the mists.

But the commandant walks back and forth from window to desk, listlessly leafing through files. Why, he thinks, should foreigners attack the Fortezza? They may be carrying out routine operations to test the rigors of the desert. The time of the Tartars has passed; they're no more than a distant legend. Who else might be interested in violating the border? There's something unpersuasive in this whole business.

They may not be Tartars, colonel, no, but they are certainly soldiers. For quite a few years deep resentments have characterized relations with the kingdom of the north. This situation isn't a mystery to anyone; war has been mentioned more than once. They are certainly soldiers. They are on horseback and on foot. Artillery will probably show up soon. Before nightfall—no exaggeration—they will arrive in plenty of time to mount an attack. The walls of the Fortezza are old, old are the rifles, the cannons, everything is absolutely obsolete, apart from the spirit of the soldiers. Don't be too trusting, colonel.

Trust! Oh, he would very much like to be incapable of trust. He wasted his life because of it. He doesn't have many years left. If this isn't the right moment, everything is probably finished. It isn't fear that slows him down; it isn't the thought of dying. It doesn't even cross his mind.

The fact is that near the end of his life Filimore was witnessing the sudden arrival of Fortune, clad in silver armor, wielding a sword stained with blood. He saw her approaching strangely with a friendly face (by this point he had almost stopped thinking of her). But Filimore—this is the truth—didn't dare move toward her and respond to her smile. He had been mistaken too many times. Now he'd had enough.

The others, the officers at the Fortezza, had immediately hurried to meet her, giving her a warm welcome. They had come forward trustfully, unlike him, anticipating the powerful, acrid stench of battle as if they had experienced it on another occasion. The colonel, however, was waiting. Until the beautiful apparition touched him with her hand, he wouldn't budge, as if superstitious. Some trivial thing—a simple nod of greeting, an admission of desire—might be enough to make the image vanish into thin air.

Hence he limited himself to shaking his head to signify, No, Fortune must be wrong. He looked incredulously around and behind himself, where presumably other people stood, those whom Fortune truly sought. But he glimpsed no one else. And it couldn't be a case of mistaken identity. He was compelled to agree that the enviable destiny was ordained precisely for him.

There had been a moment, in the first light of dawn, when the mysterious black band had appeared to him on the white ground of the desert, a moment when his heart had gasped with joy. Then the image of silver armor and bloodied sword grew slightly fainter. It was still moving toward him, but in reality it couldn't approach any closer or reduce the brief yet infinite distance.

The reason is that Filimore has already waited too long, and at a certain age hope costs enormous effort: the faith of a twenty-year-old can't be recovered. He has waited too long in vain. His eyes have read too many orderly logs; on too many mornings his eyes have seen that damn plain always empty.

And now that the foreigners have appeared, he has the peculiar impression that some mistake must have been made (it would be too sublime otherwise). There must really be some gross, underlying blunder.

Meanwhile the pendulum clock opposite the desk continued to chip away at life, and the colonel's thin fingers, withered by years, persisted in cleaning the lenses of his spectacles with the aid of a handkerchief, even though it was unnecessary.

The clock hands were approaching half past ten and Major Matti entered the room to remind the commandant of his report to the officers. Filimore had forgotten about it, and he was unpleasantly surprised: he was duty bound to speak of the foreigners who had appeared on the plain. He could no longer defer the decision. He would have to identify them officially as enemies or joke about them or steer a middle course by ordering security measures and showing his skepticism at the same time, as if the incident weren't nerve-racking. But a decision still had to be taken and that displeased him. He would have preferred to continue waiting, to remain absolutely motionless, almost as if to provoke fate to run amok.

Major Matti, with one of his ambiguous smiles, said to him, "Here we go. Looks like this is it!" Colonel Filimore didn't respond. The major said, "You can see more coming now. There are three ranks. You can even see them from here." The colonel looked him in the eye, nearly feeling fond of him for a moment. "They're still coming, you say?"

"Even from here you can see them, colonel. There are so many at this point."

They went to the window. On the visible triangle of the northern plain they spotted new narrow black bands in motion, no longer one as at dawn, but three positioned side by side. You couldn't make out where they ended.

War, war, thought the colonel, uselessly trying to dispel the thought as if it were a prohibited desire. At Matti's words his hope was aroused again, and it was now filling him with excitement.

His mind seething, the colonel suddenly found himself in the assembly room with all the officers ranged before him (except those on guard duty). Above the blue stain of uniforms gleamed the pallor of singular faces which he struggled to recognize. Young or wrinkled, they all said the same thing: eyes feverishly lit, they greedily begged him to make the formal announcement that the enemy had arrived. Standing rigidly at attention, they all stared at him with the demand that they not be defrauded.

In the heavy silence of the room only the officers' deep breathing could be heard. The colonel realized that he must speak. In those moments he felt invaded by a strange, unbridled passion. Amazed, without perceiving the reason, Filimore suddenly felt certain that the foreigners were truly enemies, determined to violate the border. He didn't precisely understand how it had happened—he who until a moment ago had been capable of conquering the temptation to believe. He felt as if he were being swept away by the tension they all shared. He knew he would speak without reserve. "Officers," he would say, "behold: the hour we have awaited for so many years has finally arrived." This is what he would say, or something similar, and the officers would gratefully listen to his words, an authoritative pledge of glory.

He was about to speak in this vein but again, from the recesses of his mind, a contrary voice was insisting. "It is impossible, colonel," this voice said. "Be wary, while you still have time. There is some mistake (it would be too sublime otherwise). There is a gross, underlying blunder."

Amid the feeling that was flooding him, this enemy voice would surface every so often. But it was late: the delay was starting to become embarrassing.

The colonel took a step forward and lifted his head as he customarily did when he was beginning to speak. The officers saw that his face had suddenly turned red: yes, the colonel was blushing like a boy because he was about to confess the guarded secret of his own life.

He had delicately blushed like a boy and his lips were about to emit the first sound when the hostile voice rose from the depths of his mind and Filimore shuddered with apprehension. He then thought he heard impetuous footsteps climbing the stairs and approaching the room where they had gathered. None of the officers noticed, focused as they all were on their commandant. After so many years, however, Filimore's hearing had been trained to distinguish the faintest sounds in the Fortezza.

The footsteps were undoubtedly approaching with unaccustomed haste. They sounded at once foreign and dreary, quite like an administrative inspection. They were coming directly, the colonel would have said, from the world of the plain. The noise now reached the other officers as well, loud and clear, inflicting a coarse wound to their sensibilities, although they couldn't say why. The door finally opened and an unfamiliar officer from the dragoons appeared, panting from exhaustion and covered with dust.

He stood at attention. "Lieutenant Fernandez," he said, "from the Seventh Regiment of dragoons. I bear this message from the city on behalf of His Excellency, the chief of the General Staff." Elegantly holding his crested helmet with his left arm curved in an arc, he approached the colonel and delivered a wax-sealed envelope to him.

Filimore shook his hand. "Thank you, lieutenant," he said. "You've clearly had a rough journey. Our fellow officer Santi will now escort you for some refreshment." Without revealing even a trace of anxiety the colonel nodded at Lieutenant Santi, the first officer his eye happened to pick out, inviting him to act as host. The two officers left and the door was closed. "Will you allow me?" Filimore asked with a thin smile, displaying the envelope to indicate that he preferred to read it right away. His hands delicately broke the seals, tore off a flap, and removed a folded sheet of paper covered completely in writing.

The officers stared at him while he read, trying to see something reflected in his face. But there was nothing. As if he were glancing through a newspaper after supper, sitting by the fire, on a lethargic winter evening. Only the blush had vanished from the commandant's lean face.

When he had finished reading, the colonel folded the sheet of paper, inserted it again into the envelope, put the envelope into his pocket, and lifted his head, signaling that he was about to speak. You could feel in the air that something had happened, that the spell in force a short while before had been broken.

"Officers," he said, his voice struggling, "this morning, if I am not mistaken, the soldiers were agitated to some extent, as you were, as I am not mistaken, because of the troops observed on the so-called Tartar plain."

His words strained to open a path in the profound silence. A fly darted back and forth in the room.

"The situation," he continued, "the situation is that troops from the kingdom of the north have been entrusted with establishing the borderline, as we ourselves had done many years ago. They will therefore not come near the Fortezza. They will probably disperse into groups, ranging over the mountains. This letter from His Excellency, the chief of the General Staff, officially communicates the information to me."

As Filimore spoke, he heaved long sighs, not expressive of impatience or grief but exclusively physical, as often happens with elderly men. He also seemed elderly in his voice, which had suddenly become hollow and limp, and in his eyes, which turned yellowish and opaque.

Colonel Filimore had sensed it from the beginning. The troops couldn't be enemies, he knew quite well. He hadn't been born for glory. He had foolishly deluded himself so many times. Why—he angrily asked himself—why did he let himself be deceived? He had sensed from the beginning that it had to end like this.

"As you know," he continued in a tone too apathetic not to seem extremely bitter, "many years ago we set up boundary stones and other signs of demarcation. There remains, however, a tract that is still not defined, as His Excellency informs me. To complete the work I shall send a certain number of men under the command of a captain and a subaltern. It is a mountainous zone with two or three parallel chains. It is superfluous to add that the best thing would be to make as much progress as possible in securing the northern border. Not that strategically it is essential, if you understand me right, because war could never break out there or offer possibilities of maneuvering—" he interrupted himself, losing his train of thought. "Possibilities of maneuvering—what was I saying?"

"You were talking about the need to make as much progress as possible," prompted Major Matti with suspect compunction.

"Ah, yes: I was saying that we would need to make as much progress as possible. Unfortunately the thing is not easy: we now lag behind those from the north. All the same...Well, we shall discuss the matter later," he concluded, turning toward Lieutenant Colonel Nicolosi.

He fell silent and seemed exhausted. He had seen a veil of disappointment descend over the officers' faces while he was speaking; he had seen them metamorphose from warriors eager for combat back into humdrum officers in a garrison. But they were young, he thought. They would still have time.

"Good," the colonel proceeded. "It pains me that I must now make a comment applicable to a number of you. More than once I have noticed that at the change of guard several platoons turn up in the courtyard unaccompanied by their respective officers. These officers evidently deem themselves authorized to arrive later."

The fly darted back and forth in the room. The flag on the roof of the fort had gone limp. The colonel was speaking of discipline and regulations. In the northern plain ranks of armed men were advancing, no longer enemies keen for battle but innocuous soldiers like them, bent not on wreaking havoc but rather on conducting a land survey. Their rifles were unloaded, their daggers blunted. Down onto the northern plain streams that inoffensive semblance of an army, while in the Fortezza everything stagnates again in the rhythm of routine days.

15

THE NEXT day at dawn the expedition departed to delimit the border in the tract of frontier that remained exposed. The huge Captain Monti commanded it, accompanied by Lieutenant Angustina and a sergeant major. Each of the three had been entrusted with the password for that day as well as the next four days. The possibility that all three might perish was most unlikely. The eldest surviving officer, in any case, would have the authority to open the jacket of the superior officers who had died or lost consciousness, to search through an inside pocket, and to remove the sealed envelope containing the secret word to get back inside the Fortezza.

While the sun was rising, approximately forty armed men issued from the walls of the Fortezza, heading north. Captain Monti wore heavy hobnailed boots, like those of the soldiers. Only Angustina wore jackboots, and the captain had eyed them with exaggerated curiosity before departing, although without saying a word.

They descended roughly one hundred meters down scree slopes and then turned right, horizontally, toward the mouth of a narrow, rocky valley that pierced the heart of the mountain.

They had been marching for half an hour when the captain spoke.

"Those"—he nodded at Angustina's jackboots—"will give you trouble."

Angustina said nothing.

"I don't want you to have to stop," the captain resumed after a bit. "They'll hurt you. You'll see."

Angustina replied, "It's too late now, captain sir. You could've told me about it before if it's like you say."

"It wouldn't have mattered," retorted Monti. "I know you, Angustina. You would've worn them anyway."

Monti couldn't stomach him. With all the airs you give yourself, he thought, I'll show you before long. And he stepped up the pace to the maximum, even on the steepest slopes, knowing that Angustina wasn't hardy. In the meantime they had gotten near the base of the walls. The scree had become more granular, and their feet were plunging laboriously into it.

"Ordinarily," the captain said, "an infernal wind blows down this gulley. But today the air feels good."

Lieutenant Angustina was silent.

"We're also lucky there's no sun," resumed Monti. "Things are really going well today."

"So you've been here before?" asked Angustina.

"Once," Monti replied. "We had to track down a soldier who ran—"

He interrupted himself because the sound of a landslide had come from the top of a gray rock wall looming over them. They heard the thud of boulders crashing against the cliffs and rebounding savagely down into the chasm amid clouds of dust. A thunderous roar reverberated from wall to wall. The mysterious landslide continued a few minutes in the heart of the cliffs but lost its momentum in the deep hollows before reaching the bottom. Only two or three stones rolled in the gravel where the soldiers were climbing.

They had all fallen silent. In the thunder from the landslide they had sensed an enemy presence. Monti looked at Angustina with a vague attitude of defiance. He hoped the lieutenant might be afraid, but he wasn't in the least. He did, however, appear ridiculously overheated from the brief march; his elegant uniform was disheveled.

With all the airs you give yourself, you damn snob, thought Monti, I want to see how you're doing in a little while. He immediately resumed the march, forcing the pace even more. Every so often he would cast a glance behind to scrutinize Angustina. Just as he had hoped and foreseen, the jackboots were noticeably beginning to torture the lieutenant's feet. Not that Angustina slowed his pace or wore a pained expression. You could tell from the rhythm of his marching and the look of serious commitment that marked his forehead.

The captain said, "Today I feel like I could keep at it for another six hours. If only the soldiers weren't here. Things are really going well." His insistence seemed ingenuous but it was actually crafty. "How goes it, lieutenant?"

"Pardon me, captain," replied Angustina. "What did you say?"

"Nothing." He smiled wickedly. "I was asking how you were doing."

"Ah yes, thanks," Angustina said evasively. And after a pause to conceal his panting from the climb he added, "What a shame that—"

"What?" asked Monti, hoping the other man would confess his weariness.

"What a shame we can't come up here more often. The area is very beautiful." And he smiled with his peculiar detachment.

Monti accelerated the pace even more. But Angustina kept up behind him. His face was now pale from exertion. Sweat trickled down the edge of his cap. Even the fabric of his jacket, on his back, was drenched. But he didn't say a word or drop back.

At this point, they had set foot among the cliffs. Horrendous gray walls rose vertically all around. The valley looked as if it would ascend to inconceivable heights.

Traces of the usual flora and fauna ceased, giving way to the motionless desolation of the mountain. Fascinated, Angustina would occasionally lift his eyes to the peaks leaning over them.

"We'll take a break farther on," said Monti, who kept an eye on him. "The place still hasn't come into sight. But, really, aren't you a bit tired? Sometimes a soldier feels he can't handle it. It's better to say so, even if it does risk a delay."

"Let's keep moving" was Angustina's reply, as if he were the superior.

"Really? I said that because anyone might feel he can't handle it. That's what I meant."

Angustina was ashen. Sweat was streaming from the edge of his cap. His jacket was completely saturated. But he clenched his teeth and did not relent. He would rather die. Trying to avoid the captain's notice, he stole glances at the summit of the gorge in search of an end to his exhaustion.

Meanwhile the sun had risen, lighting up the highest peaks, although without the fresh radiance of fine autumn mornings. A veil of fog was slowly spreading in the sky, deceitful yet uniform.

Angustina's jackboots were now beginning to hurt like hell. The leather was biting into his instep. To judge from the pain, his skin must be broken at this point.

All of a sudden, the scree ended and the valley opened into a small plateau with stunted grass at the base of a cirque surrounded by sheer cliffs. Rock walls whose height was difficult to estimate rose on each side in a tangle of towers and crevices.

Captain Monti ordered a halt, even if reluctantly, and gave the soldiers time to eat. Angustina sat on a boulder, self-possessed, although he was shivering as the wind chilled his sweat. He and the captain shared some bread, slices of meat and cheese, and a bottle of wine.

Angustina felt cold. He watched the captain and soldiers so he could follow their example if any of them unrolled their cloaks. Yet the soldiers were joking among themselves, apparently unaffected by exhaustion. The captain ate with greedy satisfaction. Between mouthfuls he gazed at a steep mountain above them.

"Now," he said, "now I've figured out where we can climb," and he nodded at the imposing wall that came to an end on the disputed ridge. "We need to go straight up from here. Fairly vertical, no? What do you say, lieutenant?"

Angustina looked at the wall. To reach the ridge at the border they really needed to ascend from there, unless they wanted to detour by some pass and go around. That would take much more time, however, and haste was of the essence. The soldiers from the north had the advantage because they had mobilized first and from their side the journey was much easier. A frontal attack on the walls was necessary.

"Up from here?" asked Angustina, observing the precipitous cliffs.

He noticed the journey would be much simpler a hundred meters to the left.

"Definitely straight up from here," repeated the captain. "What do you say to it?"

Angustina said, "Anything to get there before them."

The captain looked at him with obvious dislike. "Fine," he said. "Now we'll play a little game."

He drew a pack of playing cards from his pocket and spread his cloak on a squarish boulder. He invited Angustina to play. Then he said, "Those clouds. You look at them in a funny way but don't be afraid. They're not bad-weather clouds." And he laughed inexplicably as if he had told some witty joke.

They began to play. Angustina felt freezing cold from the wind. The captain was sheltered because he sat between two large rocks, but the lieutenant took the brunt of the air on his back. This time I'll get sick, he thought.

"Ah, this is more than you can handle!" the captain shouted, literally shouted without warning. "Good God, leaving me an ace like this! Where's your head, my dear man? You keep looking up and don't pay attention to the cards."

"No, no," responded Angustina. "I made a mistake!" And he tried to laugh, although without success.

"Tell the truth," Monti said with triumphant satisfaction. "Tell the truth: those things are hurting you. I would've sworn it since we set out."

"What things?"

"Those fancy boots of yours. They're not suited to these marches, lieutenant. Tell the truth: they're hurting you."

"I find them irksome," admitted Angustina with a disdainful tone that said talking about the matter bothered him. "They have irked me, basically."

"Ah!" The captain laughed, satisfied. "I knew it! Climbing scree in jackboots is asking for trouble."

"Look: I've played the king of spades." Angustina's reminder was icy. "Don't you have a card to answer me?"

"Yes, yes, my error," said the captain, still quite pleased. "The boots!"

In truth Lieutenant Angustina's jackboots didn't manage well on the rock walls. They tended to slip, lacking nails, while the boots worn by Captain Monti and the soldiers solidly gripped the footholds. This didn't cause Angustina to fall behind: although he was exhausted, although the sweat frozen on his back tortured him, with his redoubled commitment he managed to follow the captain closely up the broken wall.

The mountain turned out to be less difficult and less steep than it appeared when viewed from below. It was furrowed by shafts, crevices, pebbly ledges, and individual rocks roughened by innumerable grips, to which you could easily cling. Not agile by nature, the captain clambered up forcefully, in successive leaps, occasionally glancing below in the hope that Angustina might have buckled. But Angustina held fast. He rapidly sought out the widest and safest supports, astonished by how he could rise so nimbly while feeling so worn out.

As the chasm yawned below them, the final ridge seemed to draw farther and farther away, sheltered by the yellow rock face. Night was approaching more and more quickly, although a dense ceiling of gray clouds prevented any estimation of the remaining height of the sun. It began to turn cold. A bitter wind rose from the gorge and you could hear it gasping in the fissures of the mountain.

At a certain point the sergeant who brought up the rear could be heard shouting from below: "Captain sir!"

Monti stopped, Angustina stopped, and then all the soldiers down to the very last man. "What is it now?" asked the captain, as if other reasons to worry were already troubling him.

"The soldiers from the north are already on the ridge," the sergeant shouted.

"You're mad! Where do you see them?" retorted Monti.

"On the left, in that hollow, right next to that nose-shaped rock!"

They were actually there. Three tiny black figures stood out against the gray sky. They were visibly moving. Evidently they had already reached the lower tract of the ridge and in all probability they would occupy the peak first.

"Damn them," the captain said with an angry glance below as if the soldiers were responsible for the delay. Then to Angustina he added: "At the very least we need to occupy the peak. No ifs, ands, or buts. If we don't, we've had it with the colonel."

"We would need our rivals to stop for a bit," said Angustina. "The climb from the hollow to the peak doesn't take more than an hour. If they don't stop, we'll inevitably get there later."

The captain then said, "Maybe the best thing is for me to go ahead with four soldiers. A small group moves faster. You can follow behind at an easy pace or wait here if you feel tired."

This is where that swine was heading, thought Angustina. He wanted to leave me behind so he could play hero himself.

"Yessir, as you wish," he responded. "But I too prefer to come up. It's too cold to stay here."

The captain set out again with four of the quickest soldiers, forming a vanguard patrol. Angustina assumed command of the remainder, hoping in vain that he could still keep up with Monti. He had too many soldiers. If he stepped up the pace, the line grew so immeasurably long that men completely dropped out of sight.

Angustina watched the captain's small patrol disappear high above behind gray rock ledges. For a while he heard the gravel slides they released in the crevices; then not even those. Their voices too ended up fading in the distance.

Meanwhile the sky darkened. The surrounding cliffs, the pale walls on the other side of the gorge, the bottom of the precipice, all acquired a bluish tint. Small crows flew along lofty crests, emitting cries. They seemed to be calling to each other because of some imminent danger.

"Lieutenant sir," said the soldier who was following Angustina. "It will rain soon."

Angustina stopped to look at him for a moment and didn't say a word. The boots had stopped torturing him, but he began to feel intensely weary. Every meter in the climb cost him enormous effort. Luckily the rocks in that stretch were less steep and even more broken than previously. Who knows how far the captain had gone—thought Angustina—perhaps already to the peak. Perhaps he had already planted the flag and set up the border sign; perhaps he was already on his way back.

He looked above and noticed the summit was no longer very far away. Yet he didn't understand how he could make further progress, so steep and smooth was the rampart that supported it.

Finally Angustina came to a wide, gravelly ledge and found himself a few meters from Monti. The captain had climbed up on a soldier's back and was trying to scale a low vertical wall, not much taller than a dozen meters but to all appearances inaccessible. Monti had obviously persisted in his attempts for several minutes, although without managing to find a way.

He floundered three, four times, searching for a grip, seeming to find it. Then you could hear him curse and see him sink down again on the back of the soldier who was shaking the length of his body from the strain. Finally he gave up and leapt to the gravel on the ledge.

Panting from the effort, Monti shot a hostile look at Angustina. "You could've waited below, lieutenant," he said. "All of us can't climb from here; it's obvious. I'll have done something if I'm able to get up this wall with a couple of soldiers. It would've been better if you had waited below. Night is coming now and getting back down will be serious business."

"You told me to do it, captain sir," Angustina responded without the slightest interest. "You told me to do what I preferred: either wait or come up behind you."

"Fine," said the captain. "Now we have to find a way. Just these few meters remain before we reach the peak."

"What? The peak is just beyond there?" the lieutenant asked with an indefinable irony that Monti didn't even suspect.

"Barely twelve meters," swore the captain. "Damn! I want to see if I can do it. At the cost of—"

He was interrupted by an arrogant shout that came from above.

Two human heads were looking over the upper edge of the low wall. They were smiling. "Buona sera, signori," shouted one, perhaps an officer. "As you can see, there's no way to get up here. You need to come over the ridge."

The two faces withdrew, and you could hear only the confused voices of men in conversation.

Monti was livid with rage. Nothing more could be done then. The northern soldiers had now occupied the peak as well. The captain sat on a boulder on the ledge, paying no attention to the soldiers who continued to arrive from below.

Right at that moment snow began to fall, a thick, heavy snowfall, as in the dead of winter. In a few moments, almost incredibly, the gravel on the ledge had turned white, and the light suddenly grew dim. Night had fallen. Until then no one had given it any serious thought.

Without showing the slightest alarm each soldier unrolled his cloak and covered himself. "Damn it! What are you doing?" snapped the captain. "Roll up your cloaks immediately! Do you really think you're spending the night here? We must descend now."

Angustina said, "If you'll permit me, captain sir, as long as those soldiers are at the peak—"

"What? What are you saying?" asked the captain angrily.

"I don't think you can turn back as long as those northern soldiers are at the peak. They arrived first and we have nothing more to do here. But we would be disgraced!"

The captain didn't respond. He paced up and down the broad ledge for a few moments. Then he said, "But they too will leave now. With this weather it's much worse on the peak than here."

"Signori!" called a voice from above as four or five heads sprang into view on the edge of the wall. "Don't stand on ceremony. Grab these ropes and come up. You can't make it down the mountainside in the dark!"

At the same time, two ropes were thrown down to help the soldiers from the Fortezza scale the low wall.

"Grazie," responded the captain with a derisive tone. "Grazie for the thought. But we'll take care of ourselves!"

"Whatever you think," they shouted from the peak. "We'll leave them here anyway, in case you might find them useful."

A long silence followed. You could hear only the whisper of falling snow and some coughing from the soldiers. Visibility had almost completely vanished. The edge of the nearby wall could barely be discerned. From it emanated the red glow of a lantern.

Here and there soldiers from the Fortezza also lit lamps after again putting on their cloaks. A lamp was brought to the captain, should he need it.

"Captain sir," Angustina said with a weary voice.

"What is it now?"

"What would you say to a game of cards?"

"To hell with cards!" replied Monti, who understood quite well that it wouldn't be possible to climb down from the mountain that night.

Without saying a word Angustina pulled the pack of cards from the case the captain had entrusted to a solider. He spread a flap of his own cloak on a rock, put a lantern next to it, and began shuffling.

"Captain sir," he repeated. "Listen to me even if you don't feel like it."

Monti then understood what the lieutenant intended to say: Nothing else could be done in the face of those northern soldiers, who were probably mocking them. And while the soldiers were holed up at the base of the wall, exploiting every recess, or sitting down to eat amid jokes and laughter, the two officers began a game of cards in the snow. Above them the sheer rock face; below the black precipice.

"Take every trick! Slam him!" someone above shouted in jest.

Neither Monti nor Angustina lifted his head. They kept playing. The captain played reluctantly, however, flinging cards on the cloak in a rage. Angustina tried to joke but to no effect: "Magnificent! Two aces in a row. But I'm taking this one. Tell the truth: you forgot that club." He even laughed from time to time, an apparently sincere laugh.

From above you could hear the resumption of voices, then noises from stones being moved. They were probably getting ready to leave.

"Good luck!" the voice shouted to them. "Good game. Don't forget the ropes!"

Neither Monti nor Angustina responded. They kept playing without even a nod in response, giving the appearance of intense concentration.

The glow of the lantern disappeared from the peak. Evidently the northern soldiers were leaving. The cards had gotten wet in the thick snow and were difficult to shuffle.

"I've had enough," said the captain, throwing his cards on the cloak. "Enough of this farce!"

He withdrew under the rocks, carefully wrapping himself in a cloak. "Toni!" he called. "Bring me my case and find me some water to drink."

"They can still see us," said Angustina. "They can still see us from the ridge!" But since he knew Monti was fed up with cards, he resumed on his own, dissembling that the game continued.

Amid noisy outbursts at each round the lieutenant held his cards in his left hand and with his right threw them on the cloak, pretending to gather up the tricks. From the ridge the thick snow prevented the foreigners from noticing that he was playing by himself.

Meanwhile a horrible sensation of bitter cold had penetrated his viscera. He felt as if he couldn't move or even lie down. Never, as far as he could remember, had he felt so bad. On the ridge, the swaying glow of the other soldiers' lantern could still be glimpsed as it receded; they could still see him. *(At the window of the marvelous mansion stood a slender figure: it was him, Angustina, as a child, with a shocking pallor, wearing an elegant velvet suit with a white lace collar. He opened the window with a weary gesture, bending toward the spirits hanging from the windowsill as if he were on familiar terms with them and wanted to say something.)*

"My trick, my trick!" he tried to shout so the foreigners could hear him, but a feeble voice came out, hoarse and weary. "Good God, this is the second time, captain sir!"

Enfolded in his cloak, slowly chewing something, Monti was now staring attentively at Angustina with less and less anger. "Enough, lieutenant. Come to the shelter. The northern soldiers have left by now!"

"You play much better than I do, captain sir," insisted Angustina in the fiction, his voice gradually failing. "But tonight you're really not in the mood. Why do you keep looking up? Why are you looking at the peak? Are you a little nervous perhaps?"

Then, beneath the teeming snowfall, the last wet cards slipped from Lieutenant Angustina's hand and the hand itself dropped, devoid of life. It lay inert on the cloak in the tremulous light of the lantern.

His shoulders propped up against a stone, the lieutenant slowly slumped backwards. A strange somnolence was invading him. *(And in the moonlight a small procession of other spirits advanced through the air, hauling a sedan chair toward the mansion.)*

"Lieutenant," the captain shouted, "come eat something. You have to eat in this cold, even if you don't want to eat! Snap out of it!" His voice quivered with a trace of apprehension. "Come under here. The snow is about to stop."

That is precisely what happened. Almost immediately the white flakes grew less dense and heavy, the air clearer. In the glare of the lanterns you could already make out rocks as far away as thirty meters.

And suddenly, during a break in the storm, at an incalculable distance, appeared the lamps of the Fortezza. They seemed infinite, like those of an enchanted castle immersed in the jubilation of ancient carnivals. Angustina saw them and a thin smile slowly formed on his lips, numbed by the bitter cold.

"Lieutenant," the captain called again. He was beginning to understand. "Lieutenant, throw away those cards. Come under here. Get some shelter from the wind."

But Angustina was gazing at the lamps, and in truth he no longer knew exactly what they might be, whether they belonged to the Fortezza or the distant city or his own castle, where no one was expecting his return.

Perhaps at that moment a sentry on the battlements of the Fortezza had casually lifted his eyes toward the mountains and picked out the lanterns on the highest ridge. At such a great distance the malevolent rock wall was less than nothing: it made no difference at all. Perhaps Drogo himself commanded the guard, Drogo who probably, if he had so desired, could have set out with Captain Monti and Angustina. But Drogo felt their mission was idiotic: since the threat of the Tartars had vanished, the task of marking the border seemed nothing but a nuisance utterly lacking in value. Now, however, Drogo spotted the flickering lanterns on the peak and started to regret he hadn't gone. Not only in war could a worthy act be performed. He would have liked to be up there, in the dead of night, in the thick of a storm. Too late. The opportunity had been within his reach and he had let it go.

Perhaps Giovanni Drogo was gazing enviously at the distant lights, well rested and dry, wrapped in his warm cloak, while Angustina, completely encrusted in snow, could hardly summon his remaining strength to smooth out his soaked moustache and meticulously drape his cloak, not drawing it tightly around himself for greater warmth but pursuing some other arcane design. From the shelter Captain Monti stared at the lieutenant in astonishment, asking himself what Angustina was doing and where he had ever chanced to see a similar figure. He couldn't remember.

An old painting that hung in a hall at the Fortezza represented the end of Prince Sebastiano. The prince lay in the heart of a forest, mortally wounded, leaning his back against a tree, his head slumped slightly to one side, his cloak falling in harmonious folds. Nothing in the image evoked the brutal physical cruelty of death. In examining it you weren't surprised the painter had completely preserved the prince's nobility and extreme elegance.

Angustina had now begun to resemble Prince Sebastiano (not that it crossed his mind!), wounded in the heart of the forest. Angustina, unlike the prince, wasn't encased in gleaming armor, nor did a bloody helmet lie at his feet beside a broken sword. He wasn't leaning against a tree but a heavy boulder. He was lit, not by the last rays of sunset, but by a dim lantern. Still, he bore a striking resemblance to the prince: the position of their limbs as well as the folds of their cloaks were identical. And their faces wore the same expression of utter weariness.

At this point, although the captain, the sergeant, and the other soldiers were much more vigorous and cocksure compared with Angustina, they all seemed nothing but unmannerly churls. And in Monti's mind arose an envious wonder, however implausible that might seem.

The snow stopped. The wind moaned through the crags, swirling clouds of ice crystals, flickering the flames in the lanterns. Angustina didn't seem to hear it. He was motionless, leaning against the stone, his eyes fixed on the distant lamps of the Fortezza.

"Lieutenant!" Captain Monti tried again. "Lieutenant! Make up your mind! Come under here. If you stay where you are, you won't be able to stick it out. You'll freeze. Come under here. Toni has created a kind of barrier."

"Thanks, captain," said Angustina with much effort. He found speaking too difficult so he raised a hand slightly, making a sign as if to say it didn't matter, it was all nonsense, not important in the least. *(Finally the leader of the spirits made an imperious gesture toward him and Angustina, assuming his bored attitude, climbed down from the window and sat graciously in the chair. The fairy carriage moved gently to depart.)*

For a few minutes nothing was heard but the hoarse cry of the wind. Even the soldiers, gathered in packs beneath the rocks for warmth, had lost the desire to joke and struggled against the cold in silence.

When the wind subsided for a moment, Angustina again raised his head a few centimeters and slowly moved his mouth to speak, uttering only these three words: "Tomorrow we'll need—" Then nothing more. Just three words and so faint that not even Captain Monti noticed he had spoken.

Three words and Angustina's head fell forward in complete surrender. One of his hands lay white and rigid in a fold of his cloak. He managed to close his mouth. Once again a thin smile had formed on his lips. *(As the chair drew away, Angustina detached his gaze from his friend and turned to look ahead, in the direction of the procession, with a kind of curiosity that was simultaneously amused and mistrustful. Thus he withdrew into the night with an almost inhuman nobility. The magical procession slowly meandered in the sky, higher and higher, becoming a confused trail, then a slight tuft of cloud, then nothing.)*

"What did you mean, Angustina? What about tomorrow?" Monti has finally left his shelter. He forcefully shakes the lieutenant by the shoulders in an effort to bring him back to life. Yet the captain succeeds only in ruffling the noble folds of his soldierly shroud. What a pity. None of the soldiers has yet noticed what has happened.

Monti curses and only the voice of the wind responds to him from the dark precipice. "What did you mean, Angustina? You left without finishing the sentence. Maybe it was something stupid and banal, maybe some absurd hope, or maybe nothing at all."

16

AFTER Lieutenant Angustina had been buried, time resumed at the Fortezza, passing just as it did before.

Major Ortiz asked Drogo, "How long is it now?"

Drogo replied, "I've been here four years."

Winter arrived suddenly, the long season. Snow would fall. First, four or five centimeters; then, after a pause, a deeper layer; then several more, impossible to count, so that the time till spring returned seemed forever. (And yet one day much earlier than expected, much earlier, you'll hear water trickling from the borders of the terraces and winter will be inexplicably over.)

Lieutenant Angustina's coffin, wrapped in the flag, lay underground in a small enclosure on one side of the Fortezza. Over it stood a cross of white stone on which his name was engraved. Farther along lay the soldier Lazzari beneath a smaller cross of wood.

Ortiz said, "Sometimes I think we long for war, we await the best opportunity, we blame bad luck, because nothing ever happens. And yet look at what happened to Angustina."

"You mean," said Drogo, "Angustina didn't need any luck? He was fine all the same?"

"He was weak," said Major Ortiz. "I believe he was sick too. He was worse off than all of us, actually. Like us, he didn't face the enemy; he didn't even fight in a war. He died, just the same, as if he were in battle. Do you know how he died, lieutenant?"

"Yes," said Drogo, "I too was present when Captain Monti told the story."

Winter came and the foreigners left. The beautiful banners of hope, perhaps with intimations of blood, were slowly lowered and the mood was calm again. But the sky remained empty, and the eye still searched pointlessly for something on the farthest frontier of the horizon.

"He certainly picked the right moment to die," said Major Ortiz. "As if he had taken a bullet. He was a hero. There's nothing more to say about it. Even if no one fired. The odds were the same for everyone else who was with him that day. He really had no advantage—unless perhaps the ability to die so easily. Besides, what did the others do? For them it was a day more or less like any other."

"Yes," said Drogo, "just a little colder."

"Right, lieutenant," said Ortiz. "But you could have gone with them. You need only have asked."

They were sitting on a wooden bench on the topmost terrace of the fourth redoubt. Ortiz had gone to find Lieutenant Drogo, who was on duty. Day by day a close friendship was forming between them.

They were sitting on a bench, wrapped in their cloaks, their eyes gravitating spontaneously toward the north, where huge clouds were gathering, amorphous and laden with snow. The northern wind gusted occasionally, freezing the clothes on their backs. The jagged cliffs towering to the right and left of the pass had darkened. Drogo said, "It does look like we'll get snow tomorrow here at the Fortezza."

"Most likely," the major replied, showing no interest. Then he fell silent.

"It will snow," Drogo said again. "Crows keep flying past."

"We are to blame too," said Ortiz, pursuing an obstinate thought. "After all, we always get what we deserve. Angustina, for instance, was willing to pay dearly. But we weren't. Perhaps this is what really matters. Perhaps we expect too much. In the end, we always get what we deserve."

"What then?" asked Drogo. "What should we do?"

"I myself would do nothing," said Ortiz with a smile. "I've waited too long at this point. But you—"

"What about me?"

"Leave while there's still time. Go back down to the city. Get used to the garrison. You really don't seem like the sort of fellow who scorns life's pleasures. I have no doubt you'll make more of a career for yourself. We weren't all born to be heroes."

Drogo said nothing.

"You've already let four years pass," Ortiz continued. "You've gained a certain advantage through seniority. Let's admit it. But imagine how much more you would've gained from being in the city. You've been cut off from the world; nobody remembers you anymore. Return while there's still time."

Giovanni listened without saying a word, his eyes fixed on the ground.

"I've seen so many men like you," said Ortiz. "They gradually fall into the routines of the Fortezza and they remain imprisoned here, no longer capable of making a move. They're basically old men at thirty."

Drogo said, "I believe you, major sir, but at my age—"

"You're young," resumed Ortiz, "and you'll be young for a while yet. But I wouldn't put much stock in it. Just let two more years pass—two more years are enough—and going back will cost you too much effort."

"Thank you," said Drogo, who wasn't impressed in the slightest. "But here at the Fortezza, finally, one can hope for something better. It may sound absurd but even you, if you're frank, must confess—"

"That may be true, regrettably," said the major. "We all, more or less, persist in hoping. But it's absurd. Just give it some thought"— and he pointed toward the north. "A war will never come from this region. And now, after recent events, who do you expect will seriously believe it?"

While he spoke, he rose to his feet, never removing his eyes from the north, just like that distant morning when Drogo had watched him stare, enchanted, from the edge of the plateau, at the enigmatic walls of the Fortezza. Four years had passed since then, a respectable portion of any man's life, and nothing, absolutely nothing, had happened that could justify such undying hope. The days had flitted by one after another. Soldiers who might be enemies had appeared one morning on the margins of the foreign plain and then had withdrawn after innocuous operations on the border. Peace reigned over the world, the sentries sounded no alarms, and nothing augured the possibility of change. As in years past, winter advanced with the same formalities and the gusts of the northern wind produced a faint sibilance against the soldiers' bayonets. And here was Major Ortiz, still standing on the terrace of the fourth redoubt, incredulous at his own wise words, gazing once more at the northern wasteland as if he alone truly possessed the right to gaze at it, as well as the right to remain at the fort, regardless of the reason. Drogo, however, might be a splendid fellow, but he was out of place, he had made the wrong calculations, and he would do well to return.

17

THE SNOW on the terraces of the Fortezza finally softened and feet were plunging into slush. The sweet sound of water suddenly arrived from the closest mountains. Here and there along the peaks you caught sight of vertical white strips sparkling in the sun. Every so often soldiers would find themselves humming as they hadn't done for months.

The sun no longer sped past as before, eager to set. It began to slacken its pace midway in the sky, devouring the accumulated snow. It was useless for the clouds to keep hurtling from the icy north: they couldn't produce any more snow, only rain, and the rain did nothing but melt the little snow that remained. Mild weather had returned.

In the morning, indeed, you could hear the birds' voices—which everyone thought he had forgotten. In recompense crows no longer gathered on the plateau before the Fortezza, waiting for kitchen scraps. Instead they scattered through the valleys in search of fresh food.

At night, in the barracks, the wall mounts where backpacks were hung, the rifle racks, the very doors, even the beautiful solid walnut furniture in the colonel's room—every piece of wood in the Fortezza, including the most ancient—creaked in the darkness. At certain moments sharp cracks that sounded like pistol shots were audible. It seemed as if something had splintered. A solider would be awakened in his bunk and prick up his ears. Yet he managed to hear nothing but more creaking, which recurred throughout the night.

This is the season when a stubborn yearning for life revives in the aged beams. Many years ago, in happy days, it coincided with the youthful flux of heat and strength and clusters of buds sprouted from branches. Then the tree was cut down. Now, when spring arrives, a surge of life, infinitely diminished, still awakens in each of its fragments. Once upon a time there were leaves and flowers; now there is merely a vague memory, just enough to cause creaking, and then silence returns till next year.

This is the season when the men of the Fortezza begin to entertain curious thoughts that have nothing to do with the military. The walls no longer offer hospitable shelter; they rather raise the specter of imprisonment. Their bare appearance, the black lines of drainpipes, the sloping edges of ramparts, their yellow color—none of these features responds in any way to the new frame of mind.

On a spring morning an officer—from behind he can't be identified, although he could well be Giovanni Drogo—strolls in boredom through the vast laundries of the troops, deserted at this hour. He isn't required to perform inspections or checks; he wanders around just to be in motion. Besides, everything is in order, basins cleaned, floors swept. That dripping tap isn't the soldiers' fault.

The officer lingers, looking up at the high windows. They are closed. They probably haven't been washed in many years. Cobwebs hang in the corners. Nothing here comforts the human mind in any way. Still, beyond the glass you can glimpse something that resembles a sky. That same sky—perhaps the officer thinks—that same sun illumines squalid laundries as well as distant meadows.

The meadows are green and just a short while ago they were sprouting with flowers, most likely white flowers. The trees too, as is fitting, have put forth new leaves. A fine thing it would be to ride aimlessly through the countryside. A lovely girl might walk down a lane between the hedgerows, and when she passes close to your horse she might greet you with a smile. Yet how ridiculous. Can an officer from Fortezza Bastiani ever permit himself such stupid thoughts?

Through the dusty window of the laundry, however strange it might seem, you can also see a white cloud with a pleasant shape. Identical clouds sail over the faraway city at this moment. People strolling serenely along look at them now and then, happy the winter has ended. Nearly everyone's clothes are new or spruced up. Young women wear brightly colored dresses and flowers in their hair. Everyone is cheerful, as if they expect good things to happen at any moment. Once upon a time, at least, the scene was just so; who knows whether it has now changed. What if a lovely girl stood in a window and when you passed beneath it she greeted you for no particular reason—she greeted you warmly with a pretty smile? All these things are basically ridiculous, schoolboy silliness.

Through a corner of a dirty window you can glimpse a stretch of wall at an angle. It too is flooded with sunlight, but it brings no joy. It's the wall of a barracks that is in fact indifferent as to whether sun or moon is shining. What matters is that no obstacles affect the efficient performance of military duties. It's the wall of a barracks, nothing more. And yet one day, in a distant September, the officer paused to look at it as if fascinated. For him these walls seemed to harbor a harsh yet enviable fate. Although he couldn't pronounce those walls attractive, he had paused for several minutes, motionless, as if before something portentous.

An officer wanders through the deserted laundries. Some officers are on duty at the various redoubts. Others ride across the stony clearing. Still others sit in their offices. None of them can really grasp what has happened, but their faces get on each other's nerves. Always the same faces, he thinks instinctively, always the same conversations, same duties, same documents. Meanwhile tender desires ferment. He finds it difficult to fix with exactness what he would want—certainly not those walls, those soldiers, those bugle calls.

Scoot, pony. Race down the road to the plain. Run before you're too late. Don't stop, even if you tire, before you see green fields, familiar trees, human dwellings, churches, campanili.

Farewell, Fortezza. To linger longer would be dangerous. Your facile mystery has toppled. The northern plain will always be deserted. Never will enemies come; never will anyone come to assault your miserable walls. Farewell, Major Ortiz, melancholy friend, you who can no longer bring yourself to part with this fortress, who have persisted too long in your hope, like so many others. Time has outrun you. You can't start over.

But Giovanni Drogo certainly can. No commitment binds him any longer to the Fortezza. He is now returning to the plain and will once again enter into human fellowship. He will most likely be tasked with some special assignment, perhaps a mission abroad in a general's entourage. During the years when he was posted at the Fortezza, he undoubtedly lost many fine opportunities. But Giovanni is still young, and he has all the time he needs to mend his situation.

And so farewell, Fortezza, with your absurd redoubts, your long-suffering soldiers, your colonel who every morning, on the sly, scrutinizes the northern desert with a telescope. But this gesture is pointless: nothing is ever there. A salute to Angustina's grave: he was, perhaps, the most fortunate. At least he died like a true soldier—better, in any case, than in a hospital bed, the most probable scenario. A salute to his own room, where, after all, Drogo has slept the sleep of the just for hundreds of nights. Another salute to the courtyard, where even tonight the guard coming on duty will assemble with the usual formalities. The final salute is directed to the northern plain, devoid of illusions by now.

Don't give it a second thought, Giovanni Drogo. Don't turn back, now that you've reached the edge of the plateau and the road is about to plunge into the valley. It would be a foolish weakness. You know Fortezza Bastiani, someone might say, stone by stone; you certainly don't run the risk of forgetting it. The horse trots merrily. The day is splendid, the air tepid and light, the life that opens before you is still long, as if you had yet to begin. What need would compel you to cast a last glance at the walls, the casemates, the sentries pacing on the parapets of the redoubts? Thus a page slowly turns, lying flat on the left-hand side, adding to the others that have already been finished. For now the accumulation is thin; the pages still to be read can be compared to an inexhaustible stack. But another page has nonetheless been consumed, lieutenant, a segment of your life.

From the end of the stony plateau, in fact, Drogo doesn't turn to look. Without even a trace of hesitation he spurs his horse down the slope. He doesn't give any indication that he might turn his head even a centimeter. He whistles a song with passable ease, although it does cost him some effort.

18

THE DOOR to the house was opened and Drogo immediately caught the old domestic scent, as when he returned to the city as a child after spending summer months at the villa. The scent was familiar and welcoming and yet, after so much time, something depressing came to the surface. It reminded him of distant years, the sweetness of certain Sundays, pleasant dinners, lost childhood. But it also spoke of closed windows, homework, tidying up in the morning, illnesses, quarrels, mice.

"Oh, young master!" shouted the good Giovanna, elated, when she opened the door. Mamma arrived at once. Thank God she still hadn't changed.

Sitting in the parlor, as he tried to respond to an onslaught of questions, he felt happiness transform into indifferent sadness. The house seemed empty compared with earlier days. One of his brothers had gone abroad; another was on a trip somewhere; a third was in the countryside. Only his mother remained, and in a short while she too had to leave for a church service where a friend awaited her.

His room had remained identical, just as he had left it, not a book had been moved, and yet he felt as if it belonged to someone else. He sat in the armchair, listening to the noise of the carts in the street and the intermittent clamor of voices that came from the kitchen. He stayed alone in his room, his mother prayed in church, his brothers were far away—the entire world, then, was living without any need of Giovanni Drogo. Opening a window, he saw gray houses, roof after roof, as well as an overcast sky. He searched a drawer for some old school notebooks, a diary he had kept for years, certain letters. He was astonished he had written those things. He didn't remember them at all; everything referred to strange, forgotten events. He sat at the piano, tried a chord, and lowered the cover on the keyboard. What now? he asked himself.

A stranger, he wandered the city in search of old friends. He learned they were deeply engaged in business deals, major initiatives, political careers. They spoke to him of serious, important things—factories, railroads, hospitals. Someone invited him to dinner, someone else had gotten married, they had all gone their separate ways, and in four years they had grown distant. No matter how hard he tried (perhaps he himself was no longer capable), he couldn't revive conversations from the past, the jokes, the turns of phrase. He wandered the city in search of old friends—and there were many—but in the end he found himself alone on a sidewalk with so many vacant hours before nightfall.

At night he would stay out of the house till late, determined to amuse himself. On each occasion he would leave with vague hopes of love, typically adolescent, and on each occasion he would return disappointed. Once again he began to hate the street—always the same, always deserted—that led him back home alone.

A lavish ball was held around this time. Drogo, entering the impressive residence in the company of Vescovi, the only friend with whom he had reconnected, felt in the best spirits. Although spring had already arrived, the night would be long, a length of time that was nearly unlimited, and many things could happen before dawn. Exactly what might happen Drogo wasn't in a position to specify but he definitely expected several hours of undiluted pleasure. He had actually begun to banter with a girl in a violet dress and midnight hadn't yet struck. Perhaps by daybreak love would materialize. But then the master of the house approached to take him on a detailed tour: he was dragged through labyrinths and tunnels, relegated to the library, obliged to examine a collection of weapons piece by piece, and forced to listen to strategic questions, military humor, and anecdotes about the royal dynasty. Meanwhile time was passing and clocks began to race at a frightful rate. When Drogo managed to extricate himself, keen to return to the dancing, the rooms were half empty and the girl in the violet dress had vanished. She had probably gone home.

In vain Drogo tried drinking; in vain he laughed senselessly. But not even wine was of any use to him. The violins grew ever fainter. At a certain point, they truly played in a vacuum because no one was dancing. Drogo found himself among the trees in a garden, a bitter taste in his mouth. As he listened to the indistinct echoes of a waltz, the enchantment of the ball faded and the sky slowly brightened with the approaching dawn.

The stars waned. Drogo lingered among the dark shadows of the foliage to watch the sunrise. One by one the gilded carriages departed. The musicians fell silent and a servant moved through the rooms to dim the lights. From a tree, right above Drogo's head, a bird trilled, at once piercing and animated. The sky became progressively brighter. Everything slept silently in the confident expectation of a fine day. At that moment—Drogo thought—the first rays of sunlight would have already reached the ramparts of the Fortezza and the freezing sentries. His ear expected the sound of a bugle to no effect.

He crossed the lulled city, which was still immersed in sleep, and opened the door to his house, needlessly causing a racket. Inside, shafts of light were already filtering through the slats in the blinds.

"Buona notte, mamma," he said, walking down the corridor. From the room, beyond the door, a confused sound apparently responded to him, a voice that was affectionate even if suffused with sleep, as usual, as in the distant days when he would return home late at night. He continued to his own room, feeling somewhat reassured, when he realized she was speaking. "What is it, mamma?" he asked in the vast silence. "Anything wrong?" In the same instant he understood he had mistaken the clatter of a distant carriage for her dear voice. His mother hadn't really responded. Her son's nocturnal footsteps could no longer wake her as before. They had virtually become foreign, as if their sound had changed over the years.

There was a time when his steps reached into her sleep like a call that was arranged beforehand. Any other noise, even if much louder, wouldn't have been enough to wake her, whether carts down in the street or a child's sobbing, howling dogs or owls, a banging shutter or wind in the eaves, rainfall or creaking furniture. Only his step woke her, although not because he was noisy (actually Giovanni tiptoed). No special reason explained it, except that he was her son.

But now no more. He greeted his mother as he previously did, with the same inflection in his voice, certain she would be awakened at the familiar noise of his steps. But no one had responded to him, save the clatter of the distant carriage. Sheer foolishness, he thought, perhaps even a ridiculous coincidence. And yet while he got ready for bed, a bitter feeling stayed with him as if the affection of the past had weakened, as if time and distance had slowly drawn a veil of separation between the two of them.

19

LATER he went to visit Maria, the sister of his friend Francesco
Vescovi. Their house had a garden and since spring had arrived the
trees bore new leaves and birds sang in the branches.

Maria met him at the door, smiling. She knew he would come and
she had put on a blue dress, narrow at the waist, similar to another
dress that had pleased him on a day long ago.

Drogo had imagined that he would be flooded with emotion, that
his heart would pound. When, however, he was close to her and saw
her smile again, when he heard the sound of her voice as she said,
"Oh, finally, Giovanni!" (so different from what he had imagined),
he was confronted with how much time had elapsed.

In his view, he hadn't changed. Perhaps he was slightly broader in
the shoulders and tanned by the sun at the Fortezza. She hadn't
changed either. Yet something had come between them.

They went into the huge parlor because the sun was too bright
outside. The room was immersed in inviting shadow. A strip of sunlight shone on the carpet. A clock was ticking.

They sat on a couch, sideways, so they could look at one another.
Drogo stared into her eyes without knowing what to say, but her lively
gaze moved from him to the furniture to her turquoise bracelet, which
seemed very new.

"Francesco will be here in a little while," said Maria gaily. "Meanwhile you can spend some time with me. You must have so many
stories to tell!"

"Oh, nothing special, really," said Drogo. "It's always the—"

"Why are you looking at me like that?" she asked. "Do you think I've changed so much?"

No, Drogo didn't think she had changed. He was actually surprised that a girl didn't display some visible difference after four years. Nonetheless, he had a vague feeling of disappointment and coldness. He wasn't able to find the tone he used in the past, when they would talk like brother and sister and could joke about anything without hurting one another. How could she sit on the sofa so composed and speak with so much grace? He should've pulled her by the arm and said, "Are you mad? What has come over you, acting so seriously?" The icy spell would've been broken.

But Drogo didn't feel capable of doing it. Sitting before him, she was different, some other person whose thoughts he didn't know. Perhaps he himself was no longer who he was before, and it was he who had begun with a false tone.

"Changed?" replied Drogo. "No, absolutely not."

"You're just saying that because you don't find me as attractive as before. Tell the truth!"

Was it really Maria speaking? Wasn't she teasing him? Drogo listened to her words, hardly believing what she said. From one moment to the next he hoped she would drop that elegant smile, that sweet manner, and burst out laughing.

"Of course! I find you most unattractive," Giovanni would have replied in the good old days as he slid an arm around her waist, and she would have pressed against him. But now? It would've been absurd, a joke in poor taste.

"I don't think that at all," said Drogo. "You're exactly the same, I swear."

She looked at him with a smile that showed she wasn't very persuaded and then she changed the subject. "Now tell me, have you come back to stay?"

He had anticipated this question (he had planned to respond, "It depends on you," or something of the kind). But he expected it sooner, when he first arrived, as would have been natural if it was really important to her. Now, however, it had almost taken him by surprise, and it came off differently, as little more than a civility, lacking any emotional subtext.

The shadowed parlor was silent for a moment. Birdsong arrived from the garden, and from a distant room piano chords, slow and mechanical, played by someone who was learning.

"I don't know, or at least not right now," said Drogo. "I'm only on furlough."

"Just a furlough?" Maria said at once. Her voice betrayed a subtle quiver, which could be an accident, or disappointment, or even distress. But something had truly come between them, a vague, indefinable veil that refused to vanish. Perhaps it had grown slowly, during their long separation, day by day, dividing them, and neither was aware of it.

"Two months," explained Drogo. "Then I might have to return, or go to another post, or even stay here in the city." The conversation was now becoming painful to him. An indifference had seeped into his mood.

Both of them were quiet. The afternoon stagnated over the city. The birds fell silent. Only distant piano chords could be heard, sad and methodical, climbing and climbing, filling the entire house. That sound expressed a sort of stubborn effort, the difficulty of saying something that can never be said.

"That's Micheli's daughter at the piano upstairs," said Maria, noticing that Giovanni was listening.

"You also played that piece once—didn't you?"

Maria gracefully bowed her head as if to listen. "No, no, that's too difficult. You must have heard it somewhere else."

Drogo said, "I thought I remembered—"

The piano played with the same painfulness. Giovanni looked at the strip of sunlight on the carpet. He thought of the Fortezza and imagined the melting snow, the dripping on the terraces, the poverty of spring in the mountains, where it knows only tiny flowers in meadows and the scent of hay harvests transported by the wind.

"But now you'll ask to be transferred, no?" resumed the girl. "After so long you'll have earned the right. It must be so boring up there!"

She said these last words with a touch of anger, as if the Fortezza were hateful.

"A little boring perhaps. Of course I'd prefer to be here with you." This mistimed phrase flashed through Drogo's mind like a daring opportunity. It was banal, but perhaps it would be enough. Yet suddenly all his desire died out. Giovanni was in fact disgusted at the foolish words he had uttered.

"Yes, that's right," he then said. "But the days pass so quickly!"

The sound of the piano could be heard. But why did those chords keep climbing without ever concluding? Scholastically bare, they repeated, with resigned detachment, an old story long cherished. They spoke of a foggy evening amid city lights and the two of them walking beneath leafless trees down a deserted avenue, holding hands like children, unexpectedly happy without knowing why. On that evening too, he recalled, pianos were playing in houses, and notes were pouring out of lit windows. Although they were probably boring exercises, Giovanni and Maria had never heard music sweeter or more tender.

"Of course," Drogo added, joking, "you don't find any grand diversions up there, but we've gotten used to it. A little."

The conversation, in the flower-scented parlor, seemed to be slowly acquiring a poetic wistfulness that would support confessions of love. Who knows, thought Giovanni, whether this first meeting might have turned out differently after such a long separation. Perhaps we can meet again. I have two months free. You can't draw any conclusions from a brief encounter. She may still love me and I may never return to the Fortezza.

But the girl said, "What a shame! In three days I'm leaving with mamma and Giorgina. We'll be away a few months, I think." The mere idea made her burst with joy. "We're going to Holland."

"To Holland?"

The girl now launched into an account of the journey, waxing enthusiastic about the friends who would accompany her, her horses, the parties she had attended during carnival, her life, and her companions. She was oblivious of Drogo.

She now felt completely at ease and seemed more beautiful.

"A magnificent idea," said Drogo, who felt a bitter knot closing his throat. "I've heard this is the best season in Holland. They say entire fields are blooming with tulips."

"Oh, yes," agreed Maria, "it must be very beautiful."

"Instead of wheat they cultivate roses," continued Giovanni with a slight hesitation in his voice, "millions and millions of roses as far as the eye can see. And above them stand the windmills, all freshly painted in vivid colors."

"Freshly painted?" asked Maria, who was beginning to grasp the joke. "What do you mean?"

"So they say," Giovanni replied. "I've read it in a book too."

The strip of sunlight, after crossing the carpet, was now rising gradually along the marquetry of an escritoire. The afternoon was already dying. The piano's voice had grown faint. Outside in the garden an isolated bird began to sing again. Drogo stared at the andirons in the fireplace, which were exactly like a pair at the Fortezza. The coincidence provided him with a subtle consolation, as if it had demonstrated that Fortezza and city constituted one world, after all, with the same habits, customs, beliefs. Apart from the andirons, however, Drogo couldn't make out anything else they might have shared.

"Yes, it must be beautiful," said Maria, lowering her eyes. "But now that we're on the eve of our departure, the desire has left me."

"Nonsense," said Drogo deliberately, as if he hadn't caught the hint about how she really felt. "That always happens at the last moment. Packing is such a bore."

"Oh, it isn't the packing. That's not the problem."

He needed a word, a simple phrase to tell her he would be sad if she left. But Drogo didn't want to make demands. At that moment he really wasn't capable. It would've seemed like he was lying. So he said nothing and wore a vague smile.

"Shall we go into the garden for a bit?" the girl finally suggested, no longer sure of what to say. "The sun must have gone down."

They got up from the couch. She was quiet, as if expecting Drogo to speak to her. She looked at him with what remained of her love.

But Giovanni's thoughts, at the sight of the garden, flew to the meager fields that girded the Fortezza. The sweet season was on the verge of arriving there as well, and brave tufts of young grass were sprouting among the stones. Precisely at that time of year, centuries ago, the Tartars may have made an appearance.

Drogo said, "It's already quite warm for April. It will bring rain. You'll see."

This was all he had to say. Maria gave a slight, desolate smile. "Yes, it's too warm," she replied in a toneless voice. They both realized everything was over. Now they were distant again; a void opened between them. In vain they would have reached out their hands to touch. The distance was increasing with every minute.

Drogo felt he still loved Maria and her world. But all the things that once nourished his life had grown distant, transformed into a world of strangers where his place had readily been filled. At this point, he viewed it from the outside, although with nostalgia. To return to it would make him ill at ease: it involved new faces, different habits, new jokes, new expressions, to which he wasn't accustomed. It was no longer his life. He had taken another path. To come back would be stupid and futile.

Since Francesco never turned up, Drogo and Maria said goodbye with exaggerated cordiality, each of them locking their secret thoughts inside themselves. Maria grasped his hand tightly, staring into his eyes. Was it perhaps an urgent wish that he not leave like this, that he forgive her and make a fresh start at what was now lost?

He too fixed his eyes on her, saying, "Goodbye. I hope we meet again before you leave." He then left without turning back, heading toward the entry gate with martial steps. The gravel path crunched in the silence.

20

TRADITIONALLY, four years at the Fortezza sufficed to earn the right to a new post. But Drogo, who aimed to avoid a remote garrison and remain in his own city, still requested a personal interview with the division commander. It was really his mother who insisted on this interview: she said he needed to assert himself so he wouldn't be forgotten. No one, of course, would spontaneously look after him if he didn't take the initiative; he would probably wind up at another gloomy garrison on the border. His mother also pulled some strings, through friends, to ensure the general would be inclined to receive her son favorably.

The general sat in a huge office behind a broad table, smoking a cigar. It was a day like any other, perhaps rainy, perhaps just cloudy. The general was aging. He stared benignly at Lieutenant Drogo through a monocle.

"I wished to see you," he began, as if he had requested the interview. "I wanted to know how things are getting along up there. Filimore—still doing well?"

"When I left," replied Drogo, "the colonel was quite well, Your Excellency."

The general fell silent for a moment. Then he shook his head paternally. "You fellows up there at the Fortezza! You've caused trouble for us. Yes, indeed, that matter of the border. The story about that lieutenant—his name escapes me just now—that certainly didn't please His Highness very much."

Drogo kept quiet, not knowing what to say.

"Yes, that lieutenant," continued the general, talking to himself. "What is his name? A name like Arduino, I believe."

"His name is Angustina, Your Excellency."

"Right, Angustina. What was he thinking of? Compromising the borderline because of some stupid willfulness. I don't know how they—Well, let's drop it!" he concluded abruptly in a show of his own magnanimity.

"But permit me, Your Excellency," Drogo dared to remark. "Angustina is the man who died!"

"Perhaps, very well, you may be right, I can't recall at the moment," said the general, as if it were a detail without the least importance. "But His Highness was very displeased. Very much so!"

He broke off and gave Drogo a questioning look.

"So you have come here," he said in a diplomatic tone laden with innuendo, "to be transferred to the city—isn't that right? You are all obsessed with the city, you truly are, and you don't understand one learns to be a soldier precisely in remote garrisons."

"Yes, Your Excellency," said Drogo, struggling to check his language and tone. "I have in fact served four years already—"

"Four years at your age! What can four years matter to one so young?" the general shot back with a laugh. "I am not, however, reprimanding you. As a prevailing tendency, I would say, the obsession with the city is perhaps not the best means of strengthening the morale of officers."

He paused as if he had lost the thread. Then he concentrated for a moment and resumed: "In any case, my dear lieutenant, we shall try to satisfy you. Let's send for your record."

While waiting for the documents, the general continued. "The Fortezza," he said, "Fortezza Bastiani—let's see. Do you know its weak point, lieutenant?"

"I wouldn't know, Your Excellency," said Drogo. "Perhaps it's a little too isolated?"

The general wore a benevolent smile imbued with condescension.

"What strange ideas you young people have," he said. "A little too isolated! I must confess that wouldn't have crossed my mind. The weak point of the Fortezza—do you want me to tell you what it is?—it's that there are too many soldiers, too many soldiers!"

"Too many soldiers?"

"And expressly for this reason," continued the general without noticing the lieutenant's interruption, "the decision has been made to change the regulations. What are they saying about it at the Fortezza?"

"About what, Your Excellency? Forgive me."

"About what we're talking about! The new regulations, I told you," the general repeated with irritation.

"I haven't heard anything," replied Drogo, who was taken aback. "I really haven't."

"Indeed, perhaps the official announcement hasn't been made," the general admitted as he calmed down. "But I would think you knew about it all the same. Military men, in general, are adept at knowing things before everyone else."

"A new regulation, Your Excellency?" asked Drogo, his curiosity piqued.

"A reduction in personnel. The garrison will be cut nearly by half." The general's retort was brusque. "I always said there were too many soldiers. That fort needed to be trimmed down!"

The adjutant major entered just then, carrying a thick file of documents. He leafed through them on a table, withdrew one relating to Giovanni Drogo, and handed it to the general, who ran his expert eye over it.

"All in order," he said. "But the request for transfer seems to be missing."

"The request for transfer?" Drogo asked. "I didn't think it was necessary after four years."

"As a rule, no," said the general, clearly annoyed he had to provide an explanation to a subordinate. "But since on this occasion there is such a substantial reduction in personnel, and everyone wants to leave, we must give due attention to priority."

"But no one at the Fortezza knows about it, Your Excellency. No one has yet made a request."

The general turned to the adjutant major.

"Captain," he asked, "have any requests for transfer been submitted from Fortezza Bastiani?"

"About twenty, I believe, Your Excellency," the captain replied.

What a joke, thought Drogo, crushed. His colleagues had evidently kept the thing secret to get ahead of him. Had even Ortiz deceived him so basely?

"Forgive me, Your Excellency, if I insist," dared Drogo, who realized the issue was crucial. "But serving four uninterrupted years should count for more than mere formal priority."

The general's response was icy, as if he were offended: "Your four years are nothing, my man, compared to so many others who have spent entire lives at the Fortezza. I can consider your case with the greatest generosity, I can encourage your legitimate ambitions, but I cannot fail to do what is just. We must take into account qualifications and achievements as well."

Giovanni Drogo blanched.

"But then, Your Excellency," he pleaded, almost stuttering, "then I would risk being at the fort for the rest of my life."

"Qualifications and achievements must be taken into account," repeated the general impassively while he kept leafing through Drogo's documents. "I see here, for example—my eye just chanced upon a 'letter of admonishment.' Such a letter isn't a grave matter"—he continued reading—"but here the incident is rather objectionable, in my view, a sentry killed by mistake."

"Regrettably, Your Excellency, I didn't—"

The general interrupted him. "You know very well, lieutenant, I cannot listen to your excuses. I can only read what is written in your report. I am even willing to admit it was entirely an accident: it can certainly happen. But your colleagues have been able to avoid these accidents. I am inclined to do everything I possibly can. I agreed to receive you in person, you see, but now... If only you had submitted your request a month ago. Odd that you weren't informed. A significant disadvantage, obviously."

The initial tone of affability had vanished. Now the general spoke with a subtle trace of boredom and derision, modulating his voice pompously. Drogo knew he had come off as an imbecile. His fellow officers had screwed him. The general must have a very poor impression of him and there wasn't a thing he could do. The sense of injustice burned intensely in his chest, near his heart. I could just leave, hand in my resignation, he thought. After all, I won't die of hunger, and I'm still young.

The general made a familiar gesture with his hand. "Very well. Goodbye, lieutenant, and buck up."

Drogo stood at attention, clicked his heels, and backed away toward the door. At the threshold he gave a final salute.

21

A HORSE'S tread climbs back up the solitary valley. It produces a vast echo in the silence of the ravines. The shrubs on top of the ridges don't stir. The yellow tufts of grass stand still. Even clouds pass in the sky with exceptional slowness. The horse's tread rises steadily up the white road. Giovanni Drogo is returning.

It is really him. Now that he has drawn near, he can be positively identified. No particular torment can be read in his face. He has not rebelled, then, nor has he submitted his resignation. He swallowed the injustice without a word, and he is returning to his usual post. Deep down he even feels the cowardly satisfaction of having avoided abrupt changes in his life, of being able to resume his old habits unchanged. Drogo deludes himself that he will enjoy a glorious revenge at some later date. He believes he still has eons at his disposal, and so he forgoes the petty struggles of daily existence. The day will come, he thinks, when all accounts will be generously settled. In the meantime, however, others turn up unexpectedly, they avidly compete to be first, they race ahead of Drogo without paying him the least attention, and they leave him behind. He watches them disappear in the distance, perplexed, seized by unusual doubts: What if he were actually mistaken? What if he were an ordinary man who has been rightfully allotted no more than a mediocre destiny?

Giovanni Drogo climbed to the solitary Fortezza as he had that day in September, that distant day. Except now no other officer was advancing on the other side of the ravine, and at the bridge where the two paths joined Captain Ortiz wasn't coming to meet him.

On this occasion Drogo proceeded alone, reflecting on his life.

He was returning to the Fortezza to remain for an indefinite time right at the moment when many officers would be leaving forever. They had acted more quickly, Drogo thought, but you couldn't exclude the possibility that they were really better than him. This might also explain what had happened.

The more time passed, the more significance the fort lost. In days of yore, perhaps, it had been an important garrison, or at least it was considered such. Now, with its force reduced by half, it was just a security barrier, strategically excluded from every war plan. It was maintained only so that the border wouldn't be left undefended. The possibility of some threat from the northern plain wasn't acknowledged; at most a few nomad caravans could arrive at the pass. What would become of life there?

Reflecting on these matters, Drogo reached the edge of the highest plateau in the afternoon and found himself before the Fortezza. Unlike the first time, it no longer harbored disquieting secrets. As a matter of fact, it was merely a barracks on the frontier, a ridiculous fortress. The walls could hardly withstand the latest cannons for more than a few hours. With the passage of time they would be left to deteriorate. Already sections of the battlements had collapsed and a rampart had decayed into rubble, but no one made any effort to repair it.

Such were Drogo's musings as he stood at the edge of the plateau, observing the usual sentries pace back and forth on the walls. The flag on the roof hung limp. No chimney emitted smoke. Not a living being could be seen in the bare expanse.

How boring life was going to be now. Merry Morel would probably leave in the first group. None of Drogo's friends would remain. And then there would always be the usual guard duty, the usual card games, the usual jaunts to the nearby village for some drinking and mediocre lovemaking. How miserable, thought Drogo. Still, a remnant of the spell drifted along the outlines of the yellow redoubts. Mystery lingered in the slant of embankments, in the shadow of casemates— an inexpressible sensation of future things.

At the Fortezza he found many things changed. Amid so many

imminent departures intense animation reigned everywhere. Who might be destined to depart was yet unknown, and the officers, nearly all of whom had requested to be transferred, were living in anxious anticipation, forgetting the responsibilities they once had. Even Filimore—you knew for sure—was meant to leave the Fortezza, and this knowledge worked to disrupt routine duties. The restlessness even spread among the soldiers, since a large detachment, still to be determined, would have to descend to the plain. Guard duty was performed with reluctance; often the squads weren't ready when the change of guard was scheduled. In everyone the conviction had grown that such precautions were stupid and pointless.

It became obvious that the hopes of the past, the soldierly illusions, the expectation of an enemy from the north, were nothing but a pretext to give meaning to life. Now that the possibility of returning to civil society existed, those tales seemed like childish obsessions. No one wanted to admit to believing them and no one hesitated to crack jokes about them. What mattered was leaving. Everyone, among Drogo's colleagues, had marshaled influential friendships to gain favor; everyone was deeply convinced of success.

"And what about you?" Giovanni's colleagues asked him, vaguely sympathetic—those who had suppressed the momentous news to get ahead of him and eliminate at least one competitor. "What about you?" they asked him.

"I'll probably have to stay a few more months," Drogo would reply. The others rushed to reassure him: he'd be transferred too, damn right, it was undeniable, he shouldn't be so pessimistic (among similar remarks).

Only Ortiz appeared unchanged. He hadn't asked to leave. For several years he had taken no interest in the matter. The news that the garrison would be reduced had reached him last, after all the other officers, and for this reason he hadn't been able to warn Drogo in time. Ortiz was an indifferent witness to the new commotion: he attended to the affairs of the Fortezza with his typical zeal.

The departures finally began. Wagons laden with barracks furniture and fittings rumbled continually through the courtyard. The companies took turns lining up to say goodbye. The colonel came down from his office to review each company, saying a few parting words to the soldiers. His voice was brittle and spent.

Officers who had lived there for many years, who when stationed at the redoubts devoted hundreds of days to scrutinizing the solitary spaces of the north, who used to engage in interminable discussions about whether a sudden enemy attack was likely or not—most of these officers were leaving with a happy face, winking insolently at the colleagues who were staying behind. They withdrew toward the valley, sitting arrogantly erect in the saddle, at the head of their detachments. They didn't even turn back to glance at their Fortezza one last time.

Morel's departure was unique. One sunny morning when he presented his platoon to the colonel in the center of the courtyard, lowering his saber in salute, his eyes were glistening with tears and his voice trembled as he gave the orders. Drogo, leaning his back against a wall, observed the scene. He smiled amicably when his colleague rode past him, heading for the gate. It was perhaps the last time they would see one another. Giovanni raised his right hand to the visor of his cap, executing a regulation salute.

Then he went back inside the entrance of the Fortezza. The halls were cold, even in summer, and day by day they would grow emptier. The thought that Morel was gone suddenly reopened the wound from the injustice he had suffered, and he ached. Giovanni went in search of Ortiz and found him as he was leaving his office with a bundle of papers. He caught up with him, walking at his side. "Buongiorno, major sir."

"Buongiorno, Drogo," responded Ortiz, stopping. "Is there some news? Do you want something from me?"

Drogo did in fact want to ask him something. It was a general point, lacking any urgency, but it had been weighing on his mind for several days.

"Excuse me, major," he said. "Do you remember when I arrived at the Fortezza, four and a half years ago, Major Matti told me only volunteers stayed here? That if someone wanted to leave, he was completely free to go? Do you remember I told you that? To hear Matti tell it, I just needed to visit the doctor to get a formal excuse. The only problem, he said, was that it would bother the colonel a bit."

"Yes, I vaguely remember," said Ortiz with a trace of annoyance. "I beg your pardon, my good man, but at this point I—"

"One minute, major sir. You remember that to avoid doing something undesirable, I resigned myself to staying four months? But if I wanted, I could leave—isn't that correct?"

Ortiz said, "I understand, Drogo, but you aren't the only man who—"

"Then," Giovanni interrupted him, visibly agitated, "then they were just stories? It isn't true that if I wanted, I could leave? They were just stories to shut me up?"

"I don't believe this," said the major. "Don't even think it!"

"Don't tell me no, major," Drogo shot back. "Are you claiming Matti told the truth?"

"The same thing happened to me, more or less," said Ortiz, looking downward, embarrassed. "In those days I too had my mind set on a brilliant career."

They were standing in one of the long corridors. Their voices resounded mournfully along the walls now that the place was bare and empty.

"Then it isn't true that all the officers requested to come here? They were forced to stay like me—isn't that so?"

Ortiz was silent as he jabbed the point of his saber into a crack in the stone floor.

"And whoever said they wanted to stay was talking utter nonsense—right?" insisted Drogo. "Why didn't anyone have the courage to say so?"

"Perhaps it really isn't as you say," Ortiz replied. "There were some who truly wanted to remain, just a few, I concede, but there were some."

"Who? Tell me who they are!" shouted Drogo. Then he abruptly restrained himself. "Forgive me, major sir. Naturally, I wasn't thinking of you. You know what happens when people talk."

Ortiz smiled. "I wasn't referring to myself, you know. Some official decision probably kept me here as well."

The two men began to walk together. They passed before the small oblong windows covered with grating. Beyond you could see the empty plain behind the Fortezza, the mountains to the south, the dense mist in the valley.

"What about all that enthusiasm," resumed Drogo after a moment of silence, "those tales about the Tartars? Did anyone really expect an attack?"

"They absolutely expected it!" Ortiz said. "They believed the tales."

Drogo shook his head. "I don't understand."

"What do you want me to tell you?" the major said. "The situation is complicated. Up here it's a bit like being in exile. You need to find some sort of outlet, something that can give you hope. Someone got the idea that there were Tartars and he started talking about them. We'll never know who it was."

"Perhaps it was the place too," said Drogo, "the effect of seeing that desert."

"Certainly, the place too—the desert, the impenetrable fog, the mountains, you can't deny it. The place is a contributing factor."

He paused, thinking, then resumed, as if he were speaking to himself: "The Tartars, the Tartars. In the beginning, of course, it seems like sheer foolishness. Then you wind up believing it anyhow. Or at least this is the way it happened with many men."

"But you, major, I'm sorry, you—"

"It's altogether different with me," said Ortiz. "I come from an earlier generation. I no longer aspire to a career. A post with no worries is all I need. But you, lieutenant, you have your entire life ahead of you. Within a year, a year and a half, you will be transferred."

"Here goes Morel. Lucky him!" Drogo cried out, stopping at a window. You could actually see the platoon receding across the plain. The soldiers stood out distinctly on the barren, sunblasted ground. Although burdened by heavy backpacks, they were marching with aplomb.

22

THE LAST company scheduled to depart had lined up in the courtyard. Everyone was thinking that by tomorrow his new life at a reduced garrison would be definitively sorted out. The soldiers were particularly impatient to end the interminable rigamarole of farewells as well as the rage at seeing other men leave. The company had lined up and was waiting for Lieutenant Colonel Nicolosi to pass in review when Drogo, who was watching, saw Lieutenant Simeoni appear with an odd expression on his face.

Lieutenant Simeoni had been at the Fortezza for three years. He seemed like a stand-up fellow, a bit pedantic, respectful of authority and enamored of physical exercise. After advancing into the courtyard, he looked around with what seemed to be anxiety, in search of someone to whom he had something to tell. Anyone would probably do, since he had no close friends.

He spotted Drogo watching him and approached. "Come and see," he whispered. "Hurry. Come and see."

"What?" asked Drogo.

"I'm on duty at the third redoubt. I dashed down for a moment. Come as soon as you're free. There's something I don't understand." He was panting a little as if he had been running.

"Where? What have you seen?" asked Drogo, intrigued.

Simeoni said, "Wait now; wait till the company has left."

At that moment a bugle issued a triple blast, and the soldiers stood at attention as the commandant of the downgraded Fortezza arrived.

"Wait till they've left," repeated Simeoni, because Drogo was growing impatient about the mystery, apparently for no reason. "I at least want to see them clear out of here. There's something I've wanted to say for five days. But first they all need to leave."

Finally, after a few words from Nicolosi and the last fanfares, the company left the Fortezza with heavy steps, equipped for a long march. They were headed toward the valley. It was a day in September. The sky was gray and gloomy.

At that point, Simeoni dragged Drogo down long, solitary corridors as far as the entrance to the third redoubt. They crossed the guardroom and emerged on the walkway behind the battlements.

Lieutenant Simeoni drew out a telescope and invited Drogo to look at the small triangle of plain left open by the mountains.

"What is it?" asked Drogo.

"Look first. I don't want to be mistaken. Look and tell me if you see something."

Leaning his elbows on the parapet, Drogo looked attentively at the desert through the telescope, an instrument that belonged to Simeoni. He could easily distinguish stones, hollows, and sparse shrubbery, even though they were extraordinarily far away.

Bit by bit, Drogo scoured the visible triangle of desert. He was about to say no, he couldn't see anything, when at the farthest point, right where every image vanished within the perennial curtain of mist, he thought he could pick out a tiny black spot that was moving.

He was still leaning his elbows on the parapet and peering through the telescope when he felt his heart begin to pound furiously. Like two years ago, he thought, when they all believed the enemy had arrived.

"You're talking about that little black spot?" asked Drogo.

"I've watched it for five days but I didn't want to tell anyone."

"Why?" Drogo replied. "What were you afraid of?"

"If I talked, they might suspend the departures. And after cheating us, Morel and the others would make the most of the opportunity. Better we keep it to ourselves."

"What opportunity? What do you think it is? Like the other time, it'll turn out to be a reconnaissance patrol, or perhaps shepherds, or simply some animal."

"I've been observing it for five days," said Simeoni. "If they were shepherds, they would've gone away. The same thing goes for animals. There's something moving but it stays roughly in the same place."

"So what opportunity do you expect it to bring?"

Simeoni smiled at Drogo as if he were asking whether he could tell him a secret. Then he said, "They're building a road, I think, a military road. This is the real thing. Two years ago they came to study the terrain. Now they're really coming."

Drogo laughed amiably.

"What makes you think they're building a road? You can't seriously believe someone is coming again. Didn't you get enough the last go-round?"

"You're probably a little nearsighted," said Simeoni. "Maybe your eyes aren't so good. I can make it out very clearly. They've started to lay the roadbed. Yesterday was sunny and you could see very clearly."

Drogo shook his head, astounded at such perversity. Hadn't Simeoni grown weary of waiting? Was he really afraid of revealing his discovery, as if it were some kind of treasure? Was he afraid they'd take it away from him?

"Once upon a time," said Drogo, "I too would've believed it. But now you seem delusional to me. If I were you, I wouldn't say a word. They'll wind up laughing at you behind your back."

"They're building a road," replied Simeoni, looking at Drogo with pity. "It will take months, you understand, but this is it."

"Let's assume what you say is true," Drogo said. "Do you believe the Fortezza would be left undefended if a road were being built to bring artillery from the north? The General Staff would immediately get wind of it; they would've known for years."

"The General Staff never takes Fortezza Bastiani seriously. No one will believe the stories until it gets bombarded. They'll be persuaded too late."

"Say what you like," repeated Drogo. "If this road were really under construction, the General Staff would be completely in the know, you can rest assured."

"The General Staff gathers intelligence from a thousand sources, but out of a thousand only one is any good, so they don't give credence to any. In the end, it's useless to argue. You'll see if things don't turn out as I say."

They were alone on the edge of the walkway. The sentries, positioned much farther apart than they used to be, paced back and forth in their appointed sections. Drogo again looked toward the north. Rock, desert, the distant mist—it all seemed devoid of meaning.

Later, speaking with Ortiz, Drogo came to learn that Lieutenant Simeoni's famous secret was known to practically everybody. But no one gave it any weight. Many men were amazed, in fact, that a serious young man like Simeoni would have circulated these new tales.

In those days other things demanded attention. The reduction in personnel required the forces stationed along the walls to be thinned out. Various attempts continued to be made—with fewer means—to establish a security protocol that was nearly as effective as before. Several guard units had to be disbanded so others could be fitted with more equipment. Companies needed to be reassembled and assigned to different barracks.

For the first time since the Fortezza had been constructed, a number of areas were shut and bolted. Prosdocimo the tailor had to let his three assistants go because there was no longer enough work. Every so often you might enter a barracks or office that was completely empty, its walls showing white stains from furniture and paintings that had been removed.

The black spot moving at the outermost confines of the plain continued to be regarded as a joke. Hardly any men borrowed Simeoni's telescope to take a look and the few who did said they saw nothing. Simeoni himself, since no one took him seriously, avoided talking about his discovery. He even had the prudence to laugh about it without taking offense.

Then one evening Simeoni went to get Drogo in his room. Night had already fallen and the change of guard had been completed. The bare-bones squad had returned from the New Redoubt and the Fortezza was preparing for the watch, another night uselessly wasted.

"Come and see," said Simeoni. "I know you don't believe it, but come and see. Either I'm hallucinating or I see a light."

They went to observe. They climbed up to the walkway on the walls of the fourth redoubt. In the darkness Simeoni handed Drogo the telescope so he could look.

"But it's pitch dark!" said Giovanni. "What do you expect me to see?"

"Look, I tell you," Simeoni insisted. "I wouldn't want it to be a hallucination, as I've said. Look where I showed you the last time. Tell me if you see something."

Drogo raised the telescope to his right eye and pointed it toward the far north. In the darkness he saw a tiny light, an infinitesimal dot of light that was shining more or less at the edge of the mist.

"A light!" cried Drogo. "I see a tiny light. Wait." He continued to adjust the telescope. "I can't tell whether there's just one or more. Sometimes there seems to be two."

"So you've seen it," Simeoni said, triumphant. "You still think I'm an idiot?"

"What does that have to do with it?" retorted Drogo, although without much conviction. "What difference does it make if there's a light? It could be a gypsy camp or shepherds."

"It's the lamp on the construction site," Simeoni said. "For the new road. You'll see whether I'm right."

The naked eye, strangely, couldn't make out the light. Not even the sentries (including some who were highly skilled, famous hunters) managed to see anything.

Drogo was still peering through the telescope, searching for the remote light. After looking for a few moments, he lifted the instrument skyward and started observing the stars with curiosity. Infinite in number, they filled every part of the sky, a most beautiful sight. In the east, however, they grew more rare because the moon was about to rise, preceded by a hazy glow.

"Simeoni!" called Drogo, no longer seeing his companion close by. But the other man didn't respond. He must have gone down a short flight of stairs to inspect the ramparts.

Drogo looked around. In the darkness he could distinguish only the empty walkway, the outline of the fortifications, the black shadow of the mountains. The clock struck a few times. The farthest sentry on the right should have issued his nightly call by now; it would have sounded from soldier to soldier along the walls. "Stay alert! Stay alert!" Then the call would have raced down the opposite side, fading at the base of the towering cliffs. Now that the sentry posts had been cut by half—Drogo thought—there would be fewer voices to repeat the call, and the entire journey would be over much more quickly. But silence prevailed.

Suddenly Drogo's mind was flooded with thoughts of a desirable yet distant world—a villa, for instance, on the shore of a sea, a soft summer night, charming creatures sitting nearby, listening to music, images of happiness that youth allowed you to contemplate with impunity, as the farthest edge of the eastern sea glistened darkly and the sky was just beginning to whiten with the approaching dawn. The freedom to waste nights in this way, without taking refuge in sleep, without fearing the lateness of the hour, letting the sun rise, a foretaste of eternity unfolding before you, without any compulsion to agonize. Among so many beautiful things in the world Giovanni insisted on desiring this improbable seaside villa, music, squandering hours, waiting for dawn. However foolish these thoughts may have seemed, he felt they expressed most intensely the peace he had lost. For some time, in fact, an anxiety he couldn't understand had been hounding him: the impression that he was running out of time, that something important would happen and take him by surprise.

The interview with the general down in the city had left him with little hope of a transfer and a brilliant career. Still, Giovanni realized he couldn't spend the rest of his life within the walls of the Fortezza. Sooner or later he would have to make a decision. The routines eventually resumed with their usual rhythms and Drogo stopped thinking about the other men, the companions who had escaped in time, the old friends who were becoming rich and famous. He was consoled by the sight of the officers who lived the same exile as he did, although failing to consider that they may be weak or beaten men, the last example he should follow.

From one day to the next Drogo postponed his decision. He felt, after all, that he was still young, just twenty-five. Nonetheless, the same subtle anxiety hounded him. He now had to deal with the tale of the lamp on the northern plain. Simeoni might even be right.

Few men at the Fortezza spoke of it, as if it were some unimportant thing that couldn't concern them. The disappointment over the war that had failed to materialize was still too close, although none of them had the courage to confess it. And the humiliation of seeing fellow soldiers leave, of being the few and forgotten ones who remained to guard the walls, was still too fresh. The reduction of the garrison had shown quite clearly that the General Staff no longer assigned any importance to Fortezza Bastiani. The illusions, once so effortless and so deeply desired, were now angrily rejected. To avoid being mocked, Simeoni preferred to keep quiet.

On the following nights, at any rate, you couldn't see the mysterious light anymore, and during the day you couldn't make out any movement on the edge of the plain. Major Matti, driven by curiosity to climb to the ramparts, availed himself of Simeoni's telescope only to scour the desert in vain.

"You can keep your telescope, lieutenant," he said to Simeoni with indifference. "Perhaps, instead of ruining your eyesight for nothing, you should pay a little more attention to your men. I saw a sentry without a bandolier. Go and see. He must be that soldier down there."

Accompanying Matti was Lieutenant Maderna, who later told the story at mess amid huge guffaws. At this point, everyone was just trying to pass the days as comfortably as possible. Any concern about the north was forgotten.

Only with Drogo did Simeoni continue to discuss the mystery. For four days, in fact, you could see neither lights nor moving spots, but on the fifth they appeared again. Simeoni believed he could provide an explanation: the northern mist either thickened or faded according to season, wind, and temperature. In those four days it had descended in a southerly direction, enveloping the alleged construction site.

Not only did the light reappear but after roughly a week Simeoni claimed it had shifted and was moving in the direction of the Fortezza. This time Drogo objected: How was it possible, in the dark of night, without any reference point, to verify such movement, even if it had actually occurred?

"There you go," said Simeoni, digging in his heels. "You admit that if the light shifted, it can't be proven definitively. That means I have as much right to say it moved as you do to say it didn't. But you'll see: I'm planning to watch those moving dots every day. You'll see they're gradually moving forward."

The next day they started watching together, alternating in the use of the telescope. You really couldn't see anything but three or four tiny little spots, which were moving at a snail's pace. Getting a definite sense of these movements was rather difficult. You needed to take two or three reference points—the shadow of a boulder, the crest of a hill—and establish the proportional distances. After several minutes you could see the proportion differed, a sign that the dot had changed position.

What was most extraordinary was that Simeoni had been able to notice it in the first place. Then again, you couldn't exclude the possibility that the phenomenon had been occurring for years or centuries. A village might be located there, or a well where caravans stopped. And until then no one at the Fortezza had made use of a telescope as powerful as Simeoni's.

The shifting of the tiny dots almost always happened along the same line, back and forth. Simeoni thought they might be wagons for transporting stones or gravel. At that distance, he said, the men would've been too small to be seen.

Usually you could distinguish only three or four dots moving simultaneously. If you assumed three wagons were moving, Simeoni reasoned, at least another six must be stationary, loading and unloading. These six couldn't be identified since they merged with the thousands of other motionless dots in the landscape. In that section alone, therefore, some ten vehicles were being maneuvered, each probably with four horses, as was customary for heavy transport. The number of men, in proportion, must be in the hundreds.

These observations, initially made as a kind of wager or jest, became the only interesting aspect of Drogo's life. Although Drogo didn't find Simeoni particularly likable—his temperament was joyless and his conversation pedantic—Giovanni almost always spent his free time with him. Even in the evening, in the officers' quarters, the two men would stay up late, deep in discussion.

Simeoni had already arrived at an estimate: if you assumed the work was proceeding slowly and the distance was greater than what had been generally assumed, six months would be enough for the road to come within range of a cannon at the Fortezza. In all probability, he thought, the enemy would stop in the shelter of a ridge that crossed the desert longitudinally.

This ridge usually merged with the rest of the plain because it was the same color. But sometimes evening shadows or banks of mist would reveal its presence. It descended into a gulley that ran toward the north. You couldn't gauge its steepness or depth. Hence the tract of desert it concealed from anyone looking from the New Redoubt was unknown (you couldn't see the ridge from the walls of the fort because the mountains blocked it).

From the upper edge of this gulley to the foot of the mountains, where the rocky cone of the New Redoubt rose, the desert stretched flat and uniform, interrupted only by the odd fissure, piles of rubble, and small patches of canebrake.

Once the enemies' road reached the ridge—Simeoni predicted—they could easily complete the remaining section in a flurry of work, taking advantage of a cloudy night. The terrain would be smooth and compact enough to allow artillery to proceed easily.

Yet the six months that figured in his general prediction—the lieutenant added—could turn into seven, eight, or even many more, depending on circumstances. Here Simeoni listed the possible causes of delay: an error in calculating the total distance to be covered; the existence of other, intervening gullies, invisible from the New Redoubt, making construction more difficult and time-consuming; a gradual slowdown in construction, as the foreigners moved farther and farther away from the source of their supplies; complications of a political nature, which might make the suspension of work advisable for a certain period; snow, which could completely paralyze construction for two or more months; rain, which would transform the plain into marshland. These were the principal obstacles. Simeoni was keen to formulate them meticulously, one by one, so he wouldn't come off as fixated.

What if, Drogo asked, the road didn't serve some aggressive aim? What if it were being constructed for agricultural purposes? The cultivation, say, of the immense wasteland that until then had lain barren and uninhabited? Or what if the work simply stopped after one or two kilometers?

Simeoni shook his head. The desert, he replied, was too rocky to be capable of cultivation. The kingdom of the north, furthermore, possessed vast abandoned grasslands used only for grazing. That terrain would be much more propitious for such a project.

But was it beyond question that the foreigners were actually building a road? Simeoni swore that on certain limpid days, close to sunset, when the shadows grew to great lengths, the rectilinear strip of roadbed could be distinguished. Drogo hadn't seen it, however, no matter how hard he tried. Who could swear the strip wasn't a simple bend in the landscape? The movement of the mysterious black spots and the lamp lit at night were by no means probative. They might've always been there. And no one had seen them before because they were covered by mist (not to mention the inadequacy of the old telescopes that had until then been used at the Fortezza).

One day, while Drogo and Simeoni were engaged in this debate, snow began to fall. Summer isn't yet over, Drogo immediately thought, and the foul weather has already arrived. He felt, in fact, that he had just returned from the city and hadn't even had time to get settled again. And yet the calendar marked the day as the twenty-fifth of November. Entire months had been wasted.

The snow fell thick and heavy, accumulating on the terraces and turning them white. Watching it, Drogo felt his usual anxiety more acutely. In vain he sought to drive it away by dwelling on his youth and the many years that remained to him. Time had inexplicably started to race faster and faster, swallowing one day after the next. You could hardly get your bearings before night began to fall and the sun wound down only to reappear on the other side to brighten the snowbound world.

The other men, his colleagues, seemed not to notice. They performed their usual duties without enthusiasm. When the name of a new month appeared on the orders of the day, they bucked up as if they had received a bonus. Fewer months to spend at Fortezza Bastiani, they calculated. They had set their goals, whether banal or illustrious, and could be satisfied with them.

Even Major Ortiz, who was already in his fifties, watched apathetically as the weeks and months flew past. By this point, he had relinquished his lofty hopes. "Another decade or so," he would say, "and I'll retire." He planned to return to his family's home in an old provincial town—he explained—where several of his relatives lived. Drogo looked at him sympathetically, although without managing to understand. What would Ortiz do, down there among the townspeople, without any purpose, alone?

"I've learned how to be content," said the major, as he realized what Giovanni was thinking. "Year after year I've learned how to desire less and less. If things turn out well for me, I'll return home at the rank of colonel."

"And then?" Drogo asked.

"And then enough," said Ortiz with a resigned smile. "Then I'll continue to wait," he added in jest, "happy to have done my duty."

"But here, at the Fortezza, in the coming decade, you don't think that—"

"A war? Are you still thinking about a war? Haven't we had enough of that?"

On the northern plain, at the edge of the perennial mist, you could no longer see anything suspicious. Even the nocturnal light was extinguished. And Simeoni was extremely pleased with that. It showed he was right: the light had nothing to do with a village or gypsy camp; it pointed only to construction, which the snow had interrupted

23

WINTER had descended upon the Fortezza for some time when a strange communication appeared in the orders of the day, affixed as usual in a frame on a courtyard wall.

The rubric was entitled "Deplorable Warnings and False Rumors." It read as follows: "In accordance with the express instructions of the High Command, noncommissioned officers and enlisted soldiers are hereby enjoined from crediting, repeating, or otherwise disseminating alarmist rumors, devoid of any basis, concerning presumed threats of aggression against our borders. These rumors, apart from the problems they pose for obvious disciplinary reasons, can disrupt normal, neighborly relations with the adjoining state and spread unnecessary anxiety among the troops, harmful to the performance of duties. It is my wish that the vigilance that forms the purview of the sentries be conducted by normal means, and that above all there be no recourse to optical instruments for which provision is not made in the regulations and which, being often used without discernment, easily occasion errors and false interpretations. Anyone who may be in possession of said instruments must notify their respective squad leader, who will arrange to confiscate and impound them."

Next came the usual instructions for the daily changing of the guard followed by the signature of the commandant, Lieutenant Colonel Nicolosi.

Obviously the orders of the day, although formally addressed to the troops, were in reality directed to officers. Nicolosi had thus achieved a double goal: he avoided humiliating anyone and at the same time advised the entire Fortezza. From now on, of course, none of the officers would dare let the sentries see them surveying the desert with a telescope that violated the regulations. The instruments on hand at the various redoubts were old, practically unusable. Some of them had in fact gone missing.

Who had played the spy? Who had informed the High Command down in the city? Everyone thought instinctively of Matti: he alone could've done it, always ready to enforce the regulations and stifle every pleasure, every effort to catch your breath.

Most of the officers laughed about it. The High Command—they said—wasn't inconsistent in taking action two years after the fact. Who was actually thinking about an invasion from the north? Ah, yes, Drogo and Simeoni (whose conjectures had been forgotten). But the notion that the order had been issued specifically on their account—that seemed incredible. A decent fellow like Drogo—they thought—couldn't be a threat to anyone, even if he had a telescope in his hand the whole damn day. Simeoni too was judged innocuous.

Giovanni, however, felt sure the lieutenant colonel's order concerned him personally. Once again things were conspiring against him. What harm was done if he spent a few hours observing the desert? Why deprive him of this consolation? The very thought enraged him. He had already steeled himself for the wait till spring arrived. As soon as the snow melted—he was hoping—the mysterious light would reappear in the far north. The black dots would resume moving back and forth. His faith would be reborn.

His entire emotional life was concentrated in that hope, and on this occasion only Simeoni saw things the same way. The other men didn't give it a thought, not even Ortiz or the regiment tailor, Prosdocimo. It was glorious to be so alone, to nurture a secret jealously, not as in those distant days, before Angustina died, when everyone eyed each other as conspirators, as if they were plotting some sort of greedy competition.

But now the telescope had been prohibited. Simeoni, scrupulous as he was, would certainly not dare use it again. Even if the light burns once more at the edge of the perennial mist, even if the back-and-forth of tiny spots resumes, they will never know. No one could see that far with the naked eye, not even the best sentries, famous hunters who pinpoint a raven more than a kilometer away.

That day Drogo was eager to hear Simeoni's assessment of the situation. But he waited till nightfall so he wouldn't attract any notice. Someone would certainly have reported him at once. Besides, Simeoni hadn't come to the mess hall at midday, and Giovanni hadn't seen him anywhere else.

Simeoni appeared at supper, but later than usual, when Drogo had already begun. He ate very quickly, stood up before Giovanni, and dashed off to a gaming table. Was he afraid of being alone with Drogo?

Neither of them was on duty that night. Giovanni sat in an armchair beside the door to the officers' quarters, planning to corner his friend when he left. He saw how, during the game, Simeoni cast furtive looks in his direction, trying not to be seen.

Simeoni played late, much later than usual, something he had never done before. He continued to glance at the door, hoping Drogo might grow tired of waiting. Finally, when everyone left, he too had to stand and head toward the exit. Drogo approached him.

"Ciao, Drogo," said Simeoni with an embarrassed smile. "I didn't see you. Where were you?"

They had started down one of the many squalid corridors that crossed the center of the Fortezza lengthwise.

"I sat down to read," said Drogo. "I didn't notice it had gotten so late."

They walked a short way in silence, amid the flickering of the sporadic lanterns attached symmetrically to the two walls. The other officers had already moved farther off. Their confused voices could be heard coming from the distant shadows. It was late at night, and it was cold.

"Did you read the orders of the day?" Drogo suddenly asked. "Did you see that business about false alarms? I wonder what caused it. Who do you think was the spy?"

"How would I know?" replied Simeoni, practically rude, stopping at the entrance to a staircase that led above. "Are you coming up?"

"What about the telescope?" Drogo was insistent. "Your telescope can't be used anymore. Unless—"

"I've already turned it into the command," Simeoni interrupted him decorously. "That seemed like the best course. Especially since they were keeping an eye on us."

"You could've waited, if you ask me. Even a few months, until the snow was gone. No one would think twice about it. We could've gone back to watching. The road you were always talking about—how are we going to see it without your telescope?"

"Ah, the road." Simeoni's voice contained a note of sympathy. "In the end, I was persuaded you were right!"

"What do you mean I was right?"

"There wasn't any road. It must be some village or gypsy camp, as you said."

Was Simeoni so scared, then, he was ready to deny everything? So scared of getting into trouble he wouldn't dare talk about it, even to him, to Drogo? Giovanni looked into his friend's face. The corridor had become completely deserted. No voice could be heard. The two officers projected monstrous shadows that swayed from side to side.

"You're telling me you don't believe it anymore?" asked Drogo. "You really think you were wrong? What about all the calculations you made?"

"Just a way to pass the time," Simeoni said, trying to turn everything into a joke. "I hope you didn't set much store by them."

"Tell me the truth," Drogo said in a nasty tone. "You're scared. It was the order—tell the truth—and now you won't risk it."

"I don't know what's bothering you tonight," replied Simeoni. "I don't know what you're trying to say. You can't take a joke—that's what it is—you take everything too seriously. You're like a child."

Drogo didn't utter a word. He just stared at his friend. They remained in that eerie corridor a few moments, speechless, but the silence weighed too heavily.

"Well, I'm going to sleep," concluded Simeoni. "Buona notte!" He started up the stairs, which were lit at every landing by a dim lantern.

After climbing the first flight, he disappeared behind a corner. You could see only his shadow on the wall. Then not even that.

What a worm, thought Drogo.

24

MEANWHILE time was racing. Its silent beat scans life faster and faster. You can't stop, even a moment, even for a glance behind. You want to shout, "Stop! Stop!" But you know it's useless. Everything flies past—men, seasons, clouds. And clinging to rocks or standing firm on the peak of some cliff won't help. Weary fingers open, arms fall limp, inert, and once more you're dragged into the river, which seems slow but never stops.

Day by day Drogo felt the increasing force of this mysterious ruin and in vain he sought to hold it back. Reference points were lacking in the unchanging life of the Fortezza; the hours slipped past before he could count them.

There remained the secret hope for which he frittered away the best part of his life. To nourish this hope, he made small sacrifices month after month, but they were never enough. Winter, the interminable winter at the Fortezza, was only a sort of down payment. Once winter had ended, Drogo was still waiting.

When the weather turned mild—he thought—the foreigners would resume construction on the road. But Simeoni's telescope, which allowed him to see it, was no longer available. Nonetheless, as the construction advanced (how long it would take was sheer conjecture), the foreigners would draw nearer and one fine day they would arrive within range of the old telescopes that remained on hand for some sentry units.

Hence Drogo established that his wait wouldn't come to an end in spring, as he had anticipated, but several months later, still on the assumption that the road was actually under construction. He was forced, furthermore, to brood over all these thoughts in secret. Simeoni, fearful of trouble, no longer wanted to know about them. Other colleagues would have mocked him. And superiors frowned on such fantasies.

At the beginning of May, even though Giovanni scrutinized the plain with the best of the regulation telescopes, he still couldn't make out any sign of human activity. Not even the light that appeared nightly, despite the fact that fires can easily be seen from vast distances.

Little by little his confidence faded. To believe in something is difficult when you're alone and can't talk to anyone about it. Around that time Drogo noticed how men always remain distant, regardless of the affection they feel for each other, how if a man suffers, the pain is entirely his, and no other man can take upon himself the least part of it. Accordingly, if a man suffers, other men don't feel pain, even if their love is deep. This triggers loneliness.

His confidence began to weaken and grow weary and his impatience increased. He heard the hours strike closer and closer together. He was now allowing entire days to pass without even glancing toward the north (although he was fond of self-deception and would persuade himself he'd forgotten when in fact he had deliberately avoided looking, so his odds might prove slightly better next time).

Finally one night—it took ever so long—a tiny flickering light appeared within the lens of the telescope, a dim light that seemed to quiver on the verge of dying out but must've been of a respectable intensity, if the distance were calculated.

It was the night of July 7. For years Drogo remembered the wonderful joy that flooded his heart and the urge to run and shout so everyone might know of it, along with the proud effort to say nothing to anyone out of the superstitious fear that the light might die.

Every night Drogo positioned himself on the walls and waited; every night the small light seemed to draw a little closer and increase in size. On many of these nights it must've been only an illusion, born of desire, but on certain others it made an actual advance, so much so a sentry finally caught sight of it with his naked eye.

Thereafter, on the whitish background of the desert, a movement of tiny black dots began to be noticed during the day as well, just as in the previous year, except now the telescope was less powerful and therefore the foreigners must've gotten much closer.

In September the lamp assumed to be on the construction site could be perceived distinctly on clear nights, even by people with normal eyesight. Gradually the soldiers resumed their talk about the northern plain, the foreigners, those strange movements and nocturnal lights. Many said it was really a road, although without managing to explain its purpose; the hypothesis of a military enterprise seemed absurd. Besides, the work seemed to proceed with extraordinary slowness in relation to the huge distance that remained.

One night, just the same, you could hear someone talking in vague terms about war. And once again strange hopes began to churn within the walls of the Fortezza.

25

A STAKE is planted on the brow of the ridge that cuts the northern plain lengthwise at less than a kilometer from the Fortezza. From there to the rocky cone of the New Redoubt the desert unfolds uniform and compact, capable of permitting artillery to proceed without encumbrance. A stake is driven into the upper edge of the gulley, a singular human sign, which can be seen quite clearly, even by the naked eye, from the top of the New Redoubt.

The foreigners have gotten this far with their road. The momentous work is finally completed, but at what a terrible price! Lieutenant Simeoni had made an estimate, had said six months. But six months weren't enough for the construction, not six months, or eight, or ten. The road is now finished and enemy convoys can descend from the north at a fast gallop to reach the walls of the Fortezza. From where the road stops the last stretch remains to be crossed, a few hundred meters over smooth, easy terrain. Yet all this has cost dearly. It has taken fifteen years, fifteen very long years, which have nonetheless sped past as in a dream.

At a glance, nothing seems changed. The mountains have remained exactly the same. You can still see the same stains on the walls of the fort. Some new stains have appeared but their dimensions are negligible. The sky is the same. The Tartar desert is the same, if you exclude that blackish stake on the brow of the ridge as well as a vertical strip whose visibility fluctuates with the light. This is the famous road.

Fifteen years have been less than nothing for the mountains. Nor have they done much harm to the ramparts. For the men, however, they have amounted to a long journey, although no one understands how they passed so quickly. The faces are still the same, more or less. Routines haven't changed, or the turns of guard duty, or the officers' nightly conversations.

Yet if you look closely, the years have left recognizable signs in faces. And then the garrison has been further decreased in number. Lengthy segments of the walls are no longer guarded and you can gain access to them without a password. Sentries are positioned only at essential points. The decision was even made to close the New Redoubt and send a squad to inspect it every ten days. So little importance does the High Command now assign to Fortezza Bastiani.

In fact, the construction of the road on the northern plain hasn't been taken seriously by the General Staff. Some say this reflects the typical inconsistency of military leadership; others say the capital is assuredly better informed. Evidently the road turns out to lack any aggressive purpose. Though this isn't very persuasive, no other explanation has been forthcoming.

Life at the Fortezza has grown increasingly monotonous and isolated. Lieutenant Colonel Nicolosi, Major Monti, and Lieutenant Colonel Matti have retired. The garrison is now commanded by Lieutenant Colonel Ortiz. Every officer has advanced in rank, like him, with the exception of the regiment tailor, Prosdocimo, who has remained a marshal.

On a beautiful September morning, Drogo, Captain Giovanni Drogo, once again rides up the steep road that leads from the plain to Fortezza Bastiani. He was given a month furlough but after twenty days he is already returning. The city has now become completely foreign to him. Old friends have made their mark, they occupy important positions, and they greet him hurriedly like any garden-variety officer. Whenever Drogo returns, even his home, which he continues to love, fills him with pain that defies description. On most of these occasions the house is deserted. His mother's room is empty forever. His brothers are always somewhere else: one is married and lives in a different city; another is constantly traveling. The rooms no longer reveal any signs of family life. Voices echo grotesquely. Throwing windows open to the sun isn't enough.

So once again Drogo climbs up the valley of the Fortezza. He has fifteen fewer years to live. Unfortunately he doesn't feel as if he has changed a great deal. Time has moved so quickly his psyche hasn't been able to age. And although the obscure excitement of the passing hours intensifies every day, Drogo persists in the illusion that the important event has yet to begin. Giovanni patiently awaits his hour, which has never arrived. He doesn't think the future has been terribly abbreviated. Things aren't the way they were before, when the time to come could seem a vast period, an inexhaustible richness you could squander without running any risk.

And yet one day he realized that for some time he hadn't gone riding in the clearing behind the Fortezza. He realized, in fact, that he had lost the desire to do it. And in the last few months (how many, exactly?) he hadn't run up stairs two steps at a time. Nonsense, he thought. Physically he felt the same. Everything was about to start over; there wasn't any doubt. A test would've been ridiculously superfluous.

No, Drogo hasn't physically degenerated. If he started riding again and running up stairs, he would be quite capable. But that doesn't matter. The serious thing is that he has lost the desire, and after lunch he prefers to nod off in the sun instead of roving up and down the stony clearing. This is what counts; this alone records the years that have elapsed.

If only it had crossed his mind the first night he took the stairs one step at a time! True, he felt a bit tired. His head ached and he had no desire for the usual card game (besides, he had sometimes refrained from running up stairs in the past as well, when he suffered the occasional ailment). That particular night marked a sad event for him, although he didn't have the faintest inkling of it. On those stairs, at that precise hour, his youth was ending. And for no special reason he wouldn't revert to his old propensities the following day, or the day after, or later. Or ever.

*

Now, as Drogo rides up the steep road in sunlight, deep in thought, and his horse, already somewhat weary, moves at a lope, a voice calls to him from across the valley.

"Captain sir!" he heard someone shout. When he turned, he noticed a young officer on horseback perched on the road that ran along the opposite side of the ravine. He didn't recognize the soldier, but he could make out a lieutenant's stripes. He imagined it was another officer from the Fortezza who, like him, was returning from a furlough.

"What is it?" asked Giovanni, stopping after he responded to the soldier's regulation salute. What motive prompted that lieutenant to call out to him, especially in a way that was much too casual?

The soldier didn't reply. "What is it?" Drogo repeated in a louder voice, this time slightly irritated.

Sitting upright in the saddle, the unknown lieutenant cupped his hands to his mouth and replied at the top of his voice: "Nothing! I just wanted to salute you!"

To Giovanni it seemed a stupid explanation, almost offensive, something that could be construed as a joke. Another half an hour's ride before reaching the bridge, where the two roads would join. Was there any need, then, for these civilian enthusiasms?

"Who are you?" Drogo shouted back.

"Lieutenant Moro!" was the reply, or rather the captain seemed to hear that name. Lieutenant Moro? he asked himself. There was no such name at the Fortezza. Was he perhaps a new junior officer coming to assume his duties?

Only then was Drogo struck by painful echoes of the distant day when he climbed to the Fortezza the first time—memories of his encounter with Captain Ortiz (at the very same point in the valley), his longing to speak with a friend, his embarrassing conversation across the ravine.

It was exactly like that day, he thought, except the roles had been switched: he, Drogo, was now the old captain climbing to Fortezza

Bastiani for the hundredth time, while the new lieutenant was a certain Moro, whom he didn't know. Drogo understood how an entire generation had been depleted in the intervening years and how he had now passed the peak of life to join the cohort of old men where he felt Ortiz belonged on that remote day. Past forty, without having accomplished anything notable, with no children, truly alone in the world, Giovanni looked around in dismay, feeling his destiny decline.

He saw rocks encrusted with shrubbery, wet gorges, bare ridges overlapping far off in the sky, the impassive face of the mountains, and, on the other side of the valley, the new lieutenant, timid and out of his element, no doubt deluding himself that he would remain at the Fortezza just a few months as he dreamt of a brilliant career, glorious feats of arms, romantic affairs.

With one hand he patted the neck of his horse, which amiably turned back its head but of course couldn't understand him. A knot tightened around Drogo's heart. Farewell to the dreams of the distant past; farewell to the beautiful things in life. The limpid sunlight shone benignly. An invigorating flow of air descended from the valley. The meadows sent forth a pleasant fragrance. Birds' voices accompanied the music from the stream. For humanity, thought Drogo, this is a day filled with happiness. He was amazed that nothing differed in appearance from certain marvelous mornings in his youth. The horse resumed the journey. Half an hour later Drogo saw the bridge where the roads joined. Soon, he thought, he'd have to start conversing with the new lieutenant. It pained him.

26

WHY, WITH the road now finished, had the foreigners disappeared? Why had men, horses, and wagons gone back across the vast plain, back into the northern mists? Was all that work for nothing?

The squads of road workers were indeed seen drawing away, one by one, until they again became tiny dots visible only with a telescope, exactly as they were fifteen years before. The way was open to soldiers: let the army now advance to attack Fortezza Bastiani.

Yet the army wasn't seen advancing. Nothing remained but the strip of road over the Tartar desert, a singular sign of human order amid ancient desolation. The army didn't descend for the attack. Everything seemed left in suspension. No one knew how many years it might last.

Thus the plain remained motionless. The northern mists were fixed, fixed the regimented life of the Fortezza. The sentries ever repeated the same steps from this to that point on the walkway around the battlements. The soldiers' soup was the same. One day was identical to the next, repeated infinitely, like a soldier running in place. And yet the winds of time were blowing. Paying no heed to humanity, they swept back and forth around the world and laid waste to beautiful things. No one could escape them, not even newborn children who were yet to be named.

Giovanni's face gradually became covered with wrinkles. His hair turned gray, his step heavier. The torrent of life had now flung him aside, toward outlying whirlpools, although he hadn't yet reached fifty. Naturally Drogo was no longer assigned to guard duty. He occupied his own office in the command, adjacent to that of Lieutenant Colonel Ortiz.

When shadows were lengthening, the meager number of men on watch was no longer enough to prevent night from seizing control of the Fortezza. Extensive segments of wall were unguarded, and at those points rifts were opened by ruminations on the darkness coupled with the melancholy of solitude. The old fort in fact resembled a remote island surrounded by empty spaces: to the right and left stood mountains, to the south the long, uninhabited valley, and on the opposite side the Tartar plain. In the early hours strange noises never heard before reverberated throughout the labyrinthine fortifications and the sentries' hearts began to pound. The shout of "Stay alert! Stay alert!" still ran from one end of the walls to the other. But the soldiers struggled to pass it on, given the great distance that separated them.

In those days Drogo witnessed Lieutenant Moro's initial worries, viewing them as a faithful reproduction of his own youth. From the start Moro had also been frightened. He turned to Major Simeoni, who had replaced Matti to some extent. The young man was persuaded to stay four months and wound up being snared. He too had started watching the northern plain much too persistently, focusing on the new, unutilized road by which his soldierly hopes might arrive. Drogo would've liked to talk to him, to tell him to be careful, to leave while there was still time, considering Moro was a likable, conscientious fellow. But some foolishness would always intervene to prevent the conversation. Besides, chances are it would've been completely useless.

As the pages turned one after another, the gray pages of day and the black pages of night, the anxiety that time was running out mounted in Drogo and Ortiz (and perhaps other aging officers as well). Indifferent to the ruin inflicted by the years, the foreigners never budged, as if they were immortal and couldn't care less about trifling away entire seasons. The Fortezza, however, contained mere men, defenseless against the work of time, whose ultimate end was approaching. Dates that once seemed implausible, so far away, now suddenly appeared on the nearby horizon, recalling the brutal deadlines imposed by life. Whenever they came due, you could keep going only by developing a new system, finding new terms of comparison, consoling yourself with men who were worse off.

Finally Ortiz had to retire (in the northern plain you couldn't discern the slightest sign of life, not even a minuscule light). Lieutenant Colonel Ortiz handed over the reins to the new commander, Simeoni, and assembled the troops in the courtyard—except, of course, the squads on guard duty. He stumbled through a speech, mounted his horse with an orderly's help, and left through the gate of the Fortezza. A lieutenant and two soldiers escorted him.

Drogo accompanied him to the edge of the plateau, where they said goodbye. It was the morning of a splendid summer day. Clouds were passing in the sky; their shadows created strange stains on the landscape. Lieutenant Colonel Ortiz dismounted and stood with Drogo at a distance from the others. Both of them were silent, not knowing how to part. Then they uttered words that were forced and banal, so different from what they harbored in their hearts and so much more superficial.

"From now on my life will be different," said Drogo. "I almost wish I were leaving as well. I almost feel like submitting my resignation."

Ortiz said, "You're still young! It would be foolish. You still have plenty of time!"

"Time for what?"

"The war. You'll see, in less than two years." (He said as much but in his heart he hoped it wouldn't happen. In reality he wanted Drogo to leave, like him, without ever experiencing some glorious destiny. That would've struck him as unjust. Still, he saw Drogo as a friend, and he wished him well.)

But Giovanni said nothing.

"You'll see, in less than two years, really," Ortiz insisted, hoping he would be contradicted.

"Nonsense!" said Drogo finally. "Centuries will pass and it still won't be enough. The road has been abandoned at this point. No one will ever come from the north." Although these words were his, the voice in his heart said something quite different, something absurd yet resistant to the passage of time. That deeply instilled premonition of fated events, an obscure certainty that the best thing in his life was yet to begin, had remained intact from his youth.

They fell silent again, realizing the conversation was dividing them. But what could they say, after living together for almost thirty years within the same walls, dreaming the same dreams? Their two roads, after such a long journey, were now parting—one here, the other there—and they were heading off toward unknown lands.

"What sunlight!" said Ortiz. His eyes somewhat clouded by age, he gazed at the walls of his Fortezza, which he was abandoning forever. They always looked the same, the same yellowish color, the same romantic appearance. Ortiz gazed at them intensely, and no one but Drogo could've guessed how much he was suffering.

"It's really hot," replied Drogo, recalling Maria Vescovi, that distant conversation in the parlor as the melancholy piano chords wafted downstairs.

"A hot day, that's the truth," Ortiz added. The two men smiled, an instinctive gesture of agreement, as if to say they recognized the significance of those silly words. The shadow of a cloud had now reached them. For a few minutes the entire clearing turned dark. The Fortezza, in contrast, flashed with a sinister radiance, still immersed in sunlight. Two large birds were circling over the first redoubt. You could hear the sound of a bugle, in the distance, almost imperceptible.

"Did you hear? The bugle," said the elderly officer.

"No, I didn't hear it," Drogo replied, lying. He had a vague feeling the lie might please his friend.

"Perhaps I was mistaken," Ortiz admitted, his voice trembling. "We are really too far away." Then he added with difficulty: "Do you remember the first time, when you came here and were afraid? You didn't want to stay. Do you remember?"

Drogo could say only "A long time ago." A strange knot closed his throat.

Then Ortiz said something else, after catching up to his thoughts.

"Who knows," he said, "perhaps I could have served in a war. I might have been useful. In a war. But for everything else, useless. As we've seen."

The cloud had passed. It had already gone beyond the Fortezza and was now slipping across the Tartars' desolate plain, farther and farther to the north, in silence. Farewell, farewell. With the return of the sun the two men were again casting shadows. Twenty meters off, the horses of Ortiz and his escort stamped their hooves on the stones, signifying impatience.

27

THE PAGE turns. Months and years pass. The men who were Drogo's schoolmates are nearly sick of working. Their gray beards are trimmed square. They walk with composure through the city, where they are greeted respectfully. Their sons are grown men; some are already grandfathers. Drogo's old friends, contented with their careers, love lingering at the entrances of the houses they built for themselves, observing how the river of life flows. They amuse themselves by singling out their sons in the swirl of the multitude, urging them to be quick, to outstrip the others, to arrive first. Giovanni Drogo, however, is still waiting, although his hope wanes with every minute.

Now, indeed, he has finally changed. He is fifty-four. He holds the rank of major and is second in command at the scant garrison of the Fortezza. Until a short while ago he hadn't changed much; you could say he was still young. Occasionally he would ride across the clearing for the sake of his health. But it took some effort.

Then he began to lose weight. His face turned a sad yellow color; his muscles sagged. "Liver problems," said Dr. Rovina, who was now quite old, stubbornly determined to end his life there. The doctor's powders had no effect. In the morning Giovanni would awaken with a disheartening fatigue that seized him in the back of the neck. Later, when he was sitting in his office, he couldn't wait for evening to arrive so he could throw himself into an armchair or onto a bed. Liver problems aggravated by general exhaustion, said the doctor, although exhaustion would be most odd, considering the life Giovanni was leading. Anyway it was a passing thing—said Dr. Rovina—frequent at his age, lasting a bit long, perhaps, but without any risk of complications.

Thus grafted into Drogo's life was an additional wait, the hope of recovery. He didn't, in any case, seem impatient. The northern desert was still empty. Nothing augured an eventual enemy attack.

"You're looking better," his colleagues told him almost daily. But Drogo really didn't feel the slightest improvement. The headaches and the troublesome diarrhea during the early days had disappeared; no specific illness afflicted him. His overall vitality, however, was languishing.

Simeoni, the commander of the Fortezza, told him, "Take a leave. Get some rest. A city by the sea would do you good." When Drogo declined, saying that he was feeling better, that he preferred to stay, Simeoni shook his head in reproach, as if Giovanni were ungratefully refusing valuable advice that was in complete harmony with the spirit of the regulations, the efficiency of the garrison, and his personal interest. Simeoni's sense of his own virtuous perfection weighed so heavily on the other officers that he could even make them nostalgic for Matti.

No matter what he said, his words, while extremely cordial on the surface, would always carry a faint note of reprimand for everyone else—as if he alone did his duty to the last detail, he alone were the pillar of the Fortezza, he alone were equipped to remedy the infinite woes that would otherwise have sent everything to hell. Matti, in his prime, had acted in a similar way, but he was less hypocritical. Matti never held back when he displayed his insensitivity, and some of his pitiless crudity the soldiers didn't mind.

Fortunately Drogo had befriended Rovina and made the doctor his accomplice, enabling him to stay. A dark superstition told him that if illness made him leave the Fortezza now, he would never return again. This thought caused him anguish. Twenty years earlier he would've wanted to leave and settle in some garrison where life was serene yet lively, with summer maneuvers, shooting drills, riding competitions, theater, social gatherings, beautiful women. But what would be left for him now? He wasn't many years short of retirement. His career was finished. At most they would give him a position in some command to complete his service. He had only a few years left, the last reserve, and perhaps before they ended the anticipated event would occur. He had thrown away his good years; now he at least wanted to wait till the last minute.

To expedite Drogo's recovery Rovina advised him not to overtax himself, to stay in bed all day and have any business that needed to be dispatched brought to his room. All of this occurred during a cold, rainy March accompanied by huge landslides in the mountains. Entire pinnacles suddenly collapsed for unknown reasons, crashing into the chasms. Eerie voices resounded in the night for hours on end.

Finally, after a string of false starts, good weather began to appear. The snow in the pass had melted, but wet mists lingered over the Fortezza. Only a powerful sun could drive them away, so deeply had winter tainted the air in the valleys. One morning, however, as Drogo awoke, he saw a marvelous strip of sunlight gleam on the wood floor, and he felt spring had arrived.

He let himself be seized by the hope that his energy would revive in harmony with the good weather. In spring a residue of life revives even in ancient beams; hence the innumerable creaks that fill those nights. Everything seems to start anew. A surge of health and joy pours over the world.

Drogo brooded over these thoughts, recalling the writings of illustrious authors who addressed the topic, aiming to persuade himself. He rose from the bed and walked unsteadily to the window. He started to feel dizzy. But he took comfort in the thought that this always happens after spending many days in bed, even if you've recovered. In fact, the dizzy feeling disappeared, and Drogo could gaze at the radiance of the sun.

Limitless joy seemed to be diffused in the world. Drogo couldn't verify it directly because a wall stood before him. But he sensed it effortlessly. Even those old walls, the reddish earth of the courtyard, the benches of faded wood, an empty cart, a soldier slowly passing by —they all seemed happy. And what about outside, beyond the walls?

He was tempted to dress, to sit outdoors in an armchair and take the sun, but a slight shiver frightened him, recommending he return to bed. Still, he thought, convinced he wasn't deluding himself, I feel better today, truly better.

The stupendous spring morning quietly advanced. The strip of sunlight was shifting across the floor. Drogo observed it every so often without the least desire to examine the notebooks piled on a bedside table. An extraordinary silence hung in the room, undiminished by the infrequent bugle calls or the dripping cistern. Even after his promotion to major Drogo really didn't want to change his room, as if he feared it would've brought him bad luck. By now the sobbing of the cistern had become an ingrained habit and it no longer gave him any annoyance.

Drogo was watching a fly that had landed on the floor right on the strip of sunlight. Strange to see a fly in early spring; who knows how it survived the winter. He was watching it walk cautiously when someone knocked at the door.

It sounded different from the usual knocks, noted Giovanni. It certainly wasn't the orderly or Captain Corradi from the staff office, who would ask permission, or any of his other customary visitors. "Avanti!" said Drogo.

The door opened and in walked the old regiment tailor, Prosdocimo, now completely stooped, wearing a curious suit that must have been a marshal's uniform at some point. He took a step forward, wheezing a little, and made a gesture with his right index finger, referring to something beyond the walls.

"They're coming! They're coming!" he proclaimed in a whisper as if he were revealing a momentous secret.

"Who's coming?" asked Drogo, astonished to see the tailor so frantic. I'm in for it, he thought. The drivel is about to start. He'll go on for an hour at least.

"They're coming down the road, God willing, the road from the north! Everybody's gone out on the terrace to see them."

"The road from the north? Soldiers?"

"Battalions of them, entire battalions!" shouted the frail old man, beside himself, clenching his fists. "There's no mistake this time. Besides, a letter came from the General Staff telling us they're sending reinforcements! It's war! War!" he shouted. You couldn't make out if he was a little afraid too.

"You can already see them?" asked Drogo. "You can see them without a telescope?" (He had sat up in bed, invaded by tremendous unease.)

"By God, you can see them! You can see the cannons too. They've already counted eighteen of them!"

"How soon will they be able to attack? How much longer will it take them?"

"Ah, they're moving quick with the road. I'd say they'll be here in two days. Two days at the most!"

This damn bed, Drogo said to himself. I'm stuck here with this illness. The idea that Prosdocimo might be telling a tale didn't cross his mind. He had suddenly felt everything was true. He noticed even the air had changed somehow, even the sunlight.

"Prosdocimo," he said, short of breath. "Go call Luca for me, my orderly. Ringing the bell is useless. He must be down in the staff office, waiting for them to give him some papers. Hurry, please!"

"Come on, major sir," urged Prosdocimo, heading out. "Don't worry about your illness. Come onto the walls and see!"

He exited in a rush, forgetting to close the door. You could hear the sound of his steps receding down the corridor. Then silence returned.

"God, make me feel better, I implore you," murmured Drogo without managing to control his excitement. "At least for six, seven days." He wanted to get out of bed right away, at any cost. He would climb up to the walls at once, appear before Simeoni, make him understand that he, Giovanni, wouldn't be left out, that he was at his post in the command, that he had assumed his usual responsibilities as if he weren't ill.

Bang! A gust of wind in the corridor made the door slam abominably. In the heavy silence the noise echoed loud and baleful, as if it were a response to Drogo's prayer. Why wasn't Luca on his way? How long did it take that imbecile to climb two flights of stairs?

Without waiting for him Drogo got out of bed and was seized by a wave of dizziness which, however, slowly abated. He stood before the mirror, horrified to see his face, yellow and emaciated. The beard makes me look worse off than I am, Giovanni tried telling himself. Taking unsteady steps, still in his nightshirt, he wandered around the room in search of his razor. Why didn't Luca make up his mind to come?

Bang! The door slammed again, blown by the wind. "The devil take you!" said Drogo as he went to close it. At that moment he heard the approach of the orderly's steps.

Shaved and dressed punctiliously—although his uniform was so baggy he felt like he was swimming in it—Major Giovanni Drogo left his room and headed down the corridor, which seemed much longer than usual. Luca walked at his side, slightly behind him, ready to support him, since he saw how the officer struggled to stay on his feet. The waves of dizziness now returned in fits and starts, forcing Drogo to stop and lean against the wall. I'm getting too excited, he thought, the usual nervousness. But on the whole I feel better.

The dizziness eventually passed and Drogo reached the topmost terrace of the fort, where various officers were using telescopes to scrutinize the visible triangle of plain not obscured by the mountains. Giovanni was dazzled by the full radiance of the sun—he had grown unaccustomed to it. He responded confusedly to the greetings of the officers present. He felt (although perhaps it was a malicious interpretation) that the junior officers saluted him with a certain informality, as if he were no longer their direct superior, the arbiter of their daily lives in a sense. Had they decided he was already as good as dead?

This disagreeable thought was brief, giving way to his chief concern: the idea of war. The first thing Drogo noticed was a thin plume of smoke rising from the edge of the New Redoubt. The guard had been restored then, and emergency measures taken. The command was already in operation, although no one had consulted him, the second in command. On the contrary, they hadn't even warned him. If Prosdocimo hadn't taken the initiative by coming to call him, Drogo would've still been in bed, unaware of the threat.

A fit of searing, bitter anger gripped him. His eyes were clouded. He had to lean against the parapet of the terrace. He did it with the utmost control to prevent the other officers from seeing how bad off he was. He felt horribly alone, among an enemy people. Some of the young lieutenants, like Moro, were fond of him. But how could the support of subordinates matter to him?

In the meantime he heard the order to come to attention. With hurried steps Lieutenant Colonel Simeoni moved forward, red in the face.

"For half an hour I've been looking for you everywhere," he exclaimed to Drogo. "I didn't know what to do. Decisions must be made!"

He approached with exuberant cordiality, frowning, as if he were very worried and keen to get Drogo's advice. Drogo felt disarmed. His anger suddenly subsided, although he was well aware that Simeoni was deceiving him. Simeoni had imagined that Drogo couldn't move. He had stopped paying attention to the sick officer and chosen to make all decisions on his own, although he intended to inform him when everything had been carried out. Then he had been told Drogo was wandering around the Fortezza and rushed to find him, eager to demonstrate his good faith.

"I have a message here from General Stazzi," said Simeoni, pre-empting all of Drogo's questions and taking him aside so the other officers couldn't hear. "Two regiments are arriving. Do you understand? Where do I put them?"

"Two regiments of reinforcements?" said Drogo, awestruck.

Simeoni handed him the message. The general announced that as a security measure, fearing possible enemy provocations, two regiments, the Seventeenth Infantry and a second in formation, along with a light artillery unit, had been dispatched to reinforce the garrison at the Fortezza. Guard duty should be reestablished with the traditional personnel, that is to say, with a complete contingent, and quarters should be prepared for officers and soldiers. One group would naturally pitch a camp.

"Meanwhile I've sent a platoon to the New Redoubt. I was right to do so, no?" Simeoni added without giving Drogo any time to respond. "You've already seen them?"

"Yes, yes, you were right," replied Drogo with considerable difficulty. Simeoni's words entered his ears as a staccato, unreal sound. The things around him swayed unpleasantly. Drogo felt sick. A terrible exhaustion suddenly overcame him. All his willpower was concentrated in the single effort to stay on his feet. Oh God, oh God, he implored mentally, help me a little!

To mask his collapse, he called for a telescope (it was Lieutenant Simeoni's famous telescope) and started looking toward the north, leaning his elbows on the parapet, a position that helped to keep him on his feet. If only the enemy had waited a little while. A week would've been enough to enable him to recover. They had waited so many years. Couldn't they delay a few days more, just a few days?

He looked at the visible triangle of desert through the telescope. He hoped that he wouldn't see anything, that the road would be empty, showing no signs of life. This was Drogo's hope after wasting his life waiting for the enemy.

He hoped that he wouldn't see anything. But a black strip cut a diagonal across the whitish background of the plain, and this strip was moving, a dense swarm of men and convoys descending toward the Fortezza. This was different from the measly ranks of armed men when the border was demarcated. It was the northern army, at last, and conceivably . . .

At this point Drogo saw the image in the telescope start to turn with a swirling motion. It grew darker and darker and plunged into blackness. As he lost consciousness on the parapet, he fell limp as a puppet. Simeoni caught him in time. Holding the body drained of life, he felt the fleshless framework of bones through the cloth.

28

A DAY AND a night passed. Major Giovanni Drogo lay in bed. Every so often the rhythmic drip of the cistern reached him but no other sound, even though throughout the Fortezza an anxious turmoil was mounting with every minute. Completely isolated, Drogo was lying there, listening to his own body, hoping to determine whether his lost strength would ever return. Dr. Rovina told him it would in a few days. But how many days, in reality? When the enemy arrived, could he at least get to his feet, dress, and drag himself as far as the roof of the fort? From time to time he would get out of bed. Whenever he seemed to feel a little better, he would walk as far as the mirror without leaning on anything. But here the sinister image of his face, increasingly sallow and gaunt, quashed his new hopes. Befuddled by dizziness, he staggered back to bed and cursed the doctor for being unable to cure him.

The strip of sunlight had already cut a wide swath on the floor. It must have been at least eleven o'clock. Unfamiliar voices rose from the courtyard. Drogo was lying motionless, his gaze fixed on the ceiling, when Lieutenant Colonel Simeoni, the commandant of the Fortezza, entered his room.

"How goes it?" he asked in a buoyant tone. "A little better? Do you realize how pale you are?"

"I know," replied Drogo coldly. "Have they advanced from the north?"

"They have more than advanced," Simeoni said. "The artillery is already on top of the ridge and they're now putting it in position. You must forgive me for not coming by. It has become a living hell here. This afternoon the first reinforcements arrive. Only now could I find five free minutes."

"I hope to get out of bed tomorrow," Drogo said, astonished at hearing his own voice falter. "I should be able to help a little."

"No, no, don't even think of it. Concentrate on your recovery now. And don't think I've forgotten you. I actually have some good news: a magnificent carriage will come to fetch you today." Then he dared to add: "War or no war, friends come first."

"A carriage will fetch? Why fetch me?"

"To take you away, of course. You don't want to stay shut up here in this stuffy room. Your recovery will make better progress in the city. Within a month you'll be back on your feet. Don't worry about what's happening here. Most of the preparations are done now."

A tremendous rage built up in Drogo's chest. Would they send him away just when the war was finally coming, after he had thrown away the best things in life to wait for the enemy, after he had fed on that one belief for more than thirty years?

"You should've at least asked me," he responded, his voice trembling with anger. "I'm not moving. I want to stay here. I'm less sick than you think. Tomorrow I'm getting out of bed."

"Please don't get worked up. We won't do anything. If you get worked up, you'll feel even worse," said Simeoni with a forced smile of understanding. "It just seemed much better to me. Even Rovina says—"

"What about Rovina? Did he tell you to send for the carriage?"

"No, no. The carriage wasn't discussed with Rovina. But he does say you would be better off with a change of scene."

Drogo then thought of speaking to Simeoni as a true friend, opening his heart to him as he would have done with Ortiz. After all, Simeoni too was a man.

"Listen, Simeoni," he ventured, changing his tone. "You know everybody here at the Fortezza stayed because they harbored this hope. It's difficult to put into words but you know what I mean. If it weren't for this possibility—" He couldn't really explain himself: How could he make such a man see these things?

"I don't understand," said Simeoni, obviously annoyed. Had Drogo become pathetic too? he thought. Had the illness softened him?

"But you must understand," Giovanni insisted. "I've been waiting here for more than thirty years. I've let many opportunities pass by. Thirty years mean something, all spent waiting for this enemy. You can't expect—You can't expect me to leave now; you can't. I feel I have a certain right to stay."

"Fine," Simeoni shot back, irritated. "I thought I was doing you a favor and you respond to me like this. It wasn't worth the trouble. I sent two couriers expressly for this purpose. I delayed the march of an artillery battery expressly to let the carriage pass."

"But I'm really not blaming you," said Drogo. "I'm grateful to you. Your intentions were good. I understand." How painful, he thought, to have to keep things on an even keel with this swine. He added imprudently, "The carriage can stay here, in any event. I'm in no condition to take a journey like that."

"A little while ago you said you were getting out of bed tomorrow. Now you're telling me you can't even get into a carriage. Forgive me, but you don't know what you want."

Drogo tried to rectify the situation. "Oh no, it's very different. Taking a journey like that is one thing but going up to the walkway is another. I can also bring a stool with me and sit down if I feel weak." He thought of saying "a chair" but it might've seemed ridiculous. "From there I can monitor the guards on duty. I can at least see."

"Stay then, stay!" said Simeoni, as if to bring the conversation to a close. "But I don't know what sleeping quarters I can assign the officers who are arriving. I can't put them in the corridors. I can't put them in the cellar! Three beds can fit in this room."

Drogo stared icily at him. Had Simeoni gone so far, then? Did he want to pack him off to free up a room? Was this the only reason? So much for his concern and friendship. I should've seen it from the beginning, thought Drogo. I should've expected it from a scoundrel like him.

Encouraged by Drogo's silence, Simeoni insisted, "Three beds would work very well here. Two along that wall and the third in that corner. Do you see? Drogo, if you're listening to me"—he spoke precisely without the slightest compassion—"if you're really listening to me, you'll simplify my task, whereas your idea of staying here—sorry but I must say it—I don't see how you can be of any use in your condition—"

"Yes, of course," Giovanni interrupted. "I understand. Enough already, please. I have a headache."

"Forgive my insistence," said the other man, "but I'd like settle this matter at once. The carriage is now en route. Rovina approves of the departure. A room would become free. You'll recover more quickly. All things considered, keeping you here, a sick man, makes me responsible if some misfortune should happen later. You're obliging me to assume a serious responsibility. I say that in all sincerity."

"Listen," Drogo replied, although he realized how absurd it was to put up a fight. Meanwhile he stared at the strip of sunlight that was rising along the wood-paneled wall, lengthening sideways. "I'm sorry but I say no. I prefer to stay. You won't have any trouble, I guarantee it. If you like, I'll put a declaration in writing. Carry on, Simeoni. Leave me in peace. I probably don't have much time to live. Let me stay here. I've slept more than thirty years in this room!"

The other man was silent for a moment. He stared at his sick colleague with contempt. He smiled wickedly. Then he changed his tone: "What if I asked you as a superior? If I issued an order, what could you say?" Here he paused, savoring the impact his words produced. "This time, dear Drogo, you're not displaying your usual military spirit. Regrettably I must tell you that in the end you are certainly leaving. God knows how many men would switch places with you. I admit you don't like it. But you can't have everything in life; you have to be reasonable. I'm sending your orderly to pack up your things. The carriage will be here at two o'clock. We shall meet again later."

After he spoke, he rushed away, deliberately, leaving Drogo no time to voice new objections. He closed the door in great haste and hurried down the corridor, pleased with himself, in complete control of the situation.

A heavy silence remained. Plop! sounded the water in the cistern behind the wall. Then only Drogo's wheezing could be heard in the room, somewhat similar to a sob. Outside the day stood at the height of its radiance. Even the stones were beginning to grow warm. You could hear the sound of water on the sheer rock walls, far away and constant. The enemy was amassing beneath the last ridge before the Fortezza. Troops and wagons were still coming down the road across the plain.

On the battlements of the fort, everything is ready: the munitions are in order, the soldiers well prepared, the weapons checked. Every gaze is turned toward the north, even if nothing is visible because of the facing mountains (only from the New Redoubt can the whole scene be observed). Just as in those distant days when the foreigners had come to delimit the borders, hearts are suspended between alternating gasps of fear and joy. No one, in any case, has time to remember Drogo, who is dressing with Luca's help and getting ready to depart.

29

As far as carriages go, it was truly dignified, even if excessive on those rustic roads. It could've been taken as the carriage of a wealthy gentleman if the doors hadn't borne the regimental coat of arms. Two soldiers were up in the box seat, the driver and Drogo's orderly.

Amid the commotion at the Fortezza, where the first echelons of reinforcements were already arriving, no one paid much attention to a thin officer with a gaunt, yellowish face who slowly descended the stairs, headed to the entrance hall, and exited where the carriage had stopped.

At that moment you could see a long formation of soldiers, horses, and mules, originating in the valley and advancing over the sunblasted plateau. Although weary from the forced march, the soldiers quickened their pace the closer they got to the Fortezza. The band, at the head of the column, were seen removing the gray cloth covers from their instruments as if they were preparing to play.

Meanwhile some men saluted Drogo, but not many and not as they had done before. Everyone seemed to know he was leaving and therefore no longer mattered in the hierarchy of the Fortezza. Lieutenant Moro and a few other officers came to wish him a good journey. But it was the briefest of farewells, suffused with that generic affection which the young typically express toward older generations. One of the officers told Drogo that Lieutenant Colonel Simeoni, who was extremely occupied just then, asked him to delay his departure. If Major Drogo would be so kind as to wait a few minutes, the commandant would come without fail.

Yet when Drogo climbed into the carriage, he immediately gave the order to leave. He had the hood lowered so he could breathe better. And around his legs he wrapped two or three dark blankets on which the sparkle of his saber stood out.

Wobbling over the stones, the carriage proceeded across the stony plateau. This would be the last bend in Drogo's road. Turned sideways on the seat, his head rocking with every jounce of the wheels, Drogo stared at the yellow walls of the Fortezza as they sank lower and lower.

He had spent his life up there, segregated from the world. He had suffered more than thirty years of torment from waiting for the enemy. And now that the foreigners were arriving, he was being sent away. His colleagues, however, the other officers who had led easy, happy lives down in the city—look at them now arriving at the pass, with superior smiles of disdain, to garner the spoils of glory.

Drogo's eyes were fixed as never before on the yellowish walls of the Fortezza, the geometric outlines of casemates and powder magazines. Slow, bitter tears were streaming down his wrinkled skin. Everything was ending miserably and nothing remained to be said.

Nothing, exactly nothing, remained in Drogo's favor. He was alone in the world, sick, and they had banished him like a leper. Damn them to hell! But then he preferred to let go, not to think about anything any longer; otherwise an unbearable fit of anger would swell in his chest.

The sun was already on its descending route, although it still had to travel a good distance. The two soldiers in the box seat were quietly chatting, unconcerned about whether they stayed or left. They had taken life as it came without worrying themselves with absurd thoughts. The carriage, which was of excellent construction, a true carriage for the sick, swayed at every hole in the ground like a delicate pair of scales. And the Fortezza, in the entire panorama, grew increasingly small and flat, although its walls cast a strange glare on that spring afternoon.

The last time, most likely, thought Drogo when the carriage reached the edge of the plateau and the road began to plunge into the valley. Farewell, Fortezza, he said to himself. Yet Drogo was a bit stupefied. He lacked the nerve to bring the horses to a halt so he could take one more look at the ancient stronghold that only now, after centuries, was about to commence its most fitting life.

In Drogo's eyes, for a moment longer, lingered the image of the pale yellow walls, slanted ramparts, mysterious redoubts, and adjacent thaw-blackened cliffs. Giovanni imagined—although for an infinitesimal instant—that the walls were suddenly stretching toward the sky, flashing with light. Then every view was brutally cut off by the grassy rocks between which the road sank.

Around five o'clock they reached a small inn where the road ran along the side of the gorge. Above, like a mirage, rose chaotic crests of grass and red earth, desolate mountains where perhaps no man had ever laid foot. Below ran the torrent.

The carriage stopped in the open area before the inn just as a battalion of musketeers was passing by. Drogo saw their youthful faces, red from sweat and effort, eyes staring at him in amazement. Only the officers saluted him. He heard a voice among the soldiers who had drawn away: "The old codger's riding in comfort!" But no laughter followed. While they were heading into battle, he was descending to the cowardly plain. What a ridiculous officer, those soldiers were probably thinking. Unless they had read in his face that he was also on the verge of dying.

He couldn't shake off a vague, fog-like stupor. Perhaps it came from the rocking carriage, perhaps the illness, perhaps simply the pain of seeing his life end so miserably. Nothing at all mattered to him anymore, absolutely nothing. The idea of returning to the city, of dragging his feet through his old, deserted house or lying in bed for long, boring, lonely months, frightened him. He was in no hurry to arrive. He decided to spend the night at the inn.

He waited until the entire battalion had passed, until the dust raised by the soldiers had settled back down over their footprints, until the roar of their carriages was muffled by the voice of the torrent. Then he slowly climbed down from the carriage, leaning on Luca's shoulder.

At the door sat a woman intent on her knitting and at her feet slept a baby in a rustic crib. Drogo peered with amazement at that marvelous sleep, so different from that of grown men, so delicate and deep. Troubled dreams had yet to emerge in that being. The infant mind sailed through a pure and most serene atmosphere, carefree, devoid of desire or remorse. Drogo stopped to gaze at the sleeping baby. A keen sadness pierced his heart. He tried to imagine himself immersed in sleep, a singular Drogo whom he could never have known. His own physical appearance appeared before him: dozing brutishly, shaken by dark anxiety, labored breathing, mouth partly open. And yet once upon a time he too had slept like that baby, he too had been sweet and innocent, and perhaps a sick old officer had stopped to look at him with bitter amazement. Poor Drogo, he said to himself, aware of how weak that was. But he was alone in the world, in the end, and apart from himself no one else loved him.

30

HE WAS sitting in a spacious armchair in a bedroom. The evening was wondrous, sending fragrant air through the window. Drogo languidly gazed at the sky, which seemed to grow deeper and deeper blue, at the purple shadows of the ravine, at the crests still bathed in sunlight. The Fortezza was far away. Not even the surrounding mountains could be seen any longer.

That should have been a happy evening—and for men of middling fortune as well. Giovanni thought of the city at dusk, the sweet unease of the budding season, young couples in the paths along the river, piano chords from windows already lit, a train whistle in the distance. He imagined the fires of the enemy camp in the center of the northern plain, the lanterns of the Fortezza swaying in the wind, the marvelous sleepless night before battle. In one way or another, everyone had some basis for hope, however small. Everyone but him.

Downstairs in the common room a man, then two, began to sing together, some sort of popular song about love. At the highest point of the sky, where the blue was deepest, three or four stars were sparkling. Drogo was alone. The orderly had gone down to have a drink. Suspect shadows accumulated in the corners and under the furniture. For an instant, Giovanni seemed not to resist (no one, finally, could see him; no one in the world would know). For an instant, Major Drogo felt the difficult weight on his mind was about to burst into tears.

Just then from remote recesses issued a new thought, at once limpid and tremendous: death.

*

He felt as if the flight of time had stopped, as if a spell were broken. The swirling motion had lately become even more extreme; then suddenly it ceased entirely. The world stagnated in a horizontal apathy and clocks ran uselessly. Drogo's road had ended. Look at him now on the lonely coast of a gray, uniform sea. Around him stands neither house nor tree nor man, and thus it has been from time immemorial.

From the farthest frontiers he felt a progressive, concentric shadow advancing on him. It may have been a matter of hours, weeks, months. Yet even months and weeks are inconsequential when they separate us from death. Hence life had been resolved into a kind of prank. Everything had been lost through an arrogant wager.

Outside the sky had become an intense blue. In the west, however, a strip of light remained over the purple outlines of the mountains. Darkness had entered the room. Only the threatening shapes of furniture, the white of the bed, and Drogo's shining saber could be distinguished. He would, he realized, never move from there.

Thus enveloped by shadows, as the sweet songs continued below amid arpeggios from a guitar, Giovanni Drogo felt a crowning hope rising within him. Alone in the world, ill, dismissed from the Fortezza as an annoying burden, he who had lagged far behind them all, timid and weak—he dared imagine everything might not be over. Perhaps his great opportunity had truly arrived, the definitive battle that could reward an entire life.

The final enemy was in fact advancing against Giovanni Drogo. It wasn't a man like him, tormented by desire and pain, made of flesh you can wound, wearing a face into which you can look, but a being that was at once omnipotent and malign. There would be no combat atop walls, surrounded by cannon blasts and exultant cries, beneath a blue spring sky, no friends at your side, the sight of whom might lift your spirit, no acrid smell of powder and fusillade, nor the promise of glory. Everything will unfold in a room in an unknown inn, by candlelight, in the most naked solitude. This isn't a fight from which you return crowned with flowers, on a sunlit morning, amid the smiles of young women. No one is watching; no one will shout bravo.

This is a much more forbidding battle than the one that had once been his hope. Even seasoned veterans would prefer not to attempt it. Because dying in the open air, in the havoc of the fray, your body still youthful and robust, with bugles echoing triumphantly, can be a fine thing. Sadder, no doubt, is dying from a wound, after prolonged suffering, in a hospital ward. Gloomier still is breathing your last in bed at home, surrounded by affectionate tears, dim lamps, medicine bottles. But nothing is more difficult than dying in an alien, unknown region, on the common bed of an inn, old and wizened, without leaving anyone in the world.

Be valiant, Drogo! This is the last card. Face death like a soldier and your misguided life will at least end well. Avenge yourself on fate, at last. No one will sing your praises; no one will call you hero or anything of the sort. Yet precisely for this reason the effort is worthwhile. March straight across the shadow's edge, holding yourself erect as if on parade, and smile too, if you can manage it. Your conscience doesn't weigh too heavily, when all is said and done, and God will bestow his forgiveness.

This Giovanni said to himself—it was a kind of prayer—as he felt the last circle of life tighten around him. And from the bitter well of things past, from desires frustrated, from malice suffered, came a strength he would've never dared include among his hopes. With inexpressible joy Giovanni Drogo suddenly realized he was absolutely calm, even eager to resume the onslaught. Ah, you can't expect everything from life? Is that so, Simeoni? Drogo will show you now.

Be valiant, Drogo. He tried to steel himself, to stand fast, to make light of the terrifying thought. He put his whole mind to it, in a desperate impulse, as if he were setting out by himself to attack an army. Immediately ancient fears fell away, nightmares collapsed, and death lost her chilling face, transforming into a simple matter in conformity with nature. Major Giovanni Drogo, wretched human, wasted by illness and age, pushed against the immense black portal and noticed the doors yielded, opening a path to the light.

At that point, all his worrying on the battlements of the Fortezza, his scouring of the desolate northern plain, the anxieties about his career, the interminable years of waiting, came to seem trivial. Nor did he still feel the need to envy Angustina. Yes, Angustina had died on top of a mountain in the heart of a storm; he left in a manner that befitted him, truly with great elegance. But a heroic end in Drogo's circumstances, consumed by malady, exiled among an unknown people, was much bolder.

He regretted only that he had to depart in that miserable body, bones protruding, skin ashen and flaccid. Angustina had died intact—thought Giovanni—his image, notwithstanding his age, had remained that of a young man, tall and refined, his noble face pleasing to women: this was his privilege. Yet perhaps even Drogo, after crossing the dark threshold, would regain the appearance he'd once had, not handsome (because he had never been handsome) but flush with youthfulness. What bliss, Drogo said to himself at the very thought of it, like a child, since he felt strangely free and happy.

But then a doubt came to mind: What if it were all a trick? What if his courage were nothing but some sort of intoxication? What if it depended only on the marvelous sunset, the fragrant air, the lull in physical pain, the songs from the floor below, and within a few minutes, within an hour, he were forced to go back to the former Drogo, weak and defeated?

No, Drogo, banish the thought. Stop tormenting yourself. The worst is now past. Even if pain assails you, even if music no longer consoles you and fetid mists overtake this stunning night, the account will add up the same. The worst is now past; they cannot defraud you.

The room has filled with darkness. Only with great effort can the white of the bed be distinguished. Everything else is black. In a little while the moon should rise.

Will Drogo have enough time to see it or must he leave sooner? The door to the room quivers with a soft creak. Perhaps it's a gust of wind, a simple swirl of air as happens on these restless spring nights. Or perhaps it's she who has entered, her step silent, and now she is approaching Drogo's armchair. Gathering his strength, Giovanni sits up a bit and with one hand straightens the collar of his uniform. He casts another glance out the window, the briefest glance, for his last helping of stars. Then in the dark he smiles, although no one can see him.

AFTERWORD

THE ITALIAN writer Dino Buzzati is a major figure in twentieth-century literature. A proponent of the fantastic, he reworks earlier genres like the fairy tale and the Gothic in ways that connect him to such writers as Franz Kafka, Jorge Luis Borges, and Italo Calvino. Although Buzzati is recognizably a modernist, his writing possesses an extraordinary popular appeal. His fantasies are compelling narratives, told in an accessible, unpretentious style. He aims to make them believable, offering us characters who engage our sympathetic imaginations.

This approach to the fantastic reflects Buzzati's lifelong career as a journalist at the Milanese daily *Corriere della Sera*. He began working there in 1928, first as a local reporter, then as a special correspondent covering national and international affairs that included the Italian colonization of Ethiopia, battles during the Second World War, even the Giro d'Italia. Over the next four decades he also produced a steady stream of novels, short stories, stage and radio plays, librettos, poetry, and children's literature, as well as a substantial body of paintings and drawings that synthesized symbolism, surrealism, and pop art. His commitment to journalism shaped this prolific output, immersing him in current events in Italy and abroad that left traces throughout his fiction.

Buzzati's most famous work is the novel *Il deserto dei Tartari* (The Desert of the Tartars), first published in 1940. Focused on the soldiers at a frontier outpost who yearn for glory in a war against legendary invaders, the vaguely surreal narrative is unmoored from a precise time and place. It is also deeply autobiographical, a point that becomes clear in Buzzati's later comments and documents published after his death. In an interview from 1966, he linked its genesis to the period between 1933 and 1939 when he was assigned to the night shift at *Corriere della Sera*. "It was a dull, monotonous job," he recalled,

> and the months passed, the years passed, and I asked myself if things would always continue like this, if the hopes, the inevitable dreams you have when you are young would gradually atrophy, if the momentous opportunity would really come. Around me I saw men—several my age, others much older—who carried on and on, transported by the same slow river, and I wondered if I too would find myself in the same circumstances as white-haired colleagues on the eve of their retirement, obscure colleagues who would leave behind a pale memory destined to fade quickly.

Buzzati describes the main themes of his novel as "hope and the life that passes fruitlessly," and they derived not only from observing his colleagues but also from struggling with his own literary ambition. Soon after he joined the newspaper, he began expressing his wavering self-confidence in letters to a childhood friend, Arturo Brambilla, who had become a secondary-school teacher of classical languages. "Nothing pleases me more than success," Buzzati wrote in 1930, while worrying that he was an "incompetent" journalist who worked too slowly and whose writing had to be embarrassingly corrected by editors. He subsequently published two novellas: *Barnabò della montagne* (1933; Barnabo of the Mountains), in which an indecisive forest ranger fails to repel a gang of brigands, and *Il segreto del Bosco Vecchio* (1935; The Secret of the Old Forest), in which deforestation motivated by greed encounters supernatural obstacles. Neither work achieved the success he sought.

Buzzati continued to be racked by doubt. In January 1936 he wrote to Brambilla of his "profound conviction, not that I will obtain a resounding success, but that I am capable of producing a masterpiece." In February, however, he felt that "the hope of producing a literary work that is really strong, something that would suffice to recompense a life even without public success, fades from one day to the next." In December he explored his vacillation in "La nostra ora" (Our Time), a story about an enterprising civil servant named Giovanni Drogo who survives a near-fatal illness and is promoted to a managerial position only to find his days "monotonous and empty" despite his "success." By April 1938 Buzzati was writing *Il deserto dei Tartari*, mentioning setbacks to his friend but insisting that "it will have to be a serious thing, a compendium and the farthest limit of my current life." On this occasion too he called his protagonist Giovanni Drogo, although now portrayed as a military officer. Drogo and Buzzati find themselves in similar situations, waiting expectantly for the crowning achievement that will redeem their dedication to their careers.

An autobiographical impulse also lay behind Buzzati's use of a military setting for the novel, although this decision reveals the complex transformation that his experience underwent in his writing. When asked in the 1966 interview why he "had not been more faithful to the truth by setting Drogo's story in the editorial office of a newspaper," Buzzati replied that "the military environment, specifically that of a fort on the border," better exemplified the theme of a hopeful yet ultimately unproductive life. "The discipline and military rules," he explained, "were much more linear, rigid, and inexorable than those established in a newsroom." He then made a telling admission:

> The fact is that the military life conforms to my nature. The normal service as an officer cadet and second lieutenant in the reserve (at this point I don't remember exactly, but it must have been no more than sixteen months) was enough for me to feel deeply attracted and to assimilate—thoroughly, I believe—the spirit of that world which seems so discredited today.

Recalling an experience that dated back forty years, Buzzati entirely misrepresents how he felt at the time. In 1926, when he was actually performing his military service, he expressed revulsion rather than attraction. He wrote to Brambilla that the military was "a kind of prison in which you have to work incessantly from morning to night, horribly watched like a convict, always under the threat of punishment." A decade after his discharge, this negative attitude began to surface in stories he published in magazines. In "Notizie false" (1937; False News), a troop of cowardly deserters is ironically represented as proudly committed members of the royal guard; in "L'uccisione del drago" (1939; The Slaying of the Dragon), an aristocrat performs the titular feat but with such inhumanity as to strip it of any heroism. Both stories were signed with a pseudonym, "Giovanni Drogo," the character whom Buzzati clearly took to be an alter ego. By the 1960s, however, his prior criticism of the military had metamorphosed not simply into approval but into identification. This contradiction was evidently prompted by the international success of a novel that came to be regarded as his masterpiece. It also suggests the enormous extent to which the relentless routine of journalistic work had defined his identity. The trajectory of Buzzati's career effectively resolved his early insecurity about his literary aspirations, overcoming his aversion to the military as well as its analogue, the newsroom.

The 1930s was a crucial decade in Buzzati's formation as a writer. It was then, after a classical education in which he read Greek and Latin, after immersing himself in both canonical and popular works from several narrative traditions, that he first discovered the literary possibilities of the fantastic. He saw himself competing against another emerging writer, Alberto Moravia, who was depicting the decadence of the Italian middle class in realistic novels like *Gli indifferenti* (1929; *The Time of Indifference*) and *Le ambizioni sbagliate* (1935; *The Wheel of Fortune*). In 1935 Buzzati wrote to Brambilla that "realistic literature, as it is practiced today, from the classic novel of love to the sort of story that Moravia writes, has no real reason to exist." The fantastic answered Buzzati's need to "write something in which the public could not fail to be interested, even if—as in the case of Kafka—it does not read the work."

Kafka was just beginning to appear in Italian. *Il processo* (*The Trial*) was published in 1933, *La metamorfosi* in 1934, and the story collection *Il messaggio dell'imperatore* ("A Message from the Emperor") in 1935. That was the year when Buzzati read the German text of *Das Schloss* (1926; *The Castle*), which would not be translated into Italian until 1948. He told Brambilla that he found it "impressive," adding that "it is more Kafkian than *The Trial*." When Buzzati completed his own novel in March 1939, it bore a Kafka-inspired title: *La fortezza* (The Fort). By February 1940 Rizzoli had accepted it for publication. Yet since World War II had broken out after increasing political and military aggression from Germany and Italy, the editor grew concerned about the title, considering it "little suited to the public." Buzzati proposed *Il messaggio dal nord* (The Message from the North), which was obviously modeled on the Italian translation of Kafka's stories and still suggestive of recent European developments. He finally settled on *Il deserto dei Tartari*. The choice turned out to be an enticement to readers. The journalist Giulio Nascimbeni, who was seventeen at the time, later recalled that he found it "profoundly exotic."

The novel immediately found appreciative readers in Italy and elsewhere. Within a decade of publication it had been reprinted by Mondadori (1945) and translated into German (1942), Swedish (1948), and French (1949). Reviewers typically took a humanistic approach, commenting on the curious amalgam of realism and fantasy and interpreting it as an allegory or parable that signified a moral abstraction with universal application. In a 1940 review for *Corriere della Sera*, Pietro Pancrazi marveled at how the novel "moves between reality and symbol," enabling Drogo to be read not only as "an individual with a particular character" but also as "poor Adam." In France the novel was assimilated to existentialism. Marcel Brion's 1955 essay in *Le Monde* describes Buzzati's "anxious universe" as "irremediably incoherent and governed by the absurd," so that "all our attempts at revolt against the tyranny of a masked hell, a hell here below, to which man is damned in advance, are crushed, with no hope of success." For Brion, *Il deserto dei Tartari* would seem to have prefigured Jean-Paul Sartre's drama of an infernal afterlife, *Huis Clos* (*No Exit*), first staged in 1944. In the wake of such commentary, the prevalent interpretation of Buzzati's novel became what might be called existentialist humanism.

Stuart Hood's English translation, titled *The Tartar Steppe*, appeared in 1952. Anglophone reviewers greeted it with praise, citing the same formal and thematic features that intrigued their European contemporaries, notably "magic realism" as the vehicle of a "timeless story" about a "human dilemma." Hood bolstered the humanist reading. That he was successful can be inferred from Adrienne Foulke's 1952 review in *The Nation*, where after praising his work she articulated the interpretation he inscribed in his translation. "Here the human dilemma is humanely conceived," she wrote. "Men are born into a world of immensities they may not even recognize but to which they are constantly responding with unformulated fear, hope, bafflement."

As if prompted by the Eurasian landscape evoked through Hood's repeated use of "steppe" (instead of "desert" or "plain"), some reviews subtly turned the novel into a Cold War allegory in which individual freedom is compromised, if not foreclosed. Foulke believed that "Lieutenant Drogo has sensed the meaning of his surrender to apathy but can make no more than a feeble motion to break free." In *The New York Times* Frances Keene described him as "a man weighing the senseless round of a life not of his own making but to which he is subject." In *The Saturday Review* Serge Hughes saw Drogo confronting "the desperate need to affirm oneself as an autonomous entity against the forces of solitude and persecution." For these reviewers, all translators from Italian based in the United States during a period rife with anti-communism, *The Tartar Steppe* called forth a deepseated fear of totalitarian government. Hood's translation supported this response by choosing the ideologically loaded "comrade," suggestive of the Soviet bloc, to translate "compagno" (companion, friend) and "collega" (colleague). The term risks a depiction of the fort as a socialist collective, despite the rank-based hierarchy, while the fear of invasion by the "northern kingdom" hints at an anti-Stalinism.

Il deserto dei Tartari seems to have resonated with Hood's war experiences. While serving as a British intelligence officer in North Africa, he was captured by the Italian army and sent to a prison camp near Parma. He escaped in 1942, just after Italy signed an armistice with the Allied Forces, and for the next year he lived among rural workers in Tuscany, fighting with the partisan resistance against Fascist militias and the Germans. In his memoir, *Pebbles from My Skull* (1963), Hood described his "reasons" for joining the resistance. "I was suffering still from the deep trauma of capture," he wrote, "and the fear that I had somehow been lacking in a moment of test." Hood's idea of passing a "test" in combat resembles the dream of military distinction nurtured at Fortezza Bastiani, although he assigns it a political significance by mentioning his decision not to participate in the Spanish Civil War. Behind his fear of inadequacy, he continued, "shamefully tucked away, was the greater guilt that I had been content not to fight in Spain. [The partisans] were men who would give me the chance to prove myself."

In an epilogue to a later edition of his memoir, after spending years in psychoanalysis, Hood rejected the "element of romanticism" he found in it as symptomatic of his political naiveté at the time, when he was a committed socialist opposed to any form of totalitarianism. "Together with my Italian comrades," he recalled, "I looked forward to the social revolution which must, it seemed, be the outcome of their struggle." This use of "comrades" reverberates back through the military romance of *The Tartar Steppe*. Hood's translation is marked by the turmoil in his life during the war and after, as he tried to make ideological sense of his experiences.

Gradually, the interpretation of Buzzati's novel underwent a radical shift in Italy. While continuing to be read as a humanist allegory of timeless, universal truths, it came to be understood as a critique of the Italian Fascist regime presented in a symbolic form that evaded censorship. The historian Ennio Di Nolfo was among the first to advance this reading in his 1986 study, *Le paure e le speranze degli italiani: 1943–1953* (The Fears and Hopes of Italians), where *Il deserto dei Tartari* is considered "not political but rich in political meanings insofar as it expresses the dissonance and detachment of a certain type of culture and environment (many Milanese intellectuals, linked to *Corriere della Sera*) in regard to official pronouncements." To be clear, Buzzati rarely advocated or criticized a particular ideological stance, whether in public or in his writing, so that throughout his career he tended to be regarded as apolitical. In an interview he gave the year before his death, he denied that "the philosophical schemas of fascism" were connected to his main theme of heroism. *Il deserto dei Tartari*, Di Nolfo explained, "lacks the direct will to produce a political discourse." Any ideological "dissonance" can only be perceived obliquely, then, through peculiarities in the dreamlike narrative that disclose a political unconscious.

A sharp disjunction is insinuated, for example, between the Fascist regime and the goings-on at Fortezza Bastiani where Buzzati's novel is set. Fascist ideology promoted a nationalistic cult of virility and heroic military action, but the fort has succumbed to inertia as officers and soldiers alike fantasize about an enemy who seems not to exist. Although deaths occur, they result not from bravery in combat but from illness, misjudgment, and rigid enforcement of regulations. Mussolini's imperial designs led to irredentist claims in Europe and colonizing wars in East Africa, but in the novel an expedition to establish the northern border fails to carry out its mission. In contrast to the phallic nation vaunted by the regime, a limp flag is a recurrent symbol. Colors likewise carry ideological resonance. The flag of the National Fascist Party displayed a yellow fasces on a black background, and the fort is continually described as yellow. At one point, however, the colors are inverted: "on the yellow earth of the courtyard [the assembled soldiers] formed a black pattern, beautiful to see." When the novel is situated in its historical moment, these features acquire an ironic tinge that can easily seem satirical—even if this effect exceeded Buzzati's (and the censors') awareness.

The autobiographical origins of *Il deserto dei Tartari* insure that Buzzati's life is inextricably tangled in the various allusions to political and military developments. This dimension may be most evident in the very landscape. The mountains to the north of Fortezza Bastiani reflect Buzzati's love of the Dolomites in northeastern Italy, where he would enthusiastically pursue alpine sports near Belluno, the site of his family's ancestral home. During the late 1930s the area shared a border with the expanding German Reich, figured as the threatening "kingdom of the north." The vast desert before the mountains superimposes the Italian colonies in Africa while the Orientalist legend of the Tartars points to the racism of the Fascist regime's colonial policy. In a 1936 letter to Brambilla, Buzzati mentioned his "hope" of being assigned to Africa so as to escape his "usual life in the newsroom," which he continued to find "dreary and depressing"; in 1939, just after delivering his manuscript to the publisher, he actually departed for Addis Ababa. The landscape of the novel can be seen as condensing the aggressive moves made by Germany and Italy and displacing them onto the narrative of grandiose delusion—an ideological process that seems to have been motivated by Buzzati's own fears and hopes.

This sort of historical understanding has not been widely adopted in anglophone cultures. Hood's *The Tartar Steppe* has been the only English version for more than seventy years, and during that time it has sustained the initial interpretation of the novel as a work of existentialist humanism. *The Independent*, reviewing a 2007 reprint in the United Kingdom, noted that in 1939 "the looming spectre of conflict would doubtless have been even more keenly felt, and Drogo's hankering 'for a hero's death' and his impotence might both have seemed more absurd"—only to abandon any historical context: "But of course his predicament is a universal one." In a 2017 essay for *The Literary Review*, the British novelist Joanna Kavenna likewise discovered a moral that is generally applicable. "We are all as doomed as Drogo," she decided, "and yet we get up each day, we adopt our routines, we continue. We expect and hope." Although *Il deserto dei Tartari* certainly supports such readings, we may well wonder at this point whether *The Tartar Steppe* has limited the range of responses to it.

Hood's version is undoubtedly a remarkable accomplishment, not merely readable but evocative enough to have interested several generations of readers. Containing relatively few errors and omissions, it closely approximates the meaning and style of the Italian text. Much of it is written in the most widely used form of English while relying frequently on idiomatic phrasing that is even more familiarizing. For example, Hood uses "time was running short" for "erano gli ultimi istanti" (they were the final moments), "in a lather" for "tutti sudati" (all sweaty), "in the air" for "impregiudicata" (unresolved), "could not believe his ears" for "udito un'enormità" (heard an absurdity), and "seeing things" for "allucinazione" (hallucination). Such choices, at once concrete and colloquial, reinforce the realism of the narrative, inviting the reader to engage sympathetically with the characters. At times, Buzzati's plain, direct language turns more lyrical and elevated in tone, and Hood evokes these effects by resorting to poetical archaisms, words and phrases like "farewell" for "salutare" (say goodbye), "avail himself" for "approfittarne" (make use), "heroic mien" for "sguardi da eroi" (heroic looks), "halt" for "fermare" (stop), and "cast down" for "triste" (sad). The poeticisms situate the narrative in a vaguely defined past, endowing it with a romantic, fable-like quality.

In all these ways, Hood's translating works against a historically oriented interpretation. A reader might still locate an occasional allusion: an officer who remains firm in his military commitment wears "jackboots," which are called merely "stivali" (boots) in Buzzati's text but quickly came to symbolize authoritarian government, whether under Hitler or Mussolini. Yet such possibilities are rare, and they went unnoticed by reviewers. Hood encourages the humanist allegory by deepening the main theme, the hopeful yet futile wait to display battle prowess. He increases Buzzati's repetition of the keyword "speranza" (hope) by introducing it where a different Italian term appears. Late in the novel, for instance, when Drogo fails to perceive signs of enemy movement, Hood's English reads: "little by little his hopes grew fainter." But the Italian text avoids "speranze" (hopes) for "fiducia," which might be translated variously as "trust," "faith," "confidence," or "credit." Any of these choices would nuance Drogo's thinking by suggesting that he has begun to question the Fascist ideology of heroic militarism. Buzzati repeats "fiducia" in the same passage as if to underscore the change in Drogo's character—"la fiducia cominciava a stancarsi"—but Hood again replaces it: "hope began to wane." We are left to imagine that Drogo will never get over his delusions of military grandeur.

The task I set for my retranslation was to establish a basis in English for the historical interpretation without ruling out the existentialist humanism that has long been the prevalent reading. I followed Hood in balancing the two registers of the narrative, realistic and fantastic, and in employing archaism and alliteration to highlight the poetic dimension of Buzzati's prose. Yet I used Ernest Hemingway's style as a model, since Hemingway and Buzzati not only are contemporaries but share a background in the newsroom and take war as a theme. Colloquialism proved particularly useful in distinguishing among the different narrative discourses in the Italian, as the point of view shifts between the narrator, who forcefully comments on the action, and the consciousness of various characters. I avoided Hood's Britishisms, however, in favor of English that would not be difficult to understand for any anglophone reader.

I also exploited opportunities to create historical allusions while adhering to the basic meaning of words and phrases such as can be found in dictionaries. To indicate that an officer's footwear is ill-suited to mountain climbing, Hood had twice rendered the generic "stivali" (boots) with the politically marked term "jackboots." I tripled its use. The same officer is described as "obbediva al suo ambizioso stile di vita" (obeying his ambitious lifestyle). I translated this phrase figuratively as "goose-stepping in line with his ambitious aspirations," glancing at Mussolini's importation of the Nazi military march as the "passo romano."

Occasionally I retained Italian words and phrases, although not so much as to risk unintelligibility. The Italian helps to situate the narrative in a specific culture and adds a political edge in crucial scenes. When the foreign soldiers arrive first to demarcate the border, they taunt their Italian counterparts from Fortezza Bastiani with the "arrogant shout" of "Buona sera, signori" instead of "Good evening, gentlemen," which is Hood's choice. Here the retention of the Italian can serve as an ironic reminder of Mussolini's nationalist foreign policy.

Elsewhere I underlined Buzzati's latent critique of Fascist masculinism. When Drogo considers his interactions with other men at the fort—"*con i colleghi ufficiali, doveva farsi vedere uomo, doveva ridere con loro e raccontare storie spavalde di militari e donne*"—Hood's rendering of the passage signals a complacent acceptance of the male domination typical of the 1950s: "with his colleagues, he had to be a man, had to laugh with them and tell swashbuckling stories about women and the soldier's life." If we read the Italian text historically, however, it implicitly questions such attitudes, and so I foregrounded this challenge by emphasizing them: "with fellow officers, he had to act like a man, had to laugh with them and tell cocksure tales of the military and of women."

Of course the most conspicuous departure from Hood's translation appears in my title. To promote a historical approach, as well as to differentiate my interpretation from his, I needed to avoid any mention of "steppe." Otherwise its suggestion of a Eurasian landscape might be taken as an anachronistic reference to the Soviet Union. All the same, deciding to revive Buzzati's initial title, *La fortezza*, could also be limiting. Using simply "The Fort," for instance, would have emphasized the debt to Kafka's *The Castle* that so many critics have recognized. The slightly archaic "fortress," to consider another possibility, would have seemed poetical yet appropriate, taking up the fantastic register of the narrative. I sought more: an English rendering that can encompass the various associations released by the Italian. Although the primary meaning of "fortezza" is "fort," the word also signifies "strength," alluding to the cult of virility championed during the Fascist period. I chose "stronghold" because it carries all these meanings while conveying the sheer tenaciousness of the soldiers' heroic fantasies, as well as their inability to escape their debilitating obsession.

Since its first publication, *Il deserto dei Tartari* has been translated—and in several cases retranslated—into more than thirty languages. If translation interprets because it is unable to reproduce a source text, drawing on values, beliefs, and representations that already circulate in receiving situations, then the international reception of Buzzati's novel clearly implies that it has supported interpretations both diverse and disparate in appealing to heterogeneous audiences. This capacity, in the end, is testimony to its status as a classic. "The books we call classics," the critic Frank Kermode once wrote, "possess intrinsic qualities that endure, but possess also an openness to accommodation which keeps them alive under endlessly varying dispositions." Just how alive the present accommodation may be remains a question only my reader can answer.

Both the introduction and the translation benefited from the work of a number of Buzzatian specialists whom I would here like to acknowledge. Lorenzo Viganò's Italian editions with their accompanying commentary have become indispensable to any historically oriented study of Buzzati's writing. For my source text I relied on his 2021 edition of *Il deserto dei Tartari*. I also learned a great deal from Ellen Nerenberg's study, *Prison Terms: Representing Confinement During and After Italian Fascism* (2001); Robert Dean Kohen's 2014 Harvard doctoral dissertation, *Dreaming Empire: European Writers in the Fascist Era*; and Stefano Baruzzo's 2021 article, "1940, Il Deserto dei Tartari. Un Significato Storiografico," as well as our helpful email exchange.

Isabella Livorni expertly vetted my translation. All English translations, unless otherwise credited, are mine.

Karen Van Dyck gave her encouraging support—and much else.

—LAWRENCE VENUTI
New York–Landgrove–Papouri
December 2022

OTHER NEW YORK REVIEW CLASSICS

For a complete list of titles, visit www.nyrb.com.

DANTE ALIGHIERI Purgatorio; translated by D. M. Black

HANNAH ARENDT Rahel Varnhagen: The Life of a Jewish Woman

POLINA BARSKOVA Living Pictures

DINO BUZZATI A Love Affair

DINO BUZZATI Poem Strip

CAMILO JOSÉ CELA The Hive

EILEEN CHANG Written on Water

FRANÇOIS-RENÉ DE CHATEAUBRIAND Memoirs from Beyond the Grave, 1800–1815

LUCILLE CLIFTON Generations: A Memoir

COLETTE Chéri *and* The End of Chéri

E.E. CUMMINGS The Enormous Room

ANTONIO DI BENEDETTO The Silentiary

HEIMITO VON DODERER The Strudlhof Steps

FERIT EDGÜ The Wounded Age *and* Eastern Tales

ROSS FELD Guston in Time: Remembering Philip Guston

BEPPE FENOGLIO A Private Affair

WILLIAM GADDIS The Letters of William Gaddis

NATALIA GINZBURG Family *and* Borghesia

JEAN GIONO The Open Road

VASILY GROSSMAN The People Immortal

MARTIN A. HANSEN The Liar

ELIZABETH HARDWICK The Uncollected Essays of Elizabeth Hardwick

ERNST JÜNGER On the Marble Cliffs

MOLLY KEANE Good Behaviour

PAUL LAFARGUE The Right to Be Lazy

JEAN-PATRICK MANCHETTE The N'Gustro Affair

THOMAS MANN Reflections of a Nonpolitical Man

MAXIM OSIPOV Kilometer 101

KONSTANTIN PAUSTOVSKY The Story of a Life

MARCEL PROUST Swann's Way

ALEXANDER PUSHKIN Peter the Great's African: Experiments in Prose

RUMI Gold; translated by Haleh Liza Gafori

FELIX SALTEN Bambi; or, Life in the Forest

ANNA SEGHERS The Dead Girls' Class Trip

VICTOR SERGE Last Times

ELIZABETH SEWELL The Orphic Voice

ANTON SHAMMAS Arabesques

CLAUDE SIMON The Flanders Road

WILLIAM GARDNER SMITH The Stone Face

VLADIMIR SOROKIN Telluria

JEAN STAFFORD Boston Adventure

GEORGE R. STEWART Storm

ADALBERT STIFTER Motley Stones

ITALO SVEVO A Very Old Man

MAGDA SZABÓ The Fawn

ELIZABETH TAYLOR Mrs Palfrey at the Claremont

TEFFI Other Worlds: Peasants, Pilgrims, Spirits, Saints

YŪKO TSUSHIMA Woman Running in the Mountains

IVAN TURGENEV Fathers and Children

H.G. WELLS The War of the Worlds

EDITH WHARTON Ghosts: Selected and with a Preface by the Author